A NOSE BY ANY OTHER NAME . . .

I heard the voices, downstairs.

I had choices, I thought. I could nudge open Mamaw's bedroom window, jump out into the snow-covered junipers, and then—assuming that I didn't break anything—take off, without so much as ta-ta, just like my mama and daddy had done.

I could curl up under the quilt and hide.

Or, I could satisfy my growing curiosity and go meet my mama and daddy for the first time in decades. Well, for the first time, really, in a way.

No wonder my nickname's Nosey Josie. Curiosity always wins out with me. I opened the door and stepped out to the top of the stairs . . .

The Stain-Busting Mysteries
by Sharon Short

HUNG OUT TO DIE
DEATH IN THE CARDS
DEATH BY DEEP DISH PIE
DEATH OF A DOMESTIC DIVA

SHARON SHORT

Hung Out to Die

A STAIN-BUSTING MYSTERY

AVON BOOKS
An Imprint of HarperCollinsPublishers

This is a work of fiction. Names, characters, places, and incidents are products of the author's imagination or are used fictitiously and are not to be construed as real. Any resemblance to actual events, locales, organizations, or persons, living or dead, is entirely coincidental.

AVON BOOKS
An Imprint of HarperCollins*Publishers*
10 East 53rd Street
New York, New York 10022-5299

Copyright © 2006 by Sharon Short
ISBN-13: 978-0-06-079324-1
ISBN-10: 0-06-079324-4
www.avonmystery.com

First Avon Books paperback printing: February 2006

Avon Trademark Reg. U.S. Pat. Off. and in Other Countries, Marca Registrada, Hecho en U.S.A.
HarperCollins® is a registered trademark of HarperCollins Publishers Inc.

Printed in the U.S.A.

10 9 8 7 6 5 4 3 2

To my friends who are as family:
Barbara Byrd
and
The Goddesses: Barbara H., Judy, Mary Tom, Kathy,
Katrina, Mary Ann, Lucrecia, Sandy, Lee, Gilah,
Crystal, Barbara D., and Jill

1

"Now, this square was cut from your Uncle Fenwick's football warm-up jersey, after the 1970 season," Mamaw Toadfern said, as she stared at the crazy quilt spread on top of her bed, which was itself covered in another crazy quilt. The mixture of colors and shapes in both of her homemade quilts was making me dizzy.

As was her perfume—Estée Lauder's Youth Dew, also vintage 1970. I briefly wondered if Mamaw had gotten the perfume at Maxine McNally's estate auction, held the previous weekend. I'd gone and found on a card table—right next to a stack of lovely old linen and lace napkins and tablecloths—a whole box of Youth Dew. Riley—one of Mrs. McNally's granddaughters—told me no one ever knew what to get her grandmother, so they just kept sending her Youth Dew. Turned out she was allergic to it, but she wore it anyway at Thanksgiving, just to make everyone happy, and finally confessed, a year before she died, not just to her allergy but also to her complete dislike of the scent.

At least, said Riley, as I bought up the whole lot of linens—stains and all—that explained why her Mamaw McNally always sneezed through the entire Thanksgiving meal.

Anyway. My own Mamaw Toadfern now reeked of Youth Dew and I suppressed a sneeze and wondered if I was allergic, too. I hadn't seen Mamaw at the sale. But then, I hadn't seen her other than at a distance since I was about seven years old . . . and that had been twenty-two years before.

And now, here I was. At her house for Thanksgiving. Looking at a quilt that seemed to be comprised mostly of old sports clothes. And trying not to sneeze at her perfume.

Mamaw poked again, with a hot pink sparkly fake fingernail, at the square of shiny silver fabric with the navy blue number 23. "Or maybe this square was cut from your daddy's football jersey. I got their numbers mixed up all the time." She tapped navy-on-silver 47 a few squares away. "Fenwick and Henry aren't identical twins, but at least back then they looked a lot alike. Same build. You'd think the numbers would have helped me keep them straight, but with two other boys to keep track of too . . ." She shook her head. "Your daddy and your Uncle Fenwick were the stars that season. Henry set a record for interceptions and Fenwick for field goals, records that have yet to be broken in Muskrat history." She was referring to the mascot of East Mason County High School and for a moment she looked really proud, as if she'd gone back in time to the season when they'd set the records. Then she looked suddenly despairing again. "Those two were always so competitive, you know."

No. No, I didn't know.

In fact, I had no recollection of my daddy at all, considering he'd run off from my mama and me when I was two.

And yet, here I was, in *his* mama's bedroom, as she droned on sentimentally about this quilt, and I held my breath, and heard somewhere in the back of my head a high-pitched whining sound that wavered to the melody of "Over the River," as in "Over the river and through the woods, to grandmother's house we go, the horse knows the way, to carry the sleigh, through white and drifted snow, oh . . ."

At least I found the song cheery, if a bit ironic.

Because this was the first, last, and only time that this particular Thanksgiving tale would be cheery.

Oh, it included a river and woods, seeing as how I live in Paradise, Ohio, and Mamaw lives in the country, on a farm, on the other side of the Stillwater River. Her huge, two-story farmhouse sits in the midst of trees. The rest of the property is a cornfield, which she farms out.

And it included plenty of white and drifted snow. The day before Thanksgiving, we'd had a record-setting storm, which dumped almost a foot of glistening white snow throughout much of the Midwestern United States, including our little patch of the Midwest in southern Ohio.

But in this tale's case, there is no horse or sleigh, although a confused, derelict deer does figure into the telling—later on, anyway.

And grandmother is my Mamaw Toadfern, not exactly the white-haired, apron-wearing, doting grandma the song implies. In her high-heeled mules, Mamaw was at best four feet eleven inches—a good four inches shorter than me—and weighed maybe a hundred pounds. The

lines in her face were so deep and craggy they reminded me of the glacial grooves I'd once seen in a
rock at the Museum of Natural History in Cincinnati,
but still . . . she loomed as big and scary as she had the
last time I saw her, which, as I said, was when I was
about seven.

I think she still seemed scary because of her piercing blue eyes. Or maybe because at seventy-six she
wore tight black pants with those high-heeled mules,
and a tan sweatshirt appliquéd with sequined turkeys,
pilgrims, and Indians, and a big blond wig, and somehow managed to look pretty good.

Mamaw was suddenly shaking me as she hollered,
"Josie! Josie, are you okay?"

My vision cleared, the melody drifted away, and I
coughed as I peered down at Noreen Faye Wickenhoof
Toadfern. The matriarch of my daddy's family—a family I'd never known, except for a stray cousin or two, because long ago this woman had decided my daddy's
running off was my mama's fault, and forbade everyone
from talking to my mama or anyone in my mama's family (which was much smaller, consisting of only a
brother, a sister-in-law, and a nephew). Then when I was
seven, my mama ran off, too, and Mamaw chose that
time to instruct the whole family to cut me off.

I stayed briefly in the county orphanage and then my
mama's brother and sister-in-law—Aunt Clara and Uncle Horace Foersthoefel, may they rest in peace—took
me in and raised me like their daughter.

"Josie?" Mamaw Toadfern demanded, her fingers
digging so hard into my arms that I could feel her hot-
pink faux nail tips bending backward. I jerked my
arm away.

"Yeah, sorry. Got a little light-headed, there."

"Well, pay attention, girl. This here is family history, and we have a lot of catching up to do."

"That wouldn't be my fault . . ."

"What?" Mamaw snapped.

"Uh, nothing. You were saying . . . this is a square from my Uncle Fenwick's high school football jersey. Or maybe from my daddy's football jersey . . ."

"All of the squares in this quilt come from some fabric of importance to the Toadfern family history. Besides the basketball shorts, there's the paisley my poor old mama wore to be buried in—I snuck back in to Rothchild's Funeral Parlor to cut off a square from the bottom of her dress . . ." I inhaled sharply at the image, and immediately regretted it. My head was starting to pound. I never get headaches, so I blamed it on the surreal scenario and the Youth Dew. "And there's a square from Great-Aunt Fern's wedding dress, from when she ran off for the third time to get married."

Okay, this was getting even more surreal. I had a Great-Aunt Fern? She got married three times?

"The dress washed up on the shore but she never did and they never did find that rat of a husband of hers," Mamaw went on. Maybe, I thought, Mamaw was just making this up. But from the expression on her face, I didn't think so. "I was always her favorite kin, so I got what was left of her, the dress that is, and . . ."

Oh, Lord. I could not imagine cuddling up for a winter's nap under this quilt. Besides being light-headed from the perfume, I was hungry, too. My stomach growled and knotted. Dinner was delayed for at least an hour, until 2 P.M., because Uncle Fenwick and Aunt Nora, who were responsible for bringing the cranberry salad . . . and Mamaw said dinner couldn't start without Uncle Fenwick, Aunt Nora, and the cranberry salad . . . had slid in their RV off the road into some of that fabled white and drifted snow. Last report was they'd just gotten towed out and were now on their way.

And Mamaw was taking this chance lull to present me with this quilt—at least that's why I assumed she was showing it to me, pulling me from the mayhem . . . I mean, family bliss . . . going on downstairs in the tiny parlor and kitchen and dining room and family room.

There were thirty-seven people (at least, I thought that's how many I'd counted; everyone kept moving around) all crammed downstairs, all hungry. My cousins Sally and Fern were sniping at each other for reasons I didn't yet fathom, and my back was starting to ache from giving Sally's triplet five-year-old sons piggyback rides so they'd stop picking on Albert, Fern's lonely only. Meanwhile, Uncle Randolph kept complaining that he was having a sugar low and no one really liked Nora's cranberry relish anyway and why did we have to wait for Fenwick who was always late—the show off.

But now, Mamaw was pointing at a pink square, with some unsavory purplish stain in the middle of it, and saying, "Josie, this right here is really why I wanted to show you this quilt."

I sighed. Great. First time I spend any time around my Mamaw Toadfern in twenty-two years, and I'm trying to hang in there despite the Youth Dew perfume, because I'm sure this is going to be a grand, sentimental moment in which she bequeaths me a quilt made of family fabrics, and what she's really after is my stain expertise.

See, I'm Josie Toadfern, owner of Toadfern's Laundromat in Paradise, Ohio, and a stain expert. Self-taught and proud of it. Best stain expert in Paradise,

Ohio. Or in Mason County. Or in Ohio. Maybe even in all of the United States.

So, sure, I could tell my Mamaw how to get the stain out of her precious quilt. But that wasn't exactly the Hallmark moment I'd been envisioning for the past week, ever since my cousin Sally came into my laundromat and ended up screaming at me, "Josie Toadfern, you'd better get your sorry ass over the river and through the woods to Mamaw's house for Thanksgiving, or else your ass will really know what sorry is, after I give you a whipping you'll never forget!"

You can see, can't you, how I couldn't possibly turn down such an invitation?

Anyway.

I returned Mamaw's sharp gaze with one of my own. "Just tell me what the stain is," I said, "and I'll be glad to tell you how to get it out."

Mamaw's eyes went watery, as if I'd slapped her. Then she started blubbering. "I can't believe you just said that. I guess you have more Foersthoefel in you than I thought—"

"Now, just a minute here," I started. "Uncle Horace and Aunt Clara raised me and I won't . . ."

But Mamaw Toadfern didn't hear a bit of my protest. "I know just what that stain is and how it got there! Why, it's from your baby blanket, and you'd erped up some smashed eggplant, as I was a-rockin you, right downstairs in my favorite rocker, and even though you made quite a mess, I kept that baby blanket and washed it out as best I could because it was the one and only time your daddy and that woman—" I reckon she meant my mama, but couldn't bring herself to put it that way—"let me babysit you and so it has great sentimental value to me, and, and . . ."

She broke down in sobs. And I went over to hold her, muttering, "now, Mamaw, it's okay," even as I rolled my eyes and thought, geez, woman, you've only had twenty-two years of living just across the river from me, during which you've maintained stone-cold silence, until now. It wasn't like anyone had kept her from having a connection to me, except herself.

But Mamaw Toadfern was seventy-six years old, and I'd come because Sally'd insisted Mamaw was about to keel over any moment from poor health—although you'd never know it from her appearance—and wanted to see me for some special reason.

I'd guessed making peace with her kin before dying. But if this woman was anywhere close to dying, then the snow outside was also close to morphing into sand and turning the farmhouse and cornfield into a beachside resort.

Suddenly, Mamaw pushed away from me, making me stagger back. "I'm all right," she said, pulling a tissue from her pants pocket. She blew her nose, then tossed the tissue into the trashcan next to her dresser. "It's just . . . I've given away many of the quilts I've made. I stopped making them, you know, a few years ago, due to my poor arthritic hands—" she waved her fingers around, which, in addition to being hot-pink-tipped, were be-ringed on all fingers except her thumbs, and which looked pretty straight and limber to me "—and my failing eyesight—" she glared at me with her sharp, blue eyes—"but I could never bring myself to give that quilt away because it was the only piece of you I've had all these years."

She sniffled.

I forced myself not to eye roll, and waited, silently. Which, after a while, made her a bit uncomfortable, and she started shifting from foot to foot. I took note of that. You never know when such insight into a person's character will come in handy.

"So, anyway," she said, "I wanted you to have this quilt, but there was also something I wanted to tell you."

Suddenly, she stopped shifting, narrowed her eyes, and stared at me. She waited, silently.

Which, after a very short while, made me a bit uncomfortable, and I started shifting from foot to foot.

She smiled—revealing the pearliest white set of dentures I'd ever seen—when she knew she had me.

"I need to tell you a secret, Josie." Suddenly, she clasped her hands to her chest. "Something I've never told anyone . . ."

And at that moment, we heard a momentous crash outside the front of the house.

We both ran over to the bedroom window.

There, on the front lawn, amidst all the many cars parked here and there, was an RV and a cherry-red sports car, right by the clothesline still tied up between trees in Mamaw's front yard. And the vehicles' front ends had vee-ed into one another.

A tall, elegant man in a tan wool coat emerged from the driver's side of the sports car. He looked like he was laughing and cursing, all at the same time. And a petite, elegant woman in a fur coat popped out of the passenger's side.

Mamaw's hand went to her mouth. She looked at me. "Oh, my Lord. My Lord . . ."

Mamaw's bedroom door flew open and Sally rushed in. "Mamaw—they're here . . . Uncle Fenwick, Aunt Nora, and . . ."

Sally's voice trailed off, as she stared at me. Mamaw nodded at her.

"And . . . your mama and daddy, Josie. They're here, too, in the sports car . . ."

That's all it took, on top of my hunger, and Mamaw's emotional histrionics and Youth Dew perfume. I passed out, cold.

Although I vaguely remember glaring at Sally as I crumbled and saying, "Sally, I'm gonna kill you."

2

All right, I didn't *really* mean I was going to kill Sally.

After all, as she said the Sunday before Thanksgiving, she was just trying to help.

And Sally, besides being my cousin, *is* one of my best friends . . . now.

Of course, back in junior high, she often made fun of me—chanting with the other kids my hated nickname, "Nosey Josie," which I got only because I am what I like to call curiosity-gifted. And she gave me wedgies at volleyball practice. And pulled me into the boys' restroom on several occasions to dunk me in the . . .

Well. No need to elaborate on those details. That was sixteen years or so ago. Water down the drain, so to speak. I'm over it. Truly.

Anyway, somehow or another she and I have become good friends, partly because she is the only Toadfern cousin (besides Billy, but he ran off to New York, and that's a whole other story) who has had anything to do with me since Mamaw Toadfern declared twenty-two years ago that I was "dead" to the family. And no one dared to go against Mamaw's proclamation, except Billy and Sally.

In Billy's case, I think it was because he was already the black sheep of the family.

And in Sally's case . . . I'm not sure why. We've never really talked about it. I like her and feel sympathy for her since her ex, Wayne-the-No-Good-Bum, left her alone to raise their now five-year-old triplets, Harry, Barry, and Larry. But I never tell her I feel sorry for her, because I think the old Sally might come forth and give me more than a swirly.

I love her sons, my cousins-once-removed, with a partiality for Harry, who is much quieter than Larry and Barry, and who has a real love for books and drawing.

I admire how she balances as best she can raising them with running the Bar-None, a bar and restaurant that her ex-mom-in-law (who also calls Wayne a no-good-bum for ditching Sally and the triplets) sold to her for a very low price when she went into semiretirement because, she said, the busy Friday and Saturday nights were killing her. Sally's mom-in-law still helps, though, running the bar Monday through Thursday night, and keeping the triplets on afternoons and Friday and Saturday nights so Sally can work.

Plus, Sally keeps me from possibly actually killing Cherry Feinster, another friend, with whom I have a much rockier relationship. She owns the business next to my laundromat, Cherry's Chat N Curl, and half the time I'm with her, she makes me laugh, and the other half she infuriates me.

The one thing Sally and I did have in common back

in our school years was that we couldn't stand Cherry. She was on the cheerleading squad, which in itself was fine, except she also unmercifully taunted any girl who wasn't, much to the embarrassment of most of the rest of the squad.

But about five years ago she bought the barbershop next door, which had been sitting empty for two years, re-named it Cherry's Chat N Curl, renovated it, brought in two other hair designers and made a go of her business.

Since then, somehow the three of us have bonded. Maybe it's because we all own our own businesses in a town populated by a lot of people who still think that kind of thing is uppity for women (unless, of course, you're Sandy of Sandy's Restaurant—Sandy's run her business for forty years, and nobody dares cross her). Anyway, no one would have predicted our friendship, way back in junior high and high school.

But then, people . . . and relationships . . . have a way of changing and growing. Sometimes. If given the chance. Although not always.

Lessons I was about to learn the hard way—although I didn't know it the Sunday before Thanksgiving.

See, I thought I was just doing the usual good deed of opening my laundromat for a private session only for Sally. My laundromat is closed to the general public on Sundays, it being a day of rest and all, but Sunday afternoon is about the only time Sally has to do her laundry. No space for even a stackable washer/dryer in her little trailer at the Happy Trails Motor Home Court, just outside of town.

I've even given Sally a key, so she was already in my laundromat when I arrived after services at the United Methodist Church of Paradise.

I walked in through the back office/storeroom, hung my coat on the old rack that's been there since the day Uncle Horace originally opened the business, then stopped in the doorway that divides my cozy laundromat from the back room.

Sally was transferring a load from a washer to a dryer. She had four other washers and dryers going and stacks of folded towels and sheets covering one table, and stacks of her sons' clothes covering another. And she was humming "Amazing Grace."

I grinned. We all find peace in our own way. For Sally, after a long weekend running the Bar-None, it was catching up on laundry while her sons snoozed peacefully at their paternal grandparents'. (They were good people, at least, who had tried to raise Wayne-the-bum right.) The zen of laundry.

Cherry sat on a plastic chair right next to Sally's folding table. Cherry was thumbing through her latest hairstyle book.

"Now, Sally, really, you ought to let me do the highlights and a bob like this," Cherry said, tapping a page with a coral fingernail.

"Forget it," said Sally. "My ponytail is serviceable." She swished her long, brown ponytail—clasped in a green hair elastic at the nape of her neck—in a way that suggested her ponytail might actually have unexpected uses.

"Serviceable," Cherry said, with a pout and a shudder. A 'serviceable' hairstyle was, to her, like washing dyed clothes with chlorine bleach would be to me. Unthinkable.

I grinned wider. It was an argument these two had every Sunday. Cherry always just happened to "drop by," and after we helped Sally load her car up with baskets of neatly folded, clean laundry, we either went up to my apartment—there are two apartments in the second story over my laundromat, and I live in one and try, mostly unsuccessfully, to rent the other out—for a late breakfast or headed across the street to Sandy's. This was going to be a Sandy's Sunday.

Cherry poufed her hair, currently a highlighted strawberry-blond bob that curved to her face without, somehow, actually getting in her face. It was anything but serviceable . . . although it did make her look ten pounds lighter. While Sally was well toned, even skinny, from chasing three sons during the day, standing on her feet at the bar every afternoon plus Friday and Saturday night, and somehow working extra odd jobs as a carpenter, both Cherry and I always seemed to be fighting extra weight.

I fingered my hair—an ordinary bob—tucking the usual annoyingly errant strand away from my eyes. The Forelock from Hell, I call it.

"Serviceable just isn't going to give you the allure you need to capture a man—"

"I've got plenty of males running around in my life. Literally," Sally said. "Larry was chasing Barry all around the trailer yesterday and I thought it was going to rock off its cinderblocks—"

"Now, Sally, you know that's not what I mean. I mean, with your trim figure, all you need is a new hairstyle and maybe some makeup to catch you a man."

Sally just hummed louder—I think she was at the "how sweet the sound" part of the hymn—and folded her sons' underwear, which she keeps organized by initialing the inside of the waistbands with permanent laundry marker, something I'd suggested.

"Plus you need a whole new wardrobe. We could go thrift-store shopping up in Masonville . . ."

It was time for me to break in. I walked into my laundromat. "Aw, Cherry, for pity's sake, just because you're plum nuts about Deputy Dean, doesn't mean you have to try to set up every woman you know."

Deputy Dean was what Sally and I had taken to calling Cherry's latest love interest—Deputy Dean Rankle, who works for the Mason County Sheriff's Department. For some reason, it bugs her when we put the "Deputy" in front of the "Dean," so of course we do so as often as possible.

Cherry looked up from her hairstyle book and glared at me. Sally stopped humming long enough to grin and say, "Hey, there, Josie. You tell her. She's getting too hot and heavy with old Deputy Dean. Why, they've been snuggled up in the back corner booth at the Bar-None most every night this week."

I started toward one of the plastic chairs near Cherry. "Really? Well, I've noticed Deputy Dean dropping by the Chat N Curl several times this week—after hours." I waggled my eyebrows at Cherry while I added, "Let me guess. Private pedicures? What goes better with khaki sheriff uniforms . . . Handcuff-Me-Please Pink or Siren Red?"

Sally giggled, which made me grin in turn. Sally is usually not the giggling type.

Cherry glared at me. "Oh, excuse me, missy. I was under the impression that men were supposed to actually spend time with their girlfriends. At least my guy doesn't have an ex he runs off to for Thanksgiving."

I gasped.

Cherry turned her glare on Sally. "Or just plain runs off."

Sally stopped humming.

I eyed Cherry coldly. "I think you owe Sally an apology."

"Never mind me," said Sally. "She owes you an apology, Josie."

Suddenly Cherry burst out crying, put her head to her hands, letting her hairstyle book drop to the floor. "I owe you both an apology. I'm sorry. It's j-j-just you all start teasing me about Dean and I get all nervous, because I think he might really, really be the one." She emphasized those last two words.

Sally tossed me one of the boys' old cloth diapers—thoroughly sterilized and bleached since their original use, and now employed as cleaning rags—and I tossed it at Cherry.

"Stop sniveling," I said. "You're forgiven."

Cherry grabbed the old diaper, dabbed at her face while sniffling. Then she stared at the now mascara-and makeup-smeared diaper, made a face, and started to purse her lips to form an "ew."

I gave her a warning look and she thought better of complaining about her makeshift hanky. "How do I look? I bet I look terrible. And I have a date with Dean this afternoon. He's taking me to the Sir Save-a-Lot Cinema up in Masonville and then to Suzy Fu's Chinese Buffet."

"You look fine. Plus you'll end up re-doing your make-up at least twice before you see Dean."

"Okay," Cherry sniffled. "And for the record, I just do one coat of clear for Dean's pedicures."

I'm not sure who burst out laughing first—me or Sally. In any case, within a few seconds, Cherry started laughing, too. When we settled down again, Cherry and I joined Sally in taking out another load of clothes from the dryer. We all started folding.

"Um, Josie, I'm seriously wondering, though, what are you going to do Thanksgiving, with Owen gone, and all?" Sally asked gently.

I didn't even pause in midfold of a tiny blue T-shirt. "Oh, I'll be fine. I'll spend the morning at Stillwater, of course. Then, I'll, uh, I'll . . ."

I was looking forward, as always, to my visit with my cousin Guy Foersthoefel at Stillwater Farms. Guy is forty-four and a resident of a wonderful residential home, just fifteen miles north of Paradise, for adults with autism. The home is set on a renovated farm and the staff is wonderful.

Stillwater always holds a Thanksgiving breakfast—turkey omelettes! Yum!—instead of dinner, in consideration of families who have other places to go later in the day. I'd linger at the breakfast, until Guy got restless—adults with autism have an internal sense of scheduling that defies understanding at times, and Guy always let me know when he was done visiting by getting fidgety—and then I'd . . . I'd . . .

What?

Truth be told, I'd been putting off thinking about what I'd do after that.

Originally, my boyfriend Owen Collins and I had planned to have a romantic Thanksgiving dinner-for-two at my apartment. (The turkey breast was still in the freezer.) Then, maybe, we'd go over the plans I'd been sketching for converting the two apartments into one loft. My success in renting the second apartment has always been spotty at best—the most recent renters had just moved out to a small home on Maple Street—and I thought I could afford to turn my apartment into something more homey. Something that might have space for all the books I keep buying.

And then, as the candlelight flickered and we grew weary of looking at my plans, maybe we could . . .

I shook my head and told myself to focus on folding little boy T's and undies.

Owen had gone the day before to Kansas City to spend the week with his twelve-year-old, Zachariah, who lived with Tori, his mom, Owen's ex-wife. Because Owen had once served time for involuntary manslaughter, Tori had full custody of their son, and until a few months before, Owen had had no contact with Zachariah.

Owen was, understandably, excited about finally getting to spend time with Zachariah. And I was truly excited for him. Even if it meant that, by necessity, he'd also be spending time around Tori.

Dining on her turkey and dressing and pumpkin pie . . . no doubt in some cozy candle-lit eat-in kitchen of a white-picket-fenced suburban home. With a golden retriever named something like Old Pal snoozing in front of the glowing fireplace . . .

Not that I was jealous. Owen and his ex-wife were truly over each other, he'd assured me numerous times. He just wanted to see his son, and he was spending the week at a nearby Quality Inn Motel.

And of course I had no doubts that Owen, while enjoying time with his son, would long to also be with me, dining on turkey and pumpkin pie in the apartment over my laundromat. With a pothos ivy named Rocky dripping yellowing leaves from the windowsill . . .

For just a second, I hoped Tori's turkey was tepidly tasteless.

My older friend and the county's bookmobile librarian, Winnie Logan, had invited me for Thanksgiving dinner in years past, but her daughter in Chicago had just had her first child—and Winnie's first grandchild—so Winnie and her husband would be in Chicago for the holiday.

Sally always spent Thanksgiving with the Toadferns, and since I was "dead" to the family, I had no intention of haunting their holiday festivities.

Cherry had plans with her family and Deputy Dean's family.

I had other friends—none so close as Winnie, Sally, and Cherry, of course—and even customers I could have dropped a hint with, and readily been invited to Thanksgiving.

But, somehow, I didn't want to become some other family's sympathy guest . . . even though I knew no one else would see it that way.

Maybe I would just read, after my visit to Stillwater. Have the turkey and review my renovation plans by myself.

Or maybe I'd go up to Masonville and volunteer to serve at the city's annual feast for homeless and low-income individuals and families.

Yeah, I thought, starting to get excited, that could be a pretty neat way to spend the day . . .

"Well, really, Josie, Thanksgiving day is meant to be spent with family," Cherry said, interrupting my thoughts.

"That's how I'm spending the morning."

"Well I know that Guy is family, but . . ."

"What she's getting at, Josie, is that you have a whole other side to your family," Sally said. "You've kept the last name—"

"Habit!" I snapped. Which was true. Plus Toadfern was my legal last name when my aunt and uncle adopted me, and since they never saw fit to change it, neither did I.

"—but you barely know the Toadferns."

"Not my fault," I snapped again. I thumped down the T-shirt I was folding, at least as much as one can thump a T-shirt. A dryer buzzed. I started toward it, stomping my feet as I walked.

Sally turned and grabbed my arm as I walked by her, causing me to stop and whirl so that I faced her. I glared at her and jerked my arm away from her grasp.

"I know it's not your fault, Josie, everyone knows that. Believe it or not, I'm not the only one in the family who has appealed to Mamaw Toadfern . . ."

"Yeah, well, you're the only one, besides Billy, who has bothered to really have anything to do with me for the past twenty-two years. For pity's sake, I was two when Daddy ran off, and that bitter old woman we call Mamaw blamed my mama, and five years after that, when Mama ran off and I could have used some support, she totally cut me off from the family and scared most everyone else from having anything to do with me!"

My eyes pricked with tears. I was surprised by how much Mamaw's rejection bothered me, all of a sudden. I told myself it was just because I'd only driven Owen to the airport, up in Columbus, the day before.

"Now, you listen to me," Sally said. "Mamaw Toadfern's had a change of heart. She regrets her decision to cut you off years ago. And . . . and . . . she wants you to come to dinner for Thanksgiving!" Sally finally blurted out.

I narrowed my eyes at Sally, partly to try to push the tears back. "If she wants me to come so darned badly, why hasn't she called me herself? Or come on down here to the laundromat? It's not like I'm hard to find. Practically everyone in the county knows who I am and where to find me."

It was the God's truth. Sure, most everyone has a washer and dryer these days. But they don't always work. And out in the country, when the water tables are low, people come in. And home washers can't handle big comforters or throw rugs. Plus, there are still those who don't have a washer/dryer at home.

And mine's the only laundromat in the southern part of Mason County.

"Well, it's because Mamaw Toadfern is, well . . ." Sally actually paused to sniffle. I resisted an eye-roll. "She's just so unhealthy lately . . . something about her liver or her stomach or . . ."

I wasn't able to resist bursting out laughing.

"Now, Josie, that's not too kind," Cherry said. "I know your Mamaw Toadfern hasn't exactly been the ideal grandma, but—"

"Oh, Cherry, I've heard rumors for years about Mamaw's illnesses. Someone'll come in here who knows her and start talking about how Noreen Faye Wickenhoof Toadfern has been having a bout with bronchitis, or ulcers, or backaches, and how she's sure it's her time to go meet her maker, and I'll start to feel all guilty that I've never gone to see the old woman to offer up an olive branch—even though *she* rejected *me* when I was just an innocent little kid—and then I'll run into her at the Corner Market or the Antique Depot or Sandy's Restaurant—and what does she do? She gives me this long, piercing glare, sticks her nose up and her scrawny little butt out, and struts away, and—"

I stopped. I was actually starting to choke up. What

was wrong with me? I didn't care about what my old biddy Mamaw or other Toadferns who snubbed me thought . . . did I? Maybe it was the holiday season, the prospect of kicking it off without the company of Owen or any of my friends on Thanksgiving evening.

"She's having real problems lately," Sally said. "Last time I went to see her, she told me she had bleeding ulcers."

"I had a great-uncle who was kinda like your all's Mamaw," Cherry said thoughtfully. "He was a hypochondriac, too, but even hypochondriacs can get sick for real, Josie. He only lived a few weeks after about the thirtieth time my mama called me to say his doctor told him he didn't have long to live." Now she sniffled, too. "Always regretted not seeing him."

"Oh, you two, please," I said. "What is it about the Thanksgiving holiday and families and the guilties?"

"I don't know," Cherry said. "But it sure gets to me every year when I go home for dinner and Mama says at the end of the blessing, 'and God bless all our loved ones gone before us, especially Uncle Bubba, who no one believed was sick. Amen.'"

"And it's working me up that Mamaw said to me just last week when I was over to her house to fix a squeaky door. 'Now Sally,' she says, 'there's something I need to tell Josie and I know you're the only one who can get her to come to your poor old sick Mamaw's for Thanksgiving . . .'"

"No," I said.

Sally glared at me. "Josie, aren't you the least little bit curious about what Mamaw wants?"

"No," I said, lying. But I wasn't about to give in to emotional blackmail.

"Then go to make my life easier," Sally said. "Ma-maw'll never let me hear the end of it if I don't convince you—"

"No," I said again. I pointed to the stack of clean laundry. "I already *am* making your life easier, anyway."

"You're going to go, Josie," Sally said.

"No, I am not."

"Josie Toadfern, you'd better get your sorry ass over the river and through the woods to Mamaw's house for Thanksgiving, or else your ass will really know what sorry is, after I give you a whipping you'll never forget!"

Now, that was enough—really it was—for me to just toss Sally out of my laundromat—at least as soon as her last load finished drying—and tell her there was no way I was about to let her bully me into going to Mamaw Toadfern's house for Thanksgiving.

In fact, I was just mad enough that I was ready to boycott the Bar-None, at least until after Thanksgiving.

But I never got a chance to tell Sally off. Just as I opened my mouth to tell her . . . well, I can't quite remember what I was going to say, but I'm sure it was quite clever . . . there was a tap at the front door of my laundromat.

It drew my attention from Sally, and then I saw who was standing on the other side of my big pane glass window—just to the left of my logo (a toad on a lily pad bearing the phrase ALWAYS A LEAP AHEAD OF DIRT), and whatever wittily devastating response I had in mind for Sally and why I would not go to Mamaw Toadfern's for Thanksgiving dissolved to dust.

And I was left staring, gapmouthed, at the woman standing just outside my laundromat window.

"My Lord," said Sally. "I thought she swore thirteen years ago she was going to Massachusetts and never setting foot again in this godforsaken town. At least that's the phrase I heard she used for her valedictory speech at her high school graduation."

"Would you look at that? Her hair . . . it's so damned perfect. And her figure is so trim," Cherry said, a pouting note of jealousy in her voice. "You'd think she'd have at least had the decency to have gained ten pounds and gotten split ends."

I said, "She's probably still nice, too. And happily married. With two kids, a dog, and a big old house."

Then we all sighed with undisguised envy, while Rachel Burkette—the smartest, prettiest, nicest young lady ever to grow up in and then leave Paradise—stood outside waving at us.

I started toward the door.

"Wait, Josie, you're closed, remember?" said Cherry.

"Cherry!" Sally and I said in unison.

Rachel was perfect thirteen years before. She was probably perfect now. We all wanted to hate her for it, but we couldn't, because she'd be so perfectly understanding about it.

The only imperfect thing she'd ever done was her outburst at the commencement, which we'd all heard about, even though she was two years older than us and we hadn't actually been at the event.

And it gave us all the perfect excuse to heave a sigh of relief when she left town.

But now she was back and so, of course, I opened my laundromat door to her.

I swear, if it hadn't been for her showing up like that,

I wouldn't have gone to Mamaw Toadfern's for Thanksgiving and the reunion, and then—maybe—the murder and all that followed wouldn't have happened.

But I did open the door.

I was only being polite.

3

Half an hour later, we were all across the street at Sandy's Restaurant, eating our very late breakfasts. No one asks for "brunch" at Sandy's. "Brunch" is something served at fancy hotel restaurants up in, say, Columbus. At Sandy's—which is actually a double-wide trailer converted over to a faux-wood-paneled restaurant, with the back half for a kitchen and dining counter, and the front half for booths—only breakfast, lunch, and supper are served. And you can get breakfast anytime you want. But ask Sandy for brunch, and she will cross her arms across her black T-shirt emblazoned with WHO ASKED? across the chest, and glare at you from under the brim of her Nascar ball cap until you apologize and rephrase your request to breakfast.

Rachel didn't quite ask what was for brunch, but she came as close as possible, ordering fruit cocktail and toast.

No wonder she was so slender.

I, of course, ordered my usual—biscuits and gravy, a

side of sausage, and strong, black coffee. Sally had three eggs, over easy, and a stack of pancakes. Cherry just had the pancakes. We chatted as we ate, catching Rachel up on our lives. Which didn't, I'm sorry to say, take long.

Several people recognized Rachel. A few came over to say hello, politely, but a few pointedly ignored her. The only mean comment came from Bobby John Sellars, whose daughter Prissy had been salutatorian Rachel's year, and who had been so upset by Rachel's parting shots in her valedictory speech, she'd run out of the high school auditorium, barely making it to the girls' bathroom before losing her own late breakfast.

Now, there were quite a few Paradisites who didn't particularly like Rachel's daddy—Rich Burkette, one of only two lawyers in town—but Bobby John was one of the few Paradisites who didn't make any bones about it. I'd heard it wasn't just Rachel's antics making Prissy lose her breakfast at commencement all those years ago. It had something to do with Bobby John having to pay a settlement to a neighbor, represented by Rich, over a broken fence.

"Sandy, you really oughta be careful about who you let in here!" Bobby John said loudly. "Somehow, I don't think young women who run down their own home town—"

The tiny restaurant got quiet. Everyone looked at Rachel—who was turning pink—and then at Bobby John.

Sally kicked me under the table. "Say something to defend her, Josie!" she whispered.

"Why me?" I hissed.

"She invited you to breakfast," Cherry said. "We just tagged along."

"I really am fine," Rachel said, her flush deepening to red, as Bobby John continued his diatribe. "I don't need defending."

Sandy plunked a bowl of oatmeal in front of Bobby John. "Shut up and eat your oatmeal," Sandy said.

There were a few twitters in the restaurant, and I noted at the counter Caleb Loudermilk—the new editor, sole reporter, and advertising executive for the weekly *Paradise Advertiser-Gazette*—hurriedly taking notes. I frowned at him, but he pretended not to see me. Considering I was late with my Stain-Busters column, I should have been glad for that, but I also knew that Caleb—age thirty, launching a new journalism career after a stint in minor league baseball—was eager to show Arquette Publishing, the owners of numerous tiny newspapers in southern Ohio, that, really, the *Paradise Advertiser-Gazette* could be more than just the local little source of social news it had been under the previous editor, now retired. Caleb had only had his position since early November, and already he'd stirred up controversy with his "pricing exposé" of the McNally estate auction.

"I didn't order oatmeal," Bobby John protested. "I ordered two eggs over easy and sausage links!"

"Well, Maxine told me the other day your cholesterol's kicking up again, so until she tells me otherwise, you're getting oatmeal," Sandy said.

Several people groaned, sympathetically. Sandy was known to sometimes give her customers what she thought would be good for them, rather than what they wanted. I'd once come in yearning for hot fudge cake, and Sandy had instead served me chicken noodle soup because I had the sniffles.

Annoying and endearing and in this case, thankfully, she'd turned Bobby John's negative attention away from Rachel. Sandy hustled over to our table and topped off all our coffee mugs.

"You be careful now, sweetie," she said to Rachel. "I liked your speech all those years ago—especially the bits about sorry little towns breeding small minds—" she cut Bobby John a narrow-eyed look—"and Lord knows I wouldn't have minded leaving myself when I was your age—but some folks have long memories. And folks may respect your daddy, but not everyone's had a good experience with him."

Rachel nibbled on her toast—white, instead of the wheat she'd asked for. She hadn't touched her grapes, cherries, and diced peaches floating in heavy syrup. For someone who still looked, acted, and even smelled perfect (she wore just the lightest touch of gardenia perfume, which was somehow perfect with her brown suede suit and cream turtleneck), Rachel looked utterly miserable.

She shooed a syrupy grape from one side of the green Fiestaware bowl to the other. "I used to tell myself that everyone would eventually forget about my ill-thought-out comments. Deep down, I knew I was wrong. I mean, I still hear myself saying over and over the part about how Mr. Ferguson's corn silo on the edge of town was a phallic symbol of an ironically named town that gives the finger to progress."

Sally and Cherry gasped and I half choked on my swallow of coffee. When I finally got it down, I had to push down a bubble of laughter. But Rachel didn't look amused by her own wit.

"People never forget things like that in a small town," Rachel added.

No kidding. I couldn't look at Sally or Cherry, be-

cause I knew I'd start laughing. It was hard to imagine
Rachel saying something like that. She was the girl
with perfect grades, plus letters in cheerleading and
softball, and countless hours of community service at
the nursing home, and letters of recommendation
from her church's pastor and our state representative.
Which explained why Rachel had won a full scholarship to an East Coast college. Thank goodness the
scholarship committee hadn't seen a transcript of her
speech.

And no wonder Rachel's mom and dad sent her to
college early, to a camp for gifted incoming freshmen.
She hadn't, as far as any of us knew, been back to Paradise since.

"Oh, don't worry about Mr. Sellars," Cherry said.
"He's just a grump. Tell us what you've been up to all
this time and what brings you back to town."

"I'm a real estate broker. Own a brokerage, actually," she said, with a shrug, as if she found her own
career achievements boring. "I live in Atlanta now."

"Married?" Cherry asked.

"Kids?" Sally asked.

"Neither," Rachel answered. "Although I just
dumped a man who claimed neither, also, and turned
out to be the father of four and married to the best
friend of one of my clients."

Despite sharing this news, Rachel smiled—briefly
and sadly, as if at her own folly. It was her first smile, I
realized, since she'd tapped on my laundromat door
and called, "Hi, Josie. I'm in town for Thanksgiving
and hoped you'd be willing to have a cup of coffee
with me."

Now she went on, "And what brings me to town is
that Dad is retiring."

Rich Burkette was partner at the one and only law firm in Paradise—Burkette and Trunkel. Rachel was Rich and Effie's only child, although I vaguely remembered Effie had a son by her first husband, who had left her years ago. Rachel's half-brother . . . I couldn't remember his name . . . was quite a bit older than Rachel.

Another memory teased the edge of my mind. Something about Rachel, from when we were kids, a conversation we'd had. I looked at Rachel, as if staring at her would bring back the memory. She looked away from me quickly, back at her syrupy fruit, and the memory-tease fizzled.

Truth be told, all I really knew about Rachel and her family was what everyone else knew. Effie and Rich Burkette lived on the farm that had once belonged to Effie's dad. The farm was between my Mamaw Toadfern's property and the old Mason County Orphanage— now defunct—where I'd spent a few months after my mama ran off, before Aunt Clara and Uncle Horace took me in as their own.

Rich was a local attorney—powerful by local standards. Effie's first husband was all but forgotten. I had a dim memory that they had divorced and he'd run off. Her older son, by the first husband, lived elsewhere and visited now and again.

And other than Rachel's strange speech years before, and the fact that several folks found it odd that the Burkettes lived in a modest old farmhouse when they could have easily afforded to build a much finer house on the property, most everyone considered the Burkettes to be the perfect family.

"I heard about your dad's retirement party," Cherry was saying.

"Yes, it's quite a big to-do," Rachel said. "Next weekend. I came into town early to help with the preparations. We're having a local dinner next Saturday at the Run Deer Run Lodge."

We all nodded, knowing, of course, where that was. It was a local hunting lodge for good old boys, and of course Rich Burkette was a member, although he wasn't quite a good old boy, but definitely liked to hang out with them. Good for business. The lodge also rented out its facilities for wedding receptions and anniversary or birthday parties or in this case, retirement parties.

And of course, none of us at the table with Rachel had been invited. We'd never generated any money for the law firm of Burkette and Trunkel.

"Then on Sunday, we're holding a brunch at the Masonville Country Club for Daddy's clients and friends up there," Rachel went on.

Cherry, Sally, and I exchanged swift glances, then looked away from each other, stifling laughter.

"But before that, of course, on Thursday, we're having Thanksgiving, just Mom, Dad, and me, and of course Lenny," Rachel said.

We all stared at her. She read the confusion on our faces and smiled. "My older brother. Twenty-two years older, to be precise, so he's more like a beloved uncle to me than a brother," she said.

She sighed. "It's the first time I've been back to town since that awful valedictory speech. I don't know what I was thinking. Since then, Mom and Dad have come to visit me, insisting it was too much trouble—with college and my career and all—for me to visit them. We never really said the real reason was because of that speech, but . . ."

She smiled and shrugged. "They couldn't bring Dad's retirement party to me, of course. So I figured it was time to come back and let people see I'm sorry. In fact, I think I'll start now."

And before we could even discuss the wisdom of her actions, she stood up, took the few steps over to Bobby John Sellars and said—loudly enough for everyone in Sandy's to hear—"Mr. Sellars, I just want to apologize to you—to everyone—for any embarrassment I might have caused with my valedictory speech thirteen years ago. I was being young and foolish—I'm sure we all know how kids can be—" She spread her hands and smiled sheepishly, as if it was a common occurrence for valedictorians all across the land to make mean comments about their hometowns—"and of course I'm proud to have grown up in Paradise, Ohio. I tell everyone that the good Midwestern values I learned here . . ."

She glanced at me, as if for guidance. I lifted my eyebrows and did a subtle wrap-it-up gesture by twirling my index fingers around each other, hoping to project the message: stop before you get too corn-pone and cross the line to insulting again.

". . . well, they really mean a lot to me," she said, stumbling to a finish.

Now all eyes were on poor Mr. Sellars. He swallowed a lump of oatmeal, then mumbled, "That's real nice. Um, apology accepted."

There was a scattering of applause before everyone returned to their breakfasts and conversations.

Rachel sat back down with us. "There," she said. "I think that went really well, don't you?" She sounded relieved, as if she'd just checked off a particularly pesky item from her to-do list.

Cherry, Sally, and I all looked at each other—our glances communicating, she thinks it's that simple to set things right? Memories and hurt feelings run deep in a small town. She'd be better off to just let the whole valedictory-speech-gone-bad thing go.

But before we could point that out, Caleb Loudermilk was at our table.

He introduced himself, then said to Rachel, "You're obviously Rich Burkette's daughter—"

"Yes," she said, holding out her hand. Caleb shook it as if he were meeting a dignitary. We all rolled our eyes.

"Well, Ms. Burkette—"

"Rachel's fine," she said.

"Rachel. I'd love to interview you and your father about your father's retirement party and plans . . ."

"Be careful, Rachel," I said. "Caleb thinks he's a big-time investigative reporter."

Cherry giggled. "Yeah. If he can find out anything at all, he'll print it."

"Or if he can imply anything at all—" Sally started.

Rachel turned red. "I assure you our family has nothing to hide about Dad's retirement or anything else," she said to us. Then she looked up at Caleb. "I'd love for you to interview my family and me. I'm sure it would be fine. Say, Friday afternoon?"

Caleb's eyebrows shot up. He was so used to most people telling him to bug off, he was flustered at Rachel's enthusiasm. They arranged the time, exchanged phone numbers, and then Caleb said, "Perfect! In addition, since yours is a leading family in the area, I'd love to get opinions on what's happening with the old orphanage."

"Since my dad is a former county commissioner, I'm not sure it would be appropriate for him to speculate," Rachel said. "Of course, you can ask him, if you like, but don't expect a lot of commentary."

In recent issues of the *Advertiser-Gazette*, Caleb had reported that the Mason County commissioners had been actively looking for investors to purchase the county-owned orphanage—provided they had an innovative plan for the land. The orphanage had sat empty for so many years that most folks had forgotten it was for sale. But with state cuts, the county was desperate for additional funding. So far, though, no one had come forth with an offer or plan . . . except one investment firm. On condition of anonymity, one of the commissioners had shared with Caleb that the investor would attend the commissioners' meeting the fourth Monday in November . . . just a few days after Thanksgiving . . . to share a proposal for "an exciting new plan" for the property.

Of course, everyone in Paradise and Mason County was chattering with speculation about who the investor was and what the plan might be. Everything from the mundane (apartments) to the fanciful (amusement park) had been suggested.

Speculation and gossip are favorite Paradise pastimes.

"Well, our interview will focus mainly on your father's career and retirement plans," Caleb said to Rachel. Then he looked at me. "Josie, how's your column coming?"

Rachel looked at me, impressed. "You have a column?"

"Oh, it's nothing, it's just about stain tips, and . . ."

"And everyone loves it," said Sally. "She just doesn't like to admit it."

"My mother swears by Josie's Stain-Busters columns.

Clips them and puts them up on a bulletin board by her washer," Cherry said.

"I've talked to the manager of Arquette Publishing," Caleb said. "He's interested in talking to you after Thanksgiving about expanding your column to all their regional weekly papers across Ohio. That's nearly thirty, Josie. You could be weekly instead of monthly!"

I shrank down in the booth. "Now, Caleb, I never said I wanted something like that . . ."

He patted me on the shoulder. "Just get your current column in by the Monday after Thanksgiving," he said. "We'll talk about it then." Then he winked at me and sauntered off.

Damn him, I thought. I didn't need the pressure of a weekly column. I was happy with how things were in my life. I didn't want change . . . not with Owen, not with my work life . . .

"Josie, you didn't tell us Caleb is sweet on you," Cherry said.

"What? He's not! He's just . . ."

"I saw those deep brown eyes of his flashing at you," Sally said. "And you have to admit, he's kinda cute."

"Shut up," I hissed. I looked at Rachel. "In case you don't remember, Sally and Cherry are idiots. I already have a boyfriend. A very nice one. He has a PhD. Several, in fact," I added, and immediately regretted it. Why was I trying to impress Rachel?

"Yeah, a boyfriend who is out of town for Thanksgiving," Cherry started.

"Oh, Josie, how awful! And Mama has kept me up on Paradise news, so I know your aunt and uncle have passed on. Why don't you come on over to our house for Thanksgiving?"

I stared at her, thinking . . . what? Why would she want me, practically a stranger, to come to her parents' for Thanksgiving? Did I seem that pathetic?

I admit it. I panicked. I thought, perfect, Rachel's here visiting her perfect parents, and I'm all alone . . . but why should I care what she thought of that? We hadn't been close, years ago. In answer, though, the memory-tease started again, like an out-of-focus photograph. Then it faded, again, before I could figure out what I was trying to remember.

And I heard the following words tumble: "Oh, I'm having dinner with the Toadfern clan," I said. "At my Mamaw's place. You know. Just down from your folks."

Rachel gave me a genuinely happy smile. "Oh, I'm so glad to hear you've reunited with the Toadfern family!"

She knew I'd been estranged?

"Yeah," said Sally. "So am I."

I kicked Sally under the table while keeping a bright smile on my face and my eyes on Rachel.

"Josie, do you think you might have some time Thanksgiving to drop on by? Say, around four-thirty? We'll be having tea and drinks then, before a light meal of leftovers," Rachel said. She looked at Cherry and Sally and added hastily, "you gals, too."

"Oh, thanks, but I'm afraid I have plans for that afternoon," Cherry said.

"My boys will be so tired by then, I'll have to pass," Sally said.

"I'll be there," I said, a little too fast, a little too eagerly.

And Rachel looked immediately relieved. "I'll count on it," she said. She glanced at her watch. "Oh my. I'd better get going. Mama wants me to meet her up at the Masonville Country Club to discuss next

Sunday's brunch menu." She stood up. "This brunch is on me."

We watched her trot over to the register, give Sally a wad of bills, wave away any change, then rush out the door.

I looked at Sally. "Don't start with me."

Sally lifted her eyebrows, all wide-eyed innocence. "Who, me? I'm just so glad you're coming to Mamaw Toadfern's for Thanksgiving. It doesn't matter a bit to me that while the news of Mamaw being near death's door didn't convince you, saving face in front of Miss Perfect did . . ."

I kicked her under the table again. "I said, don't—" I winced as she kicked back, hard.

"Girls, stop it," Cherry said. "The real question is, what does Rachel really want?"

I glared at Cherry. "To catch up on old times, to reconnect with an old friend . . ."

Cherry rolled her eyes. "Oh please. You weren't really buddies with Rachel in high school. Think about it. Everyone thought they were, because Rachel was so nice to everyone, but no one ever, ever really got close. In case you don't recall, she and I were on the cheerleading squad together, and she never went out with any of us, no matter how many times we asked her. She always had some excuse. And she never had any of us over to her house. But she was so perfectly nice to us, we kind of thought of her as being close, but looking back, she wasn't. So, believe you me, she's up to something."

My stomach rolled over my biscuit and gravy, which had suddenly turned into a big lump. I pushed my plate away. Oh, Lord. Cherry, amazingly, was probably right.

"Don't worry, you can tell us all about it next Friday night," Sally said.

I moaned. Why was I so eager to go to Rachel's . . . and, more importantly, just what had I done . . . saying I'd go to Mamaw Toadfern's for Thanksgiving dinner? No way would Sally let me off the hook, now.

4

I don't know how I got to Mamaw Toadfern's bed after I passed out. I reckon that Sally and Mamaw Toadfern somehow got me there, or that I half-awakened long enough for them to help me to her four-poster bed.

In any case, when I came to, I was on Mamaw's bed, under the quilt that Mamaw had been showing me. I vaguely recalled that she'd also been about to share a family secret, just when Sally burst in to say that the couple that'd just careened up to Mamaw's house in a red sports car were actually my parents. Mama and Daddy . . . together.

I closed my eyes and moaned, half-hoping I'd pass back out again. I didn't. I snuggled back down under the quilt. Truth be told, its warmth—even with its faint scent of Youth Dew, even though it was forevermore stained with my ancient erp of eggplant—was comforting to me.

Still, I could hear distant chatter and dinner noises

and knew that just below me, the Toadfern clan was gathered, sharing Thanksgiving dinner.

And I was, after all, alone. And hungry. And feeling very, very sorry for myself.

Not to mention a little nervous.

After all, my parents were probably down there, too. Unless, I thought hopefully, they'd turned around and left again.

I crawled out of bed, stood still a minute to test for dizziness, and feeling none, went over to the window and peeked out.

Sure enough, there it was—the bright red sports car, its nose plowed into the nose of the motor home. The two vehicles were stuck together in a V, like some strange sports car/motor home hybrid. Would that be a motor coupe? A sports RV?

I was letting my thoughts blither as a distraction to the situation, and I knew it.

My parents.

What did I know of them? Uncle Horace never said anything at all about his much younger sister, my mama. I sensed, in the way children know such things, that she was a forbidden topic with him.

So I'd asked my Aunt Clara to tell me what she knew about my parents just once, while we were hanging laundry out on the backyard line. And all she'd said, while snapping a damp sheet to the line, was that my parents were each troubled young people when they ran off. Considering I was about twelve when I asked, I was very confused by the word "young" as a description of my AWOL parents. Then Aunt Clara said that she and Uncle Horace gave thanks to the good Lord every day for me.

After a comment like that, it seemed uncharitable to

ask more questions about my birth parents—even though I was curious and sometimes wanted to.

Much later, after Uncle Horace and Aunt Clara died, I sorted through their things and found a few pictures of my mama and Uncle Horace, from when they were kids. They looked like just average, happy kids—he about seventeen, with a protective arm around his little sister, about five.

The photo made me realize I didn't know a thing about their childhood or about my maternal grandparents.

As for my daddy's side, well, I've already made clear that—with a few happy exceptions such as Sally—my paternal kin had cast me aside at Mamaw's behest until that particular Thanksgiving dinner.

So there I was, up in my Mamaw's bedroom, knowing I should go on down and meet my parents, but feeling stuck, rooted to the floor. Maybe, I thought, if I could remember something, anything about them, that might help us get beyond, "how do you do." Saying "it's so nice to meet you" to one's own parents seemed more than a little strange.

Here's what I remembered about my mama.

When she watered the pots of flowers around our trailer, she'd use the special hose that connected to the kitchen spigot, run the hose out through the tiny kitchen window, then holler at me to turn on the tap. I'd wait for her holler on tiptoes, my eager body bent over the porcelain, rust-spotted sink, my hand at the ready on the spigot.

But sometimes she'd get to talking with Mrs. Arrowood—usually about *that* damned man, or *this* damned man (Mrs. Arrowood, despite the Mrs. and her six kids, was also without a damned man)—and by the time she'd recollect she needed to holler at me, my calves would be cramping. But then, at last—or sometimes right off—Mama's holler would spill into the kitchen and I'd turn on the spigot.

Then I'd run outside and she'd have her forefinger right over the end of the hose, to make the water spray out. This made it look like the water was coming out of the tip of Mama's finger. I liked that. It made her look powerful. Mama, the source of life-giving water.

And I think she liked it, too, because she'd hum, and forget herself, and spray the flower pots until they ran over with dirty water into our scrap of scrabbly yard that remained indifferent to greening up, no matter how much water it got.

And I remember that there was a wishing well at the entrance to Happy Trails. And if Mama was in a good mood, she'd give me a coin from a small, felt bag the color of goldenrod, and tell me to take the coin to the well and "wish us something good, Josie." I'd run to the well, trying to think of something good, and offer up the coin to the well along with my wish, which always felt more like a prayer.

And I remember the night of the fire. She'd hung out our clothes, on the clothesline that ran between our trailer and Mrs. Arrowood's. On the line were jeans and socks and graying white bras and you couldn't really tell where our clothes ended and the Arrowoods' began unless you knew that Mrs. Arrowood was much bigger chested than Mama.

That night, we'd come home in a hurry, no stopping at the wishing well. The flowers had dried, nearly dead but not quite, in their pots, and I thought about telling Mama we needed to water them, but something had put her in a tight-lipped, angry mood, and I didn't dare talk to her.

As it turned out, it wouldn't have mattered, anyway. The flowers and the clothes were all destroyed in the fire. After that, we stayed for a little while at the home of the then police chief and his wife, who took us in as a charity case. Then Mama disappeared one morning.

Here's what I remember about my daddy.

Nothing, except his scent, which was of Lava Soap.

I didn't know this, though, until just a few years ago. There was a sale at Big Sam's on Lava Soap—twenty-four-pack for the price of the twelve-pack. I bought it just because it was cheap and twenty-four packs of soap would last me a good long time. And when I opened the first bar, and the scent filled my bathroom, I thought "Daddy," and I stared in surprise for a long time at the gray soap bar, realizing that my daddy must have smelled like this soap, that maybe he'd showered with it after work, and then after his shower, he must have—might have, could have—scooped me up in a bear hug, pressing my face to his neck. But I didn't know that. I didn't remember it. I just made it up to fit the fact that the smell of Lava Soap made me think "Daddy." I was two, after all, when that damned man left.

I threw away the opened bar of soap and donated the other bars to Stillwater.

These were the sum of the memories I had of my mama and my daddy.

And, I realized, my eyes pricking, I didn't want those memories demolished by reality. It was hard to imagine the woman in the red sports car humming while watering flowers by a trailer, or the man smelling of something so ordinary as Lava Soap.

Before I knew it, I was fishing in the pocket of my khaki pants for my cell phone. I never go anywhere without it, and always have it close, on account of Guy, my cousin with autism at Stillwater.

I dialed Owen's cell phone number.

It rang a few times. Right, I thought. He probably doesn't have the phone with him. Knowing Owen, I thought with a sudden pang of longing, his cell phone is probably tossed on his hotel bed, while he's at his ex's for Thanksgiving dinner with his son.

Probably, I thought, he was also having an awkward time—long silences, unsure what to say, in the midst of his own family reunion with his son—so it was just as well he'd left his cell phone in his hotel room, so he wouldn't have the extra awkwardness of answering the phone, and really, I didn't need his comfort and encouragement just to go downstairs and meet my own mama and daddy . . .

Owen answered, third ring. "Hello?" He was breathless, laughing, giddy.

"Hey, Dad, wait'll you hear this next knock-knock joke!" I heard a young boy's voice. That would be his son, Zachariah.

"Wait until your dad's off the phone. It's probably important." That had to be Tori, his ex-wife. She was laughing, giddy, breathless, also. As if they'd all just had a rip-roaring good time with knock-knock jokes and a tickle fight.

My heart clenched.

"Oh, right," I heard Owen say, his voice a little more distant. I could imagine him holding the phone away, to address Zachariah and Tori. "Nobody more important than the two of you today."

"Hello?" he said into the phone, a note of irritation creeping into his voice.

"Tell 'em a knock-knock joke, Dad, maybe that'll get them to answer!"

More laughter. Then Owen, again, "Knock, knock . . ."

I disconnected, flipped my cell phone closed, tucked it back in my pocket. I squeezed my eyes tightly shut for a moment, telling myself, no . . . no tears.

I heard the voices, downstairs.

I had choices, I thought. I could nudge open Mamaw's bedroom window, jump out into the snow-covered junipers, and then—assuming I didn't break anything—take off, without so much as ta-ta, just like my mama and daddy had done.

I could curl up under the quilt and hide.

Or, I could satisfy my growing curiosity and go meet my mama and daddy for the first time in decades. Well, for the first time, really, in a way.

No wonder my nickname's Nosey Josie. Curiosity always wins out with me.

I opened the door, and stepped out to the top of the stairs.

5

Mamaw Toadfern's Thanksgiving table stretched all the way from the window at the front of her dining room, clear on into the kitchen.

Truth be told, her table was really her dining table adjoined on either end by several card tables of varying heights and surrounded by all manner of chairs—dining and folding and even lawn.

Even so, it looked like a Norman Rockwell Thanksgiving scene . . . at least, Toadfern style.

The tables were covered by various holiday-themed plastic tablecloths, some dotted with fall leaves, some with turkeys, in a dizzying patchwork of yellows, oranges, browns, and greens. An impressive collection of holiday candleholders graced the table. I was immediately taken with the set of him-and-her Pilgrim candleholders, with bright orange candles sticking out of the tops of their little Pilgrim hats.

And in between all the serving dishes of sweet potatoes and green bean casserole and corn and stuffing and cranberries and rolls and turkey and mashed potatoes and gravy were a scattering of at least two dozen pine-cone-and-construction-paper turkeys. These were, I realized, made in the school years of Mamaw's children and grandchildren and even great-grandchildren.

Of course, I was focusing on what was on the table because I wasn't as ready as I'd thought I was to focus on the people around the table. My Mamaw. My uncles, aunts, and cousins. My . . . parents.

At the head of the table—the end where I stood, feeling more than a little awkward, sat Mamaw. At the opposite end, disappearing into the kitchen, was Uncle Otis and his descendents, Sally and her four brothers—Manny, Leo, Clarence, and Otis Jr., and their wives and kids, seventeen in all. The table, I realized, made a left turn at the kitchen entry. I could hear Sally and her siblings and children all fussing at each other in the kitchen.

I wished I could just turn around, dash through the tiny foyer, through the living room, and into the kitchen through the other entrance. Even as Sally hollered, "Harry, put that gravy spoon down! Stop aiming it at Barry!" I thought about making a break for it. Only Uncle Otis, from his part of the Toadfern clan, was on the dining room side of the table. Uncle Otis was the oldest of Mamaw's four sons, widowed, and generally considered the family goof, Sally had said, not seeming to mind the assessment of her own father. Given that I'd helped her the previous summer get him out of a ginseng-poaching pickle—and that's a whole other story—I understood why and how she'd come to accept her daddy for the strange, lovable oaf that he was.

He tilted his chair back so far I felt sure he'd fall over backward sooner or later, and clasped his beefy hands over his ample belly, which made the buttons on his flannel shirt bulge ominously. He stared at me as if he wondered what I was doing there. I'm not sure, Uncle Otis, I thought.

Next were Uncle Randolph and Aunt Suzy, and two of their children—Bennie and Fern. (Billy, the only cousin besides Sally to pay attention to me despite Mamaw's warnings, lives in New York.) Uncle Randolph was skinny opposite to Uncle Otis. He looked a bit lost in his too-large dress shirt while Aunt Suzy gazed around with an air of faint disapproval for her husband's family. Fern's husband, Roger, and their son, Albert, sat next to Bennie and Fern. Albert, who was about seven, was happily picking his nose even as his mother swatted at his hand and glared at him. I feared for Albert making it to age eight, but he was the only one who looked happy in that branch of the Toadfern clan.

Then there were two people I hadn't met yet—Uncle Fenwick and Aunt Nora, I guessed, from descriptions Sally had given me. They'd never had kids. Aunt Nora was a thin, birdlike woman, who twitched and had a long, wattled neck, buggy eyes, and a teased-up tuft of hair for her do, giving her an unfortunate resemblance to the appliquéd turkeys on her sweater. Uncle Fenwick was paunchy, balding, dressed in a nice pale blue Oxford shirt, and looked as though he'd really like to stab something—or someone—with his fork.

Maybe, I thought, his twin brother, right next to him. Daddy. Fit and handsome in an expensive-looking gray suit, sporting a gold watch and cuff links, and a tanning-booth tan. He was balding in exactly the same pattern as Uncle Fenwick, but he hadn't tried to disguise it with an extreme comb-over or hide the gray with coloring. His salt-and-pepper hair was neatly trimmed and looked distinguished.

Next to him was a woman. Mama. Matching shade of tan, a honey-blond coif, artfully done makeup, long perfect red nails, and a knit teal suit with cream trim and gold anchor buttons.

They no more resembled what I'd have envisioned my parents to be like than the him-and-her Pilgrims with the orange candles in their heads. Not that I'd actually wasted any time envisioning my parents. I'd always thought of Aunt Clara and Uncle Horace as my parents, in spirit anyway, and besides, I'd always somehow known that my birth parents were never coming back.

And yet—here they were. And they were staring at me, along with all the other relatives I just described (except, of course, Sally and her siblings who were, lucky them, in the kitchen).

What could I say? I opened my mouth, hoping something reasonable would come out, when Sally popped out of the kitchen, carrying a plate.

"Josie!" she cried. "You okay? You came to and seemed fine, but you said you wanted to rest. I was getting right worried about you! But here, I've saved you a plate."

I grinned at her gratefully, but my smile quickly faded as she sat the plate between my daddy and Uncle Fenwick. Until then, I hadn't noticed the chair wedged between their seats.

My parents stood up. The perfect couple. The perfect parents—at least in the looks department—as if I'd gone to a rent-a-parent shop and said, them! I'll take that elegant pair who looks so nice and wealthy and sophisticated . . . never mind that I don't resemble them at all in style or fashion or . . .

But did I see a bit of my eyes in Daddy's flashing blue gaze?

A bit of my smile in Mama's soft grin?

"Well, do look at her, Henry! Why our baby girl's just all grown up!" Mama exclaimed, breaking my brief moment of reverie.

What was with the "our baby girl's grown up" line? That was the kind of thing doting parents said when their child returned from, say, a semester at college, or a job across the country. Of course I'd grown up! What did they think had happened to me in the two-plus decades since they'd seen me?

I was about to grab my plate and zip around through the living room to the kitchen, when they both moved at once, and somehow embraced me in a sandwich hug.

"Awww, ain't that sweet?" I heard Mamaw snuffling, even as I gasped for breath between my parents, nearly overcome by Mama's patchouli fragrance and Daddy's aftershave, which didn't smell at all like Lava Soap. "It's just so great to have the whole family together—well, except Billy, of course—all my sons back together for the first time in years! It's such a nice surprise!"

I frowned. There was just something too glib about how Mamaw said that last sentence. Had she been surprised by my parents' return . . . really?

"Now, now, let the girl go," Sally was saying. "Let her eat!"

And so I found myself, a few seconds later, staring at a plate heaped with Thanksgiving food, sitting between Daddy and Uncle Fenwick, and across from Mama and Aunt Nora, and realizing that everyone else was on pumpkin pie and whipped cream.

"We'll wait for you to get started, Josie," Mamaw urged. "Right, everyone?"

Uncle Fenwick, who sat across from me, had a forkful of pumpkin pie just to his lips. He dropped the fork with a clatter back on his plate. Aunt Nora jumped, and one of the turkeys on her sweater suddenly lit up. I stared at her chest. I hadn't noticed before, but the largest turkey, right in the center, had tiny lights—red, yellow, and orange—around the feathers.

I felt light-headed again. "Oh, no, that's okay," I said.

The table went quiet again.

"No one ever argues with Mamaw Toadfern," said cousin Fern, hmmphing.

Unfortunately for her, she said it just as Sally was scooching along behind her, back to the kitchen to check on her kids, who were hollering something about one of their cousins drinking all the Big Fizz Cola. Sally swatted Fern on top of the head. "Well, Josie's just now rejoined the family, so cut her some slack," Sally said. Then she looked at me. "Eat," she said.

I started to cut into my turkey. Unfortunately, my place was right where two tables came together unevenly, and I didn't have enough space on either side for my plate. So as I cut . . . and cut some more . . . well, sawed, really . . . into the turkey . . . my plate wobbled up and down. My mashed potatoes and gravy slid dangerously to the edge of my plate as I kept sawing turkey.

"I reckon it's a little dry this year," Mamaw sighed.

She was right, I thought, as I finally finished cutting a piece and started chewing. This turkey was drier than the construction paper turkeys gracing the center of the table—and probably less tasty. If I could get down this bite, maybe I could dip the next one into gravy . . .

"Oh, no it's perfectly fine," said Aunt Nora. "I didn't even need gravy on mine."

So no dipping the turkey into gravy to moisten it up. I chewed. Everyone stared at me. Oh, Lord. They were awaiting their pumpkin pie, and I had a whole mound of food to plow through!

I chewed some more. The lump of turkey in my mouth seemed to get bigger . . . and drier. Mamaw smiled at me encouragingly.

I smiled—mouth closed, of course—and kept chewing. Now Uncle Fenwick, across the table from me, got a knowing look on his face. Aunt Nora started fiddling with a feather of the turkey on her sweater. The wattle of the turkey on her sweater flashed red. The turkey in my mouth seemed to just get bigger.

Mama gazed at me. "Look, dear," she said to Daddy. "Josie has my hair. The texture, at least. Not the style."

"But she has my eyes," he said, proudly.

I suddenly felt like I was two.

I stared straight ahead. That didn't help, because I was staring right into the turkey carcass.

"It was a beauty," Mamaw said. It took me a second to realize she was talking to me, about the turkey. "I always boil down the carcass, for soup. And save the wishbone, for two people I pick to pull. Whoever gets the longest piece gets a wish."

I looked at Mamaw. This description of her plans for the poor turkey's carcass wasn't helping me. I kept chewing, chewing, chewing. Mamaw's smile took a downturn toward grimness.

I had to swallow. Did any of these people know the Heimlich, I wondered? Would any of them use it on me if I choked on Mamaw's turkey?

Finally, I swallowed. I smiled at Mamaw. "Excellent," I said. "Best turkey I ever had."

Several folks, looking relieved, started on pie.

She grinned, obviously pleased. "Well, finish that up and you can have seconds!"

I managed not to groan as I eyed my plate. The cranberry salad looked moist. Maybe that would wet my throat enough so that I could take another bite of Mamaw's dry turkey. That would be better than immediately gulping down half the water in my glass.

I took a bite of the cranberry salad. Hmm. This was actually good. A mixture of Jell-O, cranberries, pecan bits . . .

"Any boyfriends I should know about?"

I looked at my daddy. Had he really just asked that? He was grinning at me, apparently eager for the answer.

"Actually, I'm dating a professor. He's quite a catch," I said, with a preening tone.

Fern harrumphed. My face went hot. What had Sally said about me . . . and my rocky relationship with Owen . . . to our only other girl cousin? Not that I could imagine her confiding in Fern, but . . .

"Really. So where is he? I ought to meet this fella, if you're so serious about him," Daddy said.

What? Who was he to make such a comment?

Mamaw giggled. Everyone else ate pumpkin pie quietly. The silence grew uncomfortable.

"He's out of town on business," I finally said.

"Now, Henry, don't be ridiculous," Mama said.

Thank you, I thought. At least one of my parents was apparently going to be sensible about this whole, awkward reunion . . .

"She doesn't need to get saddled down with a man at

her age. She has plenty of time for that. She should focus on developing a career," she said. "Sell off that old laundromat."

I bristled. "I like my laundromat," I said. "It provides a steady enough income for me, a service for the community . . ."

"Oh, you don't have to be nice just because my big brother once owned it," Mama said, in a pooh-poohing tone. "It's time you sold that place—let people drive up to Masonville to do their wash like I used to do— have a real career."

"I do have a real career," I said, through gritted teeth. What was this? I'd skipped from age two right into the they-nag-you-because-they-care part my friends complained about. "I'm a stain expert."

Now Fern giggled. Her mother, Aunt Suzy, elbowed her, into silence.

"I am," I said defensively. "I even have a monthly column in the local paper, which is going weekly throughout southern Ohio soon."

Oh, crap. Now, why had I said that? I hadn't really agreed to that. And yet, here I was, trying to show off in front of the Toadferns, just like I'd tried to show off in front of Rachel Burkette at Sandy's Restaurant.

Sally popped her head through the entry. "I heard that," she said. "It's a great idea, isn't it, everyone?"

There were uncomfortable murmurs of agreement. Sally popped back into the kitchen.

"Well, maybe that will be enough to get you out of this backwater and somewhere important," Daddy said. "No offense, of course, to everyone who's stayed around here."

He grinned across the table at Uncle Fenwick, who glared at him.

"I like it here," I said. "You may have forgotten, but my cousin Guy Foersthoefel lives in a residential home near here . . ."

"It's nice to see," said Uncle Fenwick, wiping his mouth with exaggerated care, so hard that the paper napkin started to shred, "that amazingly enough the loyalty gene didn't skip Josie, after all."

"Still feeling loyal to the plumbing business?" Daddy asked.

"I've done well enough for myself. We have a nice house up in Masonville," Uncle Fenwick said stiffly.

"Wow. Sticking it out in the plumbing business got you all the way up to Masonville. Guess you don't remember the days when you said you couldn't wait to see the world and have some adventures," Daddy said.

Aunt Nora coughed nervously. Uncle Fenwick tossed his paper napkin dangerously close to the female Pilgrim candleholder. "You can't even get through one hour—after we haven't seen you for how many years—without starting. You always did think you were better than me!"

"Now, Fenwick, you shouldn't hold it against your brother that he's finally successful, financially. You look like you're doing well enough." Mama reached across the table and patted his arm, dropping her head slightly to look up at him from under her thick, dark eyelashes. "In fact I'd say you're still a fine figure of a man . . ."

"May!" Daddy snapped.

Mama snatched her hand back, but still smiled flirtatiously at Uncle Fenwick, who turned red.

Aunt Nora moaned and grabbed Uncle Fenwick's arm where Mama had touched him. "Please, no . . ."

Mamaw frowned at Mama, who just shrugged and stopped smiling. I lifted an eyebrow. Hmm. This was interesting. Apparently, there was some history I didn't know about.

I took another bite of the delicious cranberry salad. Better to concentrate on that, I thought. Something about it was different . . . that wasn't, couldn't be . . . bourbon in there, could it? In any case, it was yummy . . .

A loud snore startled me. I looked down at the end of the table and saw that Uncle Otis, still tilting back dangerously in his chair, had fallen asleep, his mouth hanging open.

"My dear Billy's not here," said Aunt Suzy, her voice trembling.

"Thank God," said Bennie. "He'd probably embarrass us all." He scowled. "Just like he did in school."

His mother, Suzy, burst into tears. "I miss Billy!" she wailed.

"At least you have kids," Aunt Nora said. "We were never able to have any." She looked at Uncle Fenwick, as if perhaps this was his fault.

I forked up some potatoes and nearly toppled the plate on the wobbly seam between the two tables. The second the potatoes hit my tongue, I nearly blanched. They were oversalted and underwhipped. Stick to the cranberry sauce.

"Now, dear, it was the Lord's will," Uncle Randolph said. "Everyone, perhaps we should have another prayer to calm us down. We need to settle our minds for the Lord's second coming. The time is upon us, I fear, considering the news from the Middle East . . ."

"Randy, you haven't changed a bit," Daddy said, laughing. "You always were so pompously righteous . . ."

"And we should think you've changed?" Uncle Fenwick said. "You and May—all fancied up as if you're successful—"

"That's because we are, dear," said Mama, again with a flirtatious tone.

Uncle Fenwick turned even redder. "Oh really? You're successful now? Prove it!"

"Quite simple," said Daddy, calmly. "We came back not just to reunite with our dear family—" he gestured to us all.

Fern rolled her eyes. Her husband Roger looked at her desperately. "You said it wouldn't be like this this year," he hissed. Their son, Albert . . . he would be my first cousin once removed, I calculated quickly . . . started hiccuping and whining to go into the kitchen with the other kids. I didn't blame him.

I lifted my other eyebrow, and took another bite of the heavenly cranberry salad. What had I been missing all these years?

"You know, a little prayer would have gone a long way to help you and Fenwick with your terrible sin of fighting," Uncle Randolph said. "You two always thought you could get away with everything and when you couldn't, you'd just blame each other."

Uncle Otis suddenly jolted awake as his chair started to tip too far back. "Is there a fight going on?" Uncle Otis rubbed his eyes, and looked confused.

"Go back to sleep, Daddy," Sally hollered from the kitchen. "And stop tilting your chair."

Uncle Otis just shrugged, tilted back again, and closed his eyes.

"Is he drunk?" Aunt Suzy whispered to her husband. She nervously took a sip of her iced sweet tea.

"Of course not," Sally called, sounding annoyed.

I grinned. Good old Sally. She had the loyalty gene in spades, too.

"We came back," Mama said, as if that line of conversation hadn't been hopelessly derailed, "for a business proposition."

"Oh, right, like the two of you would have any money for such a thing," Uncle Fenwick said.

Daddy lifted his eyebrows. Now I knew where I got that gesture. I immediately lowered mine. "And I suppose you're getting rich, cleaning out other people's potties?"

"Yes," Mama said, raising her voice. "We're going to buy the old orphanage!"

I gasped, and looked at her. The Mason County Children's Home, just on the other side of the Burkettes' acreage, had sat empty for years. And now, my parents were going to purchase it?

"At least I've worked hard for a living! You thief!" Uncle Fenwick hollered at Daddy. "You were supposed to share!"

Huh? What was *that* all about? Everyone else— except Mama, Daddy, and Aunt Nora—looked confused, too.

Aunt Nora moaned, clutched at her throat. Her chest turkey's gobble flashed red again.

"FleaMart. It's the latest concept in flea market marketing," said Mama, somewhat weakly. I could tell she'd meant her announcement to be triumphant, and was more than a little annoyed that the fight between Daddy and Uncle Fenwick was ruining her grand announcement. "And Henry and I came up with it. Instead of the standard flea market, organized by vendor, you have departments, organized by type of flea market find. All the antique lamps in the lighting fixtures department, for example, or the linens in the linens department. Vendors bring their items to us, sell them to us at a reduced price, and we do any refurbishing needed, and re-sell. We have investors and our first FleaMart down in Benton, Arkansas, and it's been quite successful, so when we learned through our real estate broker that the old orphanage was up for sale, we jumped at the chance."

I stared at Mama, horrified. About a quarter of the businesses in Paradise are antique stores. And some of the owners are my best customers, and friends. I help them get old linens and vintage clothing stain-free for re-sale. This FleaMart could easily put them out of business.

"You're . . . you're the ones who are trying to buy the old orphanage?" I asked.

"We learned about the opportunity from our real estate broker, who also happens to be from here. Rachel Burkette."

I stared in amazement. How did Rachel know my parents? Hadn't she said she lived in Atlanta . . . but Mama had just said she and Daddy had opened a FleaMart in Arkansas. Where had my parents been all these years? How had they found each other? And how had they connected up with Rachel?

But I didn't have time to ask the questions. Uncle Fenwick was saying again, this time in a low, dangerous voice, his face red, his words grating out between his teeth, "You were supposed to share, Henry . . ."

"Now, boys, don't start," Mamaw said.

"Oh, my, this is great cranberry salad, Aunt Nora," I said. "I'd love the recipe!"

The whole table . . . the whole house . . . went still. Even my parents stared at me in horror.

Uncle Fenwick grinned, meanly. "Like father, like daughter. Wanting to take what's not rightfully hers . . . A thief."

"Now, Fenwick," started Uncle Randolph. "Josie couldn't possibly know that Nora's recipe is top secret. Really, we should all pray for forgiveness. I'll lead us. Dear Lord, please shine your love down upon—"

"That's right," said Daddy, "Josie couldn't know, could she, because you all cut her off—"

I looked at him. What? He didn't really have any right to accuse . . .

"You're the one who abandoned her!" said Uncle Fenwick.

"I really miss Billy," cooed Aunt Suzy.

"Shut up, Mama," said Bennie.

"That's no way to talk to our mama!" Fern said, smacking her brother in the arm.

"I'm sorry," I said. "I didn't mean to ask for Aunt Nora's recipe, if it's secret. It's just it's so good . . ."

Aunt Nora clutched her chest and the turkey flashed frantically. "My recipe certainly is a secret! I keep it in a bank safety box. Only Fenwick and our attorney know where the box is and I get the recipe out just once a year at Thanksgiving . . ."

I stared at her.

Sally popped out from the dining room again. "Anyone want seconds on pie?" She stared down at our end of the table, assessed the situation, and flashed me a sympathetic look. "Oh. Never mind." Uncle Otis was still snoozing through all this, even as he tilted dangerously back in his chair. Sally gently tipped his chair so it was fully back on the floor, and retreated into the kitchen, where we heard her holler, "Manny, put Harry down! If you keep swinging him like that, you'll make him puke!"

Which should have been enough to break the tension at our end of the table, but Uncle Fenwick pointed at Daddy, and said, "I stand by what I said before. You're a thief and you took off with everything!" Now everyone looked confused. "If you'd shared like you were supposed to, I wouldn't have been stuck all these years cleaning other people's messes! I hate the plumbing business!"

Aunt Nora looked hurt. "But Fenwick, I thought you loved it. It's been good to us. It got us that nice RV . . ."

"Which he ruined!"

"You weren't looking where you were going," Daddy said. "Just like always."

"What?! You . . . you bastard!"

Uncle Fenwick didn't seem to realize that by calling his twin brother a bastard, he was calling himself one, too. Mamaw gasped and glowered at her sons.

"I should kill you for that! I ought to kill you," Fenwick went on.

Daddy stood. "Think you're enough of a man to? What are you going to do . . . shoot me with your hunting rifle? Stab me with a hunting knife?"

Suddenly, he whipped something out of a pocket inside his jacket. It was a hunting knife, I realized, with a staghorn handle. The blade, which looked to be about five inches long, was thankfully covered in leather.

"I have a whole set of these vintage knives out in my sports car, which *you* hit. The knives were supposed to be gifts to all the men in the family when we go hunting tomorrow—"

"We brought vintage hankies for the ladies," Mama

piped up, but Daddy went on as if he hadn't heard her: "—but if you want to have it out now, we can, although I'm warning you, I'd be glad to cut you down dead faster than . . ."

"Really, this is *great* cranberry salad," I half said, half hollered, desperately hoping to stop this ugliness. But I came down too hard with my spoon, just on the side of the plate that was tipped on the higher table, and turned my plate into a catapult that launched a glob of cranberry salad right onto Uncle Fenwick's chest.

The whole table went quiet again.

After a second, Aunt Nora clutched her chest, making her turkey's waddle flash red frantically. "That's . . . that's his favorite shirt . . ."

"Oh, I'm so sorry, Uncle Fenwick," I said, meaning it. "I know how to get that out . . . I really am a stain expert . . ." I dipped my paper napkin into my water glass and reach for his chest. First, scoop off as much as possible. "Let's see . . . the cranberry's both a fruit and sugar stain . . ."

Uncle Fenwick swatted my hand away. He grabbed his own napkin, and in so doing, grabbed up one of the paper turkeys.

"Hey," Daddy said, apparently forgetting their mutual death threats. "That one was mine! I made it in third grade!"

Uncle Fenwick stood up. "I've had enough!" He tossed down the napkin and pine cone/construction paper turkey, and unfortunately, they landed on the he-version of the Pilgrim candleholder. The pine cone turkey knocked over the boy Pilgrim, right onto the turkey carcass, which, dry as it was, immediately flared. Then the turkey grease at the bottom of the serving plate went up in flames.

"My carcass! My carcass! For the soup!" shrieked Mamaw.

"I'll take care of it!" Aunt Suzy tossed the contents of her glass onto the flame, but the flame surged and caught on the tablecloth.

"My, my, I thought she just had iced tea. Was that alcohol in her glass?" Mama asked primly.

"My carcass! My carcass!" Mamaw kept shrieking.

"Water, everyone, just toss water!" Fern hollered.

Wow, I thought. From Norman Rockwell Thanksgiving scene, to flaming turkey carcass and family hollering, in less than twenty minutes.

Still, I tossed my glass of water onto the flaming table. Everyone else did, too, except Uncle Fenwick and Daddy, who just glared at each other.

And that's how I left the Toadfern Thanksgiving dinner, with most everyone pouring water on the flaming turkey carcass.

They seemed to have the flames under control.

Plus I was due to visit the Burkettes next door.

And, truth be told, I just wanted to get away from my family on Thanksgiving.

I've been told, since then, that that's not an uncommon impulse.

6

After I left Mamaw Toadfern's, I realized that I still had about two hours before I was supposed to arrive at the Burkette's at four-thirty.

I didn't think showing up that early would impress the Burkettes, which, to both my chagrin and surprise, I found I wanted to do.

The afternoon was so beautiful—the sky a shade of blue that somehow looked cold, the snow-covered fields sparkling—that I thought about taking a walk along the old towpath that ran behind the Toadfern and Burkette properties as well as the old orphanage. The bike/hike trail followed along where a canal once ran . . . and then a train line . . . and a telegraph line. Some of the old telegraph poles still stood, but the train and canal lines were long gone, converted by the county into a recreational path.

I loved to bike or hike on it in the warmer months, starting at the little canal museum just outside of Paradise, where there was a convenient way to access the path. I usually managed to stick out fifteen miles, because at that point was Gratis, a town even tinier than Paradise, and boasting one sole industry: a wonderful ice cream parlor that catered to towpath hiker/bikers.

But, of course, in November that parlor would be closed. Not many people would want to hike in that weather, as beautiful as it was, especially with the report that another snow and ice storm was on its way. Plus, I didn't have the proper boots with me.

I went back to my apartment instead. I thought about calling Owen again, and then thought better of it. Let him call *me*, I thought.

Then I considered the wisdom of roasting a turkey breast in my oven while I was at the Burkette's. My oven had never given me any problems. On the other hand . . .

I shrugged off my worries. I hadn't had a real Thanksgiving dinner at Mamaw Toadfern's. I didn't really want to stay at the Burkette's and dine on their leftovers for the evening meal. And I was feeling a wee bit sorry for myself.

So I occupied my time in preparing the turkey to roast, popping it in my oven, and setting out a few other items from my cabinet for side dishes. So the potatoes would be instant, the gravy from a jar, the green beans and cranberry sauce from cans.

That made me think about Aunt Nora's wonderful cranberry relish, and the cranberry stain in Uncle Randolph's shirt, and I started to feel even sorrier for myself.

Defiantly, I set my table with a blue Fiestaware plate that I'd just acquired at the McNally estate sale, and stuck a yellow candle in one of my only slightly chipped Candlewick candleholders (purchased at the

Antique Depot), and even added a vintage linen napkin to the setting. So there. I didn't need Owen or the silly Toadferns to have a wonderful Thanksgiving. Right?

I'd already had a great time with Guy, whom I'd see again the next day at the mysterious meeting at Still-water, and I'd have a quick maybe half-hour visit with the Burkettes, and then I'd come home to my cozy apartment and have a wonderful dinner for one and curl up with a book and never have to deal with my parents or the Toadferns or my strange feelings of wanting to impress the Burkettes again. A few days later, Owen would be back, and we'd work things out.

That, at least, is what I told myself my future held, as I left my apartment, already wonderfully scented from the roasting turkey, and headed out to the Burkettes.

Hey. We're all allowed an occasional fantasy.

Rachel answered the door before I even stopped knocking.

"Josie! I'm so glad you're here!" She sounded posi-tively relieved.

She took my coat and hung it on a beautiful antique coat tree, then ushered me into the living room.

This was like a surreal alternate reality to the scene I'd left a few hours earlier at the Toadferns'. The layout to the farmhouse was basically the same, but the living and dining rooms were filled with expensive furniture.

I could see through the living room to the din-ing room, and the mahogany table covered with care-fully stacked china, ready for the corner hutch, and surrounded with matching chairs. There were no pinecone-and-construction-paper turkeys or Pilgrim candleholders. Just one centerpiece—an elaborate florist's arrangement of flowers in fall colors.

There had been no flaming turkey carcasses at their dinner, I was certain. For one thing, the house didn't smell of singed meat and grease.

Instead, the living room was pungent and toasty from the blaze in the fireplace, around which the family members sat serenely.

Effie sat on the couch, working on a needlepoint project. She was, I quickly calculated, probably seventeen years or so older than my mama, but she looked just as young. She, like my mama, had made an effort to dress in a more sophisticated way than you'd expect in Paradise—even at Thanksgiving—but somehow the tweed suit and careful makeup and carefully curled bouffant looked natural on her. Compared to Effie, the style on my mama looked like something she was just trying on for dress up.

Rich Burkette, still decked out in a suit and tie, sat next to his wife on the couch. He looked up from a book he was reading—a Lincoln biography, I noted from the title.

Another man—Rachel's much older half-brother Lenny, I guessed—sat apart from everyone else in an overstuffed leather chair. His tie was loose and he stared into the fire as if it were a portal to another world.

Now this—other than Lenny's distant gaze—really was a Norman Rockwell tableau, and it should have impressed me, but instead I felt . . . sad. Not out of a shoulda-known-the-Burkettes-would-outclass-the-Toadferns jealousy, which kind of surprised me. But because, somehow, the scene seemed empty. Like maybe it just needed a pinecone turkey or two to spruce up the utter perfection into something a little more real. I could understand Lenny's impulse to try to gaze away.

I tugged at my somewhat short brown corduroy skirt—a hand-me-over from Cherry—and worried that my cream poly-cotton turtleneck was too casual next to Rachel and Effie's cashmere.

At least, I thought, stains were easier to get out of poly-cotton . . .

"Mama, Daddy . . . you know Josie Toadfern, of course," Rachel said nervously.

Simultaneously, Rich put his book down on his lap, and Effie put her needlepoint on her lap. Then they looked at me as if I'd just teleported in from Mars. We knew of each other, of course. But even in a town with a population of just under three thousand, there are divisions. The Burkettes were from the small division that never had occasion to visit my laundromat—not even to wash throw rugs or comforters.

Rachel then said, "Josie, did you ever meet Lenny?"

"I moved to Indianapolis when she was seven," Lenny said.

My eyebrows went up at that. He knew my life that well? That seemed odd, and a little creepy . . . then I recollected that my daddy also had an eyebrow-lifting gesture. I lowered my eyebrows.

"You look so much like your mother did when she was younger," Lenny said, staring at me. He was a rather small, gently featured man, but there was something both compelling and piercing about his eyes. "Although she was prettier . . ."

"Lenny and your mother were friends—just friends—back in high school." I jumped, looked at Effie Burkette. She was a petite, thin woman, her face tense, her neck a bit stringy. She added, "Would you care for some spiced wassail, dear?"

"Wassail?" I snapped the word.

"Well, if you don't care for it," Effie started, sounding disappointed.

"Oh, no, it's just . . ." I stopped. I couldn't exactly say, it's just I'm a little peeved—not to say creeped out and confused—about your son's comment about my mama being prettier. And by the fact he keeps staring at me. At least, I didn't think I should say all that five minutes into the visit.

Rich chuckled. "Effie just can't resist making it year after year," he said. "Even though no one particularly cares for it and I always tell her sherry's the thing after a fine meal. It's her down-home ways, I guess." He chuckled again, held up his glass, and patted her on the knee.

Down-home ways? There was nothing down home about this refurbished farmhouse—or anyone in it. Even in the way everyone spoke. There was a clipped edge to their tone, not the soft twang of most Paradisites' speech. Paradise may be in Ohio, but it's in southern Ohio, much of which is in the Appalachian Mountain Range, and most of which has an Appalachian down-home feel, especially outside of the urban areas.

Rich was from northern Ohio—an area Southern Ohioans thought of as having a more industrial, East Coast feel—and of course Lenny and Rachel had lived outside of Paradise for a long time, but Effie was a Paradise native who rarely traveled. Yet, it was as if she had distanced herself from her roots in speech and style without ever actually leaving.

So what was Rich's "down home" comment about? Was Rich really trying to make an endearing statement about his wife . . . or a subtle put-down?

Effie's reaction only added to my confusion. She

stiffened, but smiled at her husband. "Tradition, dear," she said, somewhat shrilly. She smiled at me. "It was my mother's recipe."

Huh? I knew this was Effie's father's old farmhouse, and that her mother had died when Effie was just a few years old. I knew this in the way that people always know everyone's biography in a small town. And I was real sure that Effie's mama didn't make something as fancy as wassail every year. Like my Mamaw, Effie's mama would have been the "down home" kind of cook. Hopefully her turkeys turned out moister. In any case, she'd have served cider from the jug.

"I think it's really quite tasty," Rachel said.

"A way to usher in the Yuletide season," Lenny added. "I'll go get you some, Josie."

Rachel, Lenny, and Effie, I realized, all had mugs. Rich was the only one with a glass.

By the time I'd settled in with Rachel on a couch, Lenny came back with a mug—an elegant off-white that matched everyone else's. I'd have been willing to bet that theirs was the only house in the Paradise area that didn't have the Paradise Chamber of Commerce mug, which included advertising from several establishments, including my laundromat.

I sipped the wassail, and immediately forced myself not to spit. It was hot and far too sour. And too strongly laced with bourbon. I decided to sip slowly.

I asked Lenny where he lived and what he did. He was a high school history teacher in the Indianapolis school system, he said. And basketball coach, his mother added. You'd think, she went on, that with a nice job like that, and he was such a good-looking boy, he'd have found a nice girl to settle down with.

He blushed, looked embarrassed, and said, "Oh, Mama, you're the only girl for me!"

Effie actually giggled and said, "He always says that."

"Another down-home tradition," Rich said.

Ohhh-Kaaay, I thought.

"The truth is, I've just been too busy all these years to settle down. And by myself, I make enough to meet all my needs, plus each spring and summer, I and a partner run a yard maintenance company," Lenny said. "In August, I take off and go to Europe."

"Sounds wonderful," I said. It did. I hadn't traveled beyond Ohio and Kentucky, and never for more than a night away. I wanted to be close, for Guy.

As if sensing my thoughts, Effie said, "So how is your cousin—Guy? Am I remembering his name right?"

I smiled at her. "Yes, you are, thank you. He's doing very well."

Effie perked up. "Oh! So he's over his, his condition."

I stiffened a little, then reminded myself, as I always did, to be kind to people who didn't understand about autism. Even though it was a fairly well-known condition, through movies such as *Rain Man*, over the past few years, old mistaken beliefs and myths still persisted.

"No," I said. "Autism is not something that can be cured. But Guy, like many adults with autism, has been helped to be the best person he can be, to live as independently as—"

"How sad," Effie said, staring off into the distance. "To have a child less than perfect. I wonder what his mother did . . . Clara seemed like such a nice lady."

"Mother—" Rachel started.

"That's okay," I said, trying to keep my tone even. "She didn't do anything. That was a common myth, especially years ago, that autism was somehow the mother's fault. It's a condition, like many others, that has its origins in the genes . . ."

"Well, now, my little darling is too busy watching over me and the house to keep up with such things," Rich said—again, both implying an endearment, while subtly putting his wife down.

Rachel stiffened.

"I remember how much your mama loved her nephew," Lenny said. "She talked about Guy all the time. I think she felt defensive about Guy and her brother—your Uncle Horace—because their parents were embarrassed about Guy."

I stared at Lenny. How did he know so much about my family?

He smiled at me. "I'm the same age as your mother. As Mother said earlier, we were in high school together—"

Effie coughed. "Yes. They were friends. And May was like a daughter to me. Anyway, I'm just so glad my children turned out perfectly."

I thought, I should have stayed at the messy, nutty, turkey-torching Toadfern house and played with my nephews.

Maybe, I thought, I could go back. It wasn't that late. It sure wasn't late enough that Harry, Barry, and Larry were being tucked in.

"Well, this has been delightful," I said. More like dull . . . and somewhat pointless, except I'd learned that as nuts as the Toadferns were, they were a sight more interesting. Perfect wasn't all it was cracked up

to be. "Rachel, thank you for inviting me." I started to
stand up.

Effie stood up, too. "Thank you for coming, dear."
She sounded relieved that I was leaving. "I'll take your
mug . . ."

Suddenly, she started to swoon.

Lenny was on his feet in a split second, grabbing his
mother's arm, while Rich just watched, looking amused.
"Mama, you okay?" his voice, filled with worry, had re-
verted to the Paradise twang I was familiar with.

"Fine, fine, dear—just a little dizzy." She looked at
me, gave a little twittering laugh. "It's just a new
blood-pressure medicine. And all the excitement over
Rich's retirement parties . . ."

"Don't go just yet, Josie," Rachel said anxiously. "I
was, um, hoping to talk with you. Maybe we could take
a walk on the old canal path?"

"Oh, dear, Josie wouldn't want to ruin her nice
shoes," Effie said.

I glanced down at my shoes, tan suede flats that had
seen better days and didn't quite live up to Effie's description of nice, but I didn't fancy a trip up to Masonville
to the PayLess Shoe Outlet to try to replace them.

"Maybe another time," I said, edging back out of the
room, as Lenny was saying to his mother that she
should sit down and he'd go fix her a cup of tea.

"We have hiking boots," Rachel said. "We used
them earlier but they're dry enough and I'm sure my
pair would fit you and I could just wear extra socks and
use Lenny's . . ."

She looked so pathetically hopeful and pleading that
of course I said yes.

Besides, her desperation reignited my curiosity
about why she'd really brought me out there.

*   *   *

And so I found myself walking alongside Rachel across their backyard. I'd ended up in Lenny's hiking boots—with extra socks—because Rachel's were too tight. And I had to admit that in the soft gray twilight, the snow looked lovely, like a tender blanket protecting the earth until spring came again. It had snowed at least another inch and a half since I'd left Mamaw Toadfern's. And it was still snowing again, a prickly cold snow that warned of ice later. We'd have at least a half foot of both snow and ice by the next morning. Driving up to Stillwater would be tricky, I thought, but I wouldn't miss the mysterious meeting for anything . . .

"Thank you so much for coming with me on this walk," Rachel said, breaking into my thoughts of Guy and Stillwater. "I needed to get out of that house!"

I looked at her. "You couldn't go on a walk by yourself?"

"Of course," Rachel said, bristling a little. "But then mother gets so worried if I'm off by myself. 'You never know what you'll stumble across,' she always says. I went earlier with Lenny, but I know he'll want to fuss over Mama until he's reassured she's just lightheaded from her blood-pressure medicine."

I glanced around. If they'd come this way, their footprints were well filled in by now.

Rachel suddenly ducked, then stopped, looking around, confused. I looked around, too, and saw we were between two clothesline poles.

Rachel looked a little sheepish. "I forgot . . . of course . . . Mama took the clothesline down for the winter."

I guessed she and Lenny hadn't come this way on their walk. And then I remembered the clothesline that was still tied between two trees in front of Mamaw Toadfern's house. Effie—not Mamaw—would be organized enough to take in her clothesline for winter, although I was surprised she used a clothesline at all.

We started walking again, crossing from backyard to corn stubbled field. Even in the thick boots, I could feel the sharp spikes pressing into the soles of my borrowed boots.

"So why did you want me to come for a walk with you? To tell me you're representing my parents in their attempt to purchase the old orphanage?"

Rachel looked at me, startled. "You found out?"

"They told me—everyone, really—after they showed up unexpectedly at my Mamaw Toadfern's."

"They were supposed to keep it confidential until the county commissioners' meeting, after my dad's retirement party—"

"They're not the most reliable people in the world." Rachel winced at the sarcasm in my voice. I would like to say I felt badly about that, but I didn't. I went on. "So how did you happen to connect up with them?"

Rachel shrugged, hurried on. "Coincidence, I guess. The commissioners needed someone to represent the property and it wasn't selling locally, so my dad suggested my name—and some others—who specialize in investment real estate deals across the country. Then one day, I received a call from Henry Toadfern. He was interested in the property. I knew the town wouldn't like what your parents have planned for the property, but business is business, and it's better for the orphanage to be used for something, rather than sitting there abandoned. And I had no idea they were coming in for the weekend. They really don't need to be here for the negotiations next week."

I felt an immediate tug of "warning, warning!" in my solar plexus. Her story didn't add up. How had my dad found out about the property in the first place . . . unless he or Mama had stayed in touch with someone in Paradise.

But before I could ask more, we'd stopped where the Burkette property bordered the orphanage property on one side, and where the towpath ran behind both properties. On the other side of the orphanage was Mamaw Toadfern's farmhouse.

We'd stopped near an old wooden shed, its red paint now a mere smudge on the weathered wood. The shed was shielded from the path by a line of trees, and though I'd passed it many times in the summers on my bike or walking, I'd forgotten about it.

Now, the sight of the old shed brought a rush of memory, the memory that had been edging around my mind at Sandy's Restaurant just a few days before.

The summer I stayed at the orphanage, before Aunt Clara and Uncle Horace took me in, I'd sneak out at night, taking with me a book and my sheet and something I'd saved back from dinner and a flashlight, telling myself I was going to run away, find Mama, maybe even Daddy.

I'd get as far as an old shed on the far edge of the property, a shed that I knew marked a clearing to the old towpath. But then, I'd lose my courage and climb up a ladder that leaned against the back of the shed, and lie on the flat roof in the cooling evening, and sometimes read by the flashlight, and sometimes just close my eyes and listen to the summer bugs' sweet chorus.

And one night, another young girl climbed up that ladder and sat down beside me. It turned out the shed wasn't on the orphanage property as I'd thought, but on the Burkette's farmland.

The young girl was Rachel, and she'd climb up there and tell me stories about her family—her perfect family. Her daddy. Her mama. And her big brother, who was much older and lived somewhere else, but always brought her her own special box of chocolates when he came to visit.

And how she had a room all to herself, and she got to redecorate it whenever she wanted . . .

"The ladder's gone." My voice sounded distant, as if someone else spoke the words. "The ladder's gone," I repeated, and that was enough to bring me back to the present.

"I'm sorry, Josie, so sorry." I looked back at Rachel and saw she was crying. She had been remembering, too, I realized.

I sighed. "You were a little girl, Rachel. Just about my age. I was, what, seven. So you were . . ."

"Nine."

"Okay, nine. Who knows any better at nine?"

"But I did," she said. "At some level, I knew it was cruel . . . telling you stories about my perfect family, and you from the orphanage . . ."

I smiled. "It gave me something to dream about, Rachel. Maybe I'd end up with a perfect family after all. And it probably kept me from eventually taking off down this path, because sooner or later I would have gotten my courage up, and then Aunt Clara and Uncle Horace might not have had a chance to adopt me, and God only knows what might have happened to me if I'd taken off down this path."

Funny, all the times I'd biked down the path, I hadn't thought about that—or about those evenings listening to Rachel's melodic voice talk about her perfect family.

She gasped, and the sound caught in her throat. "Oh, God, Josie. I don't deserve that. We're not the perfect family! Anything but that!"

I looked at her, curiously. "What do you mean? Everyone looks up to your family. Everyone is so polite . . ."

"And so tense! The pressure is always on to be just so, just perfect, just right—or God knows Daddy'll say something—nothing outright—but just something that will devastate us. It was like that when I was a kid, like that with Mama, especially when Lenny would come home to visit, for some reason. All those 'down home' comments . . . why doesn't he just come out straight with it and call her a hick and say he feels so much superior to her?

"And whenever I'd bring someone home from school, it was the same. There'd be some subtle comment, and my friends would be left just a little confused, feeling put down but not quite sure why, and then there would be a distance at school the next day . . . so somewhere around the fourth grade I just stopped asking friends over.

"I felt like all the attention was on me. To look perfect. Get perfect grades. No one was ever good enough to be my friend. And I know Lenny feels the same way. He's not my daddy's son, after all, and through subtle comments, Daddy makes sure none of us ever forget that, or that Mom had a 'past' as he calls it—like she's the only woman to ever get divorced and have her ex run off.

"But there were never any fights in our house—nothing overt. And yet it was always there . . . this pressure from Mother for me to be perfect, to not displease Daddy.

"I think that's why I just went nuts during my commencement speech. I knew I was leaving and didn't want to come back, to where I was expected to be so perfect . . ."

And yet she'd gone off and, from what I'd seen and she'd said, tried to recreate another perfect life. Was that one reason she'd taken on my parents as clients—however they'd actually found her? To rock the perfect boat again?

She stopped, stared down at her boots. "I'm sorry. I'm doing it again, being a self-centered little brat. I just wanted to come out here, apologize to you, get some sense of closure, I guess . . ."

"I think you're being kind of hard on yourself." Truth be told, I felt sorry for Rachel. All those years ago, I thought she'd had the perfect family and the perfect life.

Maybe I'd gotten the better deal, after all.

"I'm glad I listened years ago," I said. "And I'm glad to listen now."

Of course, that came as much from my desire to satisfy my own curiosity as anything . . . but I didn't tell her that.

I started through the tree line to the path. "Come on," I said, tagging her on the arm as I passed her. "Let's go look at the old telegraph poles. Somehow, they always make me feel better."

"The *what*?" She caught up with me. We stepped onto the towpath. It glistened with unbroken snow. Our footprints appeared to be the first on the path. I stared up at the snow swirling down. It was like being in a snow globe.

"You mean you never went exploring in the woods behind your house?"

The towpath had only been converted to a paved hiking/biking path in the past ten years.

"No. I was told not to."

We started walking down the path.

"And you didn't disobey? That's sad . . . you really were the perfect child." She stared at me. I elbowed her. "Oh, come on," I said. She laughed, finally.

"There are a few old telegraph poles still standing just a few yards farther. And there's something about that . . . the layers, you know, of time . . . the canal, and the telegraph, and just a few yards to our right, the old train line . . . all those layers make me feel better."

"Why?"

"It's a reminder. Time passes. Things change. Life moves on. Doesn't that help put your problems in perspective?"

She seemed to think about that. "I guess, yes—oh look!"

She pointed, and we both gazed at a telegraph pole, just visible through the bare branches of the trees.

We walked to the edge of the path. This telegraph pole was falling apart—the top crossbeam had rotted and slipped, and criss-crossed the bottom crossbeam. One of the metal conductors—they looked like bells on either end of the two beams—had long ago fallen off. Of course, there were no longer any wires connecting this pole to the next.

"There's one in better shape, farther down, but we'll have to go off the path to see it."

"Fine with me!" Rachel said, sounding eager. I smiled, glad she was feeling better.

We walked a few feet down the path and I looked for the sparse trail that led off the official path.

There were what looked like two sets of footprints, partially filled in with the new snow, that imprinted the snow from the opposite direction, along the boundary of the orphanage property.

Had someone cut across the orphanage property to the path, or come to it from Mamaw Toadfern's? I couldn't see that far, especially through the swirling snow.

Besides, I was more intrigued by the fact that the footprints went off the path and into the woods, right where the better-preserved telegraph pole was.

I looked back at the path, squinted at the footprints. The duo that had gone off the path at that spot hadn't returned on it. Whoever it was must have cut through the woods and picked up the path elsewhere, which didn't make sense unless they were hunters. Hunting was prohibited this close to the path and private property, but that didn't mean laws were always obeyed.

On the other hand, I knew my uncles—and Daddy—were supposed to go hunting the next day. That was the most popular time for hunting around Paradise—the Friday and weekend after Thanksgiving. It was unlikely anyone would be hunting at twilight on Thanksgiving evening, so I felt safe stepping off the path into the woods, to see the old telegraph pole.

But the minute I saw it, I stopped short, my mind and body going cold with shock.

There was the telegraph pole . . . and Uncle Fenwick. A length of clothesline looped around the lowest rung on the telegraph pole, and then around his neck. The old rung had given way under his weight, and the bottom of his boots just brushed the frozen ground.

The ladder, which I'd remembered always being on the side of the Burkette's shed, lay on the ground nearby, as if Uncle Fenwick had kicked it away in his suicide attempt.

But it was clear that this was not suicide. Someone had wanted to make it look like Uncle Fenwick had tried to kill himself, and when the rung broke, must have realized this wasn't going to work, because Uncle Fenwick had also been stabbed.

His winter jacket was open, revealing his undershirt and several stab wounds, from which blood bloomed and spread into the thin cloth of his undershirt, like grotesque flowers.

On the heels of that realization came the awareness that Rachel was behind me, stammering "Oh my God, oh my God," repeatedly; that I was shaking and it had nothing to do with the cold; and that I was about to throw up.

I couldn't do a thing about Rachel or the shaking. I whirled around, let myself get sick, and then dug my cell phone out of my pocket and called the police.

7

She came, seemingly, from out of nowhere.

One minute I was blissfully floating in gray nothing-ness. At least, I think I was. Ever notice how you never really remember dreamless sleep? Anyway, the next moment I was aware, in my dream state, of being in fog, which for me is a sure sign that I'm just about to ease into a dream.

Usually—even on nights when I fall asleep concen-trating on a name or image that I hope will generate a pleasant dream (George Clooney, George Clooney . . .) —my dreams are anxiety driven. I'm back in high school, late for a French test, unable to find the class-room because I've only just remembered I signed up for French in the first place.

Or I'm in my laundromat, and I'm trying my best to help Purdey Whitlock, the Baptist minister's wife who is complaining that the washer door is stuck, and when I finally open it, dozens of her husband's white dress shirts spring forth, stained with red lipstick, and Mrs.

Whitlock starts screaming, because her sole shade of lipstick is tangerine.

Or . . . and this is when I know I'm really troubled deep down . . . Mrs. Oglevee appears from out of nowhere.

Mrs. Oglevee was my junior high history teacher. Theoretically, she retired on the day I graduated junior high school. But to earn extra money, she became a substitute, and showed up with alarming frequency in my high school classes—everything from gym to English lit to home ec. And French.

She was saving money to go on a Mediterranean cruise and had just purchased tickets when she keeled over dead of a heart attack. This did not make Mrs. Oglevee a very happy ghost—or whatever she was— when she showed up in my dreams.

Tonight, she was in an exact copy of my Mamaw Toadfern's Thanksgiving outfit—the black pants and the turkey-Pilgrim-motif sweatshirt and the high-heeled mules. She had a drum strapped around her neck and was hitting it, but not with drum drumsticks. With turkey-leg drumsticks.

I moaned.

This did not cause Mrs. Oglevee to stop, or even pause, in her drumming with the turkey-leg drumsticks. In fact, she drummed so hard, grease flew everywhere.

I groaned.

This only caused her to start tapping her right foot in rhythm with her drumming.

I finally found my voice. "Could you please just go away, Mrs. Oglevee? I've had a rough night."

To my amazement, Mrs. Oglevee stopped drumming and tapping. Usually, she never listened to my requests. But her drum disappeared, a rocking chair appeared behind her, and she plopped down into it, still holding the turkey drumsticks. She bit into the one she held in her left hand.

"Sorry," she said around a mouthful of turkey. "Long day. First chance I've had to enjoy Thanksgiving."

I stared at her as she took another bite, this time from the drumstick in her right hand.

"What?" she said, around another mouthful, glaring back at me. See? I annoyed her, even in my dreams. "Thanksgiving is always a time of great stress and drama for lots of people. Family get-togethers, you know. I don't understand why people who usually don't get together—or get along—congregate once a year and then are surprised when things don't go well. So, this is really my busiest season."

She stopped suddenly, looking like she wished she hadn't made that last comment, and lit back into the drumstick with gusto.

I gaped at her. "What? You mean to tell me you show up in other people's dreams, too?"

She didn't say anything, finished off her drumsticks and tossed the bones over her shoulder, where they disappeared into the fog. I decided this was a good opportunity to ask her as directly as I dared about whether or not she was really a ghost.

"Or . . . or . . . for some people do you actually show up when they're awake?"

Mrs. Oglevee licked off her fingers. Then she said, "I really can't say. Confidentiality issues. Part of my agreement."

I rolled my eyes. No one had ever felt comfortable confiding in Mrs. Oglevee when she was alive. I couldn't imagine what the Almighty would have been thinking, assigning her to some afterlife counseling role. Assuming she was with the Almighty. I'd never been quite sure where Mrs. Oglevee was residing in the afterlife.

But then, Mrs. Oglevee adjusted her glasses, started rocking, and gave me a piercing look. "Start talking," she said. "I'm on a schedule."

And so . . . I started telling her about the reunion with my parents and Toadfern kin. The surreal visit at the Burkettes. The conversation with Rachel Burkette about our childhoods, and our meetings at the shed, years ago.

I told her about Uncle Fenwick, stabbed, but also made to look as though he'd tried to commit suicide, with the clothesline and the ladder nearby. I told her my theory, that someone had threatened or forced Uncle Fenwick into hanging himself, and then Uncle Fenwick had fought back at the last minute, and the killer stabbed him, left him to die from a combination of bleeding to death and hanging, then panicked and ran off.

I told her how Rachel had started screaming hysterically, how I'd fumbled with my cell phone and finally managed to call 911, how the snow had really picked up. How finally officers from both the Paradise Police Department and the Mason County Sheriff's Department showed up.

I told Mrs. Oglevee about answering the questions of John Worthy, Paradise's chief of police, and about going with him to Mamaw Toadfern's house to break the news to her and Aunt Nora, and how both women had been shocked and hysterical and how, somehow, it didn't surprise me that for all their goofiness, the members of the Toadfern clan rallied around and calmed and comforted Mamaw and Aunt Nora. Even my mama and daddy.

And I told her about them, too.

And then I told her how, finally, I'd driven home, and discovered my apartment smelled of burned turkey—the roast had been in there far too long—and how I'd thrown the wasted turkey out, run the kitchen fan, and put away the other side-dish fixings I'd left out on the counter.

Then I took a quick, hot shower, stumbled into bed and a blessed dreamless slumber . . . until Mrs. Oglevee showed up.

"And it's a good thing I did, too," she said, annoyed again. Which disappointed me. I thought I'd woven a moving tale, well told. I thought Mrs. Oglevee had been wiping a tear from her eye—but maybe it was just turkey drumstick grease.

"I can see," she went on, twisting her mouth into a prim little line, as she always did when she thought I wasn't paying attention in class, "that you are just going to walk away from this murder of your poor Uncle Fenwick."

"Well, yeah," I sputtered. "It's . . . it's not any of my business."

"That's not like you. Whatever happened to Nosey Josie?"

I shuddered at her use of my hated, old nickname and used my favorite line for defending my proclivity for interest in news: "I prefer to think of myself as curiosity-gifted."

"Your gift seems to be coming unwrapped," she snapped.

"What? You've always told

business, to stop poking my nose in where it shouldn't be. Now you think I should investigate Uncle Fenwick's murder?"

Mrs. Oglevee glared at me. I gave her a sly look, thinking of something that might get her to leave me alone. "Besides, Chief John Worthy is working with the sheriff's department on the investigation."

As I'd expected, her look softened. It was all I could do not to roll my eyes. Chief John Worthy—my ex-high-school sweetheart and current nemesis—had always been Mrs. Oglevee's teacher's pet.

"Dear Johnny," she said, wistfully. "He was always so sweet and respectful—"

"A suck-up," I muttered.

"What was that?" Mrs. Oglevee snapped.

"Nothing, ma'am."

"Hmmph. Don't back talk. Besides, I have a point of view you can't share, and I'm telling you, this is one time your natural nosiness is needed."

"You don't think old Johnny's up to the job this time?"

"I think blood is thicker than water!"

This time I did roll my eyes. "Oh, please. This is the first time I've seen the Toadferns in years. Most of them except Sally—"

Mrs. Oglevee interrupted me with a grunt of disgust. If anyone could annoy her faster and more deeply than me, it was Sally. Of course, with Sally, it was intentional, because she found Mrs. Oglevee's reactions amusing.

"Most of them except *Sally*," I repeated, emphasiz-
____ ____ _een downright rude and ignored me
____ _hy should I investigate Uncle

Fenwick's murder when no one—least of all the officials—wants me to?"

"Because, my dear, you might just learn some things about your family—and yourself—that can help you personally."

There was a shrill sound, and Mrs. Oglevee jumped. "Oh! I had more to tell you, but time's up." A gigantic alarm clock—the old-fashioned antique kind with two bells on top—fell into her lap and shrilled again. She peered at it. "Yes, time for the next appointment."

Mrs. Oglevee stood up, and the rocking chair and alarm clock disappeared. Mrs. Oglevee started fading into the mist that suddenly rolled in around her.

I frowned. "Wait—Mrs. Oglevee—wait, I don't understand why I should investigate Uncle Fenwick—wait—it's a bad idea—wait—"

But only Mrs. Oglevee's Chesire cat–like smile remained in the fog, and then there was that shrilling sound again, and I snapped to, and realized my phone was ringing.

Guy, I thought, suddenly wide awake. I sat up in bed, turned on my nightstand light, and stared at my digital clock: 1:16.

I grabbed up the phone. "Toadfern's Laundromat, I mean Toadfern residence, I mean Josie . . ."

"I woke you. I'll call tomorrow . . ."

Owen! I sat up straighter, but still wasn't fully awake. "No, now's fine," I said, rubbing my eyes. "It's just that Mrs. Oglevee doesn't make sense . . ." I shook my head, trying to come fully awake. I looked at the time again, then felt a little chest squeeze of panic.

Owen's plan was to start driving home Friday morning after Thanksgiving, so we could spend some time together over the weekend. Had he decided to leave early—real early—for some reason? Was he stranded somewhere?

"Owen, are you okay?" I was wide awake by then, and straining to hear sounds of highway traffic in the background.

There was silence for a moment on his end. Not the sound of even a single eighteen-wheeler rushing by.

"I'm fine," he said finally. "I actually had a great day—a really great day. How was yours?"

He asked the question hastily, as if he'd suddenly remembered that I would have had a day, also. There was so much I could tell him . . . but I suddenly went cold. Something didn't feel right. "It was fine," I said.

"Oh, good," Owen said, sounding relieved—not at the fact my day was fine, I realized, but that I wasn't going into great detail. He, of course, had no idea how I'd spent my Thanksgiving. When he'd left the previous weekend, I'd been as vague with him about my plans as I'd been with Sally before she manipulated me into going to Mamaw Toadfern's. He hadn't seemed overly concerned about how I'd spend the holiday.

"Listen, Josie, I really am sorry to call you so late—"

"Well, as long as it's to mutter sexy sweet nothings in my ear in the middle of the night," I joked—and immediately regretted my interruption.

Owen cleared his throat. "I'm not going to get back until early next week. Something came up and I have a busy day tomorrow or I'd have waited to call you at a decent hour—aw, hell, Josie, I might as well just get to it."

I didn't say anything. So get to it, I thought, going cold again.

"I ran into Roger Muller, an old college friend—I think I've mentioned him to you? Anyway, he told me that one of his colleagues in the local community college's philosophy department has to take an extended leave of absence for the rest of the school year due to illness. The college is looking for someone to take over his classes starting in January—and, well, Josie, I applied. I put in my application just a few hours after hearing about the opening—"

"When was this?" I snapped. "A few hours ago?"

Now there was a moment of silence on Owen's end. Then: "What? No, of course not—"

"Of course not. So why are you calling me now, past one in the morning?"

"I—I couldn't sleep and I thought you'd want to know and I didn't think you'd mind and—"

"Owen, when did you put in your application?"

Silence, again. Finally: "Tuesday. Look, Josie, I know how that sounds but . . . I don't know if I'll get the job, and my interview is Monday morning, and I couldn't sleep, so I thought I'd call you, and . . . Aw, hell. Look, Josie, it's a chance to be around my son all the time. It could grow into a permanent job, if Victor, the guy who's on extended leave, doesn't get better—"

"Ooh, let me make a voodoo doll of poor Victor and start poking pins in him."

"Josie, I didn't mean it like that. It's just, I want to be around my son more, and—"

"I respect that, Owen. But you've only been back in touch with him for a few months." The minute I said it, I frowned. Was I just being selfish? Still, I plunged on. "And I know you want to get closer to him, but what about your job at the community college here? Your volunteer teaching at the prison here? Your . . .

your commitments . . . here." Meaning, I thought, our relationship.

Owen sighed. "You're angry that I didn't call earlier this week and talk to you about it, aren't you?"

"No kidding."

Now Owen turned cold. "You know, I don't know that this conversation would have been any better—or that you'd have liked my decision any better—if I'd called two days ago."

"That's just it, Owen," I said, sighing. This was a man with doctorates in philosophy, religious studies, and literature—and yet, I had to spell out the obvious for him. "You didn't want to discuss this with me—as a friend, or as anything else. You just made the decision and called to inform me at your convenience—which happens to be in the middle of the night. Well, I'm sorry you can't sleep, but I'm tired. Good luck on your interview."

I hesitated, giving him another chance to say something—anything—to convince me that he really hadn't meant to shut me out of at least talking with him about a decision that big. He didn't take the chance. "Good night," I finished primly, without a waver in my voice.

Then I hung up and burst out crying like a big baby.

Ten minutes later, I was in my kitchen hiccupping, and licking peanut butter from a spoon. Cherry had once told me that she'd read in a chick magazine that that was a great cure for headaches. I, thank the good Lord, never get headaches, but she swore it worked, so I figured the cure might work for my hiccups. And snuffles. And a confused, breaking heart.

It didn't.

In fact, my apartment still smelled of burned turkey,

and I realized that other than Aunt Nora's cranberry relish and Effie Burkette's wassail, I hadn't had a real Thanksgiving dinner at all.

Which might seem like a petty concern, given Uncle Fenwick's murder and the fact that my relationship with Owen seemed to be falling apart, but it made me tear up, anyway.

So I plunged the spoon—a big serving spoon, mind you, not some wimpy little teaspoon—into the wide-mouthed jar and ladled out another spoonful of peanut butter.

I was on my first lick of the new spoonful when my doorbell rang.

Now, my apartment is just one of two units on the second story over my laundromat. I've lived in my one-bedroom unit for nine years since I sold my aunt and uncle's house and put the proceeds into trust for Guy, and I've rented the other unit off and on. More off, than on, truth be told. The most recent renters, a nice couple, had just moved the previous week into a small house because they were expecting their first child the following spring. I'd been thinking about just expanding the entire second story into one nice, luxury apartment for me.

Anyway, the only person living above my laundromat was me, and it's not like strangers—the few times there are any in Paradise—would wander up the exterior staircase on the side of my laundromat, into the exterior door, which I always forget to lock, and down a dark hall to knock on my door for help.

So, I quickly calculated who it could be that I knew.

Cherry, I thought. Ha. I knew things wouldn't go well with her deputy sheriff beau. She was, again, moving too fast for her own heart's good.

Like I had with Owen, a needling voice whispered.

I swallowed my peanut butter, took another lick, and headed to the door. I had a fresh jar of peanut butter at the back of the cabinet. Cherry and I could lick peanut butter spoons until we were sick, and cry our hearts out about our awful boyfriends. Perfect for what was sure to be a sleepless, heartbroken night . . .

Except when I opened the door—it wasn't Cherry standing there.

It was my mama.

And she'd already cried all of her makeup off. Her face was mascara streaked. "Oh Josie," she wailed, "it's your daddy."

I jammed my spoon back into my peanut butter jar, and put my hand on my hip.

"Let me guess. He's taken off to interview for a job at some school of antiquing knowledge. Maybe a university of antiquities. Maybe—"

"What?" She looked confused for a second, then burst out sobbing. "No, honey—your daddy's been arrested! For Fenwick's murder!"

8

It took a lot more than peanut butter to calm my mama down.

She plunged right past me, flopped down on my couch, and demanded vodka and cranberry juice.

I told her I didn't have either, and there wasn't anyplace open in Paradise that sold either at that hour.

She suggested I call my friends to see if they had vodka and cranberry juice. I pointed out I wanted my friends to *stay* my friends, so, no, I wasn't about to call them at 1:00 A.M. with such a request.

Then she started wailing something about Paradise being a godforsaken place, and I told her that according to Pastor Micah at the Paradise Methodist Church, there was no such place. Then I told her that if she wasn't going to calm down, she could just get off my couch and go back to wherever she was staying. I waggled my peanut butter-slicked spoon at her as I said it.

Then she started wailing that she couldn't get back to the Red Horse Motel because she thought she'd stripped the gears in Daddy's and her cherry red sports car, which still ran despite its fender-bender with Uncle Fenwick's RV, and which she'd left in front of the Antique Depot—or some such junk shop, she said.

Antique shop, I corrected her, bristling. Then I told her to hush up, or she'd have to walk back to the Red Horse.

That seemed to stun her and I half expected her to snap, don't sass your mama! in that impatient, flustered tone I suddenly remembered as her usual tone when I was little. But she got quiet and shrank back into the couch.

I went into my kitchenette and put on a kettle of hot water.

I got out one of my TOADFERN'S LAUNDROMAT—ALWAYS A LEAP AHEAD OF DIRT! mugs, a promotional giveaway left over from years before, when I took over the laundromat and changed its name from Foersthoefel's to Toadfern's to really make it mine. Then I got out another mug, this one imprinted with GLEN ARM INN, a souvenir from a romantic getaway overnight I'd shared not too long before with Owen.

My heart panged. But my only other two mugs in my sparsely outfitted kitchen were filled with sudsy water and sitting in the sink.

I stuck my peanut buttery spoon in one of the mugs, suddenly so nervous that I didn't even want peanut butter, recapped the peanut butter jar, and put it back in the cabinet, and pulled out the honey and box of chamomile tea bags.

I squirted honey from the top of the plastic bear container into each of the mugs and plopped a chamomile bag in each mug. By the time I'd tucked away the honey and tea bags, the kettle of water was whistling. I finished making our mugs of tea and carried them the few steps into my living room. I gave Mama the Toad-fern's Laundromat mug.

See, Mama, I thought. Your baby made good, after all, even if you did just up and leave.

But she didn't even glance at the mug. She'd kicked off her shoes, spit-washed the mascara from her face, and tucked her legs up on my couch. She'd taken off her fur coat and turned it around backward, and spread it over her, like an afghan. I eyed the afghan I keep folded over the back of my couch. The afghan is a sky blue and sea-foam green crocheted creation I'd purchased from the Antique Depot. Maybe I should offer it to Mama, I thought. But I resisted the gesture.

She closed her eyes and inhaled the steam from the tea and suddenly looked at peace. She took a long sip, opened her eyes, and smiled at me.

"Thank you. That's better after all than cranberry juice and vodka," she said. "Chamomile tea and honey—it's just what I used to make you, you know, whenever you were ill. It's what my mother always made me."

And suddenly I remembered that was true. Not the part about my grandmother having made the beverage, too—that was news—but that my mama had served this to me when I was sick, and just the smell of it made me feel better.

But I took a sip, then said, "Hmm. I don't recall."

A flash of sadness crossed my mother's face, and I instantly regretted my comment.

But Mama shrugged and said, "I'm not surprised. You were so young when I left you with Chief Hilbrink and his wife. How are they?"

She didn't know, I thought. As a kid, at least for the

first few years, I imagined she had checked up on me, would be back anytime for me, have a great explanation. But then I became, emotionally, Uncle Horace and Aunt Clara's daughter, and Guy's sister, and got caught up in just living my life. I stopped imagining.

But still, the fact that she hadn't checked at all shocked me. She looked in great health. And like she'd lived a blessed life for quite a few years. So there'd been nothing to stop her from checking.

"Chief Hilbrink died three months after you left," I said. "Mrs. Hilbrink left to live with her sister in California and I lost touch with her. I lived in the orphanage for several months because the Toadferns wouldn't have me and Uncle Horace didn't want me, either, at first. But Aunt Clara put her foot down and they adopted me."

Mama sipped her tea and nodded. "Mmmm," was her only acknowledgment, and I wasn't sure if it was of the tea or my story.

"Uncle Horace died when I was still in high school, and Aunt Clara passed away a few years after that. I inherited the laundromat and now I'm Guy's guardian."

Again, she sipped and nodded.

I sat my mug down too hard in frustration, and some of the tea sloshed out on top of my stack of magazines, which were from the bookmobile.

"Damn it," I hollered, and trotted into the kitchenette for a paper towel, then came back and blotted up the tea before it could soak into Nicole Kidman's lovely face on the cover of *People*—a magazine that is one of my secret pleasures. Underneath the stack of magazines, though, were books, including *Pride and Prejudice*. Which I was re-reading. Truly.

I sat back down and glared at Mama. "So. How have you been?"

She smiled at me, ignoring my sarcasm. "The tea was lovely. I feel so much calmer now," she said, putting her empty mug on the coffee table. She cleared her throat. "So. Your daddy is in jail for murdering his brother Fenwick. I know that must shock you."

I met her gaze with a most unshocked look. After all, I was still reeling from the shock of my parents' sudden appearance and the shock of finding Uncle Fenwick hung out to die. After all of that, my daddy—whom I barely knew, after all—in the role of murderer didn't seem so shocking. Plus, I recollected, I'd witnessed their fighting and threats at the Toadfern Thanksgiving dinner.

"Maybe I should just start at the beginning—about what happened after you left," Mama said.

Or maybe, now that she was calm, I should just drive her back to the Red Horse. But—I admit—I was curious. I decided I'd listen to what she had to say—just to satisfy that curiosity—and *then* drive her back to the Red Horse. And then I'd never have to deal with my mama and daddy again. It would be as if they'd never reappeared.

Why do I allow myself to believe such things?

"It took a while after you left for all of us to calm down Mamaw Toadfern and Nora," Mama said.

"Understandably," I said.

"Yes. Although Fenwick always was such a gruff, resentful man. I really never did see why he was Mamaw Toadfern's favorite—or why Nora doted on him so."

She looked at me as if expecting some agreement that Uncle Fenwick had just not been very lovable.

Well, how would I know? I didn't have any memories of him. And for all I knew, he would have been very enjoyable if Mama and Daddy hadn't shown up.

"The truth is," Mama went on, "I don't know if they ever did calm down. I said something pleasant—about how God works in mysterious ways and maybe somehow this was all for the best—"

That startled me. She'd said *what*?

"—and you'd have thought I'd said something truly awful, like Fenwick deserved it or something, and the next thing I knew, Nora was screaming at me, and so was Mamaw Toadfern, that I always had been an insensitive troublemaker, and if it weren't for me, Henry and Fenwick would have gotten along, and Henry said, well, we certainly didn't need to put up with this kind of treatment—that's not what we'd come back for—and I said, of course not, we came back for a business deal, and it was only because we have good manners that we dropped by at all, and so we left and went back to the Red Horse Motel." She wrinkled her nose. "Awful accommodations, really, but the only place in town, of course. I think they have mildew problems."

"It's owned by the Rhinegolds—good customers and friends of mine," I said. "I've gotten to know them very well over the years. And I don't think they have mildew problems."

"Hmmm. Well. You might suggest they update the décor. Anyway, we'd finally gotten back and had started getting ready for bed when there was a knock at the door. It was Chief Worthy." She shook her head. "Handsome fellow. Seems to me you and he are the same age. I didn't notice any wedding band. But please tell me you aren't dating him."

"I'm not," I said, "although I did back in high

school, until I found out he was two-timing me. At which point I dumped him and . . ."

. . . and ran home and cried on Aunt Clara's shoulder, until she'd had enough of my sniffling and fed me hot chocolate and cookies and told me I deserved better in life.

Is that what she'd say about my situation with Owen? I wondered. I had a feeling it was . . .

"Well, I'm not surprised he cheated on you. His father was a two-timing twit, too," my mother was saying.

My eyebrows went up at that. "I always thought Mr. Worthy was a fine, upstanding citizen."

My mother hmmphed. "You've got to look past surfaces, you know. C. J. Worthy was a successful businessman, owned a plumbing company locally. Your daddy and Uncle Fenwick worked for him, before Fenwick started his own business. C.J. was a terrible flirt with me at cookouts he used to have. Made his wife— a dowdy little thing—very jealous. And it didn't make the Worthys very happy that Fenwick started a rival business up in Masonville. But that was after both Henry and I left Paradise."

I hadn't known that my daddy had been a plumber once. I realized I'd never actually thought about what he might have done for work. All I knew was that he'd left when I was little and that my mama always called him "that good for nothing."

But something else struck me about what my mama was saying. She'd heard about Uncle Fenwick starting his own plumbing company. That meant she'd stayed in touch with someone in Paradise all those years. New plumbing companies in small towns in Ohio wouldn't have made the news anywhere outside of the immediate area, so she couldn't have learned about it—

wherever she'd been all those years—from any other source than someone in Paradise.

Uncle Horace and Aunt Clara? No, I didn't believe that. Someone from the Toadfern family? No, that didn't seem likely, either.

But she'd kept up on Paradise news with someone . . . and yet hadn't known what had happened to me right after she left. Who had she stayed in touch with?

I filed the question away, telling myself it didn't matter and I didn't care.

"Anyway," Mama went on, "that little brat John Worthy came to our room with some other officers and said they had to question us. Worthy said they'd gotten an anonymous call about the fight Henry and Fenwick had at dinner, that Henry had threatened to stab Fenwick. Like a fool, Henry admitted it. Worthy asked him if he had a knife. Henry showed him the collection of antique hunting knives he'd brought up as gifts and to sell to a local dealer. We really do have some knowledge of the flea market business, you know. Anyway, Worthy took all the knives. I don't understand why."

While I had been at Mamaw Toadfern's after the murder, John Worthy had only said that Fenwick had been murdered—not how.

"Uncle Fenwick was stabbed," I said. I didn't see any reason to bring up the fact that someone had first attempted to hang poor Uncle Fenwick from a telegraph pole.

Mama blanched. "Oh. Well, Henry is being held in the Paradise jail. Given that it's the holiday weekend, I don't know if I'll be able to get him out by Monday. I called our lawyer down in Arkansas, but he just looks over our real estate contracts and can't practice here in Ohio, anyway. He gave me the name of a Columbus attorney to call tomorrow morning . . . but, oh, Josie . . . we need your help! We need you to find out whoever the killer is!"

She burst out crying, reverting to the sobbing persona who'd appeared at my door just a half hour before, and yet studying me between her fingers, with a look in her eye that told me she was watching my face to see if the sobbing was having an effect on me.

I stared at the woman on my couch . . . this woman who was my mama, but yet, who wasn't, who wavered between being just like the woman I remembered as Mama and this other manipulative creature she'd reinvented herself into . . . and I thought why? Why would they want my help . . . and why would I want to give it?

The question must have showed on my face because she said, "I read about your involvement in solving the murder of Tyra Grimes." She was referring to a nationally known domestic diva/media mogul who'd come to our town and been murdered the past spring. Unfortunately, there had been several local murders since then, and I'd gotten involved in those, too, because of my curiosity-giftedness (as I like to think of the trait everyone else calls "nosiness"), but those cases hadn't made national news.

"Josie," my mama said, sniffling, making her eyes wide, "we—your daddy and I—need your help. In finding out who set your daddy up as his brother's murderer. I imagine it was one of the Toadferns—but who? And that twit Worthy hates us, so he's just all too willing to look no further than an anonymous phone call. Henry needs to get out of jail and have this wrapped up so we can go ahead with our FleaMart plans for the orphanage . . . and I need Henry to get out of jail because I miss him!"

Now, I have to admit I was tempted, then and there, to say, sure I'd help, simply because I was curious: why did John Worthy hate my parents? Did it have to do with his daddy having flirted with my mama, way back when? Maybe that had something to do with how meanly he'd treated me, ever since we broke up, way back in high school? But if he'd known about anything between my mama and his daddy, he'd never mentioned it, either while we dated or after.

Maybe he just had an airtight case against my daddy, and Mama didn't want to admit it.

After all, it sounded like there was some pretty good evidence against my daddy in the killing of Uncle Fenwick. I shuddered before finishing off the last of my now lukewarm tea, and fixing my gaze on Mama.

"No," I said. "I can't help you with this." I stood up. "I'm going to get on my tennis shoes and coat and drive you back to the Red Horse Motel. I recommend that in the morning you also call Elroy's Filling Station to have your car towed to his shop, before your car gets impounded."

I picked up Mama's mug from the end table, turned, and stepped toward the kitchen—and stopped at her next words.

"We're your *parents*, Josie! Doesn't that mean anything to you?"

There were all kinds of answers—mostly angry—that came rushing to my mind all at once. Foremost—I was your kid. Didn't that mean anything to you? Oh, wait, I know the answer . . . *No*!

But Uncle Horace and Aunt Clara had reared me better than that. Maybe it had been a bad idea to give in to Sally's wheedling and attend the Toadfern Thanksgiving Family Reunion. If I'd known my long-gone parents would have wheeled into Mamaw Toadfern's driveway, would I have gone?

I wasn't sure. When I was little, my curiosity made me wonder about them from time to time. Why had they left? What were they like? What were they doing? Was it somehow my fault they'd left? I'd asked Aunt Clara that once, and she'd sternly told me no, I must never think that, and I'd believed her, and after that the questions about my parents started to fade and other questions about the world and life and my role in it took over.

So, I guess I had long ago stopped trying to imagine what my parents were like, but now that I'd met them, I was disappointed. They were self-absorbed and arrogant, seeming completely unaware that by leaving Paradise as they each had, they'd hurt a lot of people— and that by returning with a plan to build a FleaMart, they were going to hurt a lot more people.

I turned and looked at my mama, thinking about her question. *We're your parents . . . doesn't that mean anything to you?*

"Yes, it does," I said slowly, carefully. "I'm thankful that I'm alive, that you two created me, that you gave birth to me. Thank you for that."

Mama hmpphed, rolled her eyes in a gesture that was similar to my own eye-rolling habit.

"No, really, I do thank you for that. And I don't know what I can really say beyond that, except . . . I'm not the right person to help you and Daddy with this situation. You need to follow your attorney's advice."

I took the mugs into the kitchen, filled them with soapy water and set them next to the other soapy-water-filled mugs. I'd wash them all in the morning.

Then I went into my bedroom and slipped on my

sneakers and my coat, grabbed my purse and keys from the dresser, and went back out to the living room.

But Mama was sound asleep, snoring.

At least, she seemed to be. Maybe she was just playing possum, managing to somehow look sad and lost and vulnerable all at once, knowing at some level I'd fall for it, even though I had every reason in the world to shake her awake and take her back to the Red Horse Motel and never have another thing to do with her and Daddy.

But instead, I felt sorry for her. Had she manipulated me like that when I was a kid? I wasn't sure. Maybe.

It was too late at night—or too early in the morning—to try to figure that one out. Instead, I unfolded the afghan and spread it over Mama.

Then I went back to my room, shut the door, took off my shoes and coat and fell at last into blessed, dreamless sleep.

9

Mama, as it turned out, was next to impossible to wake up.

Right after I woke up at 7:55 A.M.—fully wide awake, right before my alarm went off at 8:00 A.M., which is how I always wake up, even after a night of less sleep than usual—I padded out to my living room. I lightly shook Mama. She moaned.

I decided to give her a few minutes. I showered, then dressed in jeans, black boots, an off-white turtleneck, and an ordinary burgundy cardigan that did *not* feature a single flashing turkey. I fluffed my short cropped do, and put on moisturizer, a dash of beige eye shadow, and a single coat of Cover Girl mascara, the brand that comes in the hot pink and lime green tube, because Cherry swears by it.

After all that, Mama still wasn't awake. So I pressed a cold, wet washcloth to her face. She flailed.

So I had breakfast as loudly as possible, clattering

around in my kitchenette as I made a pot of coffee, washed the previous night's mugs, and had a bowl of Cap'n Crunch cereal with chocolate milk. My breakfast rowdiness didn't rouse her, so I gave her yet a few more minutes of sleep while I brushed my teeth and dabbed on lip gloss. Then I called Elroy's Filling Station and left a message about having Mama's car towed there.

Then I came out and stood over her and sang "Rise, and shine, and give God the glory, glory," in the loudest, most nasally voice I could muster—just as a counselor once did to me at Ranger Girl Camp Wren-E-Na-No-Tikki. That experience is what gave me the ability to come fully awake a few minutes before whatever my alarm is set for.

But Mama just wriggled down further under the afghan.

I gave up, left a note on the coffee table: "Called Elroy's Filling Station and left message to tow your car there. I'm downstairs in my laundromat. Josie."

Then I shrugged on my coat, let myself out of my apartment—slamming the door extra hard—and went out to the balcony landing. I stood there for a few seconds and stared at more snow swirling. Then I glanced down at my van, the lone vehicle in my laundromat's parking lot. From the look of my van's roof, about another half inch had fallen. If this kept up, by Sunday night, I'd have to call Chip Beavy, the grandson of one of my most beloved customers, and hire him to do one of his many odd-job specialties, in this case, plowing.

And if we really ended up with a doozy of a snowstorm in the next few days as predicted, I'd drive my van around to my more elderly customers and gather up their laundry to do at no extra charge. The last thing

I wanted was a senior citizen falling and breaking a hip while struggling to bring a basketful of dirty laundry to my laundromat.

Truth be told, I knew I could leave my laundromat open and unattended that day and the next, and just have a few customers. Not too many laundromat customers over Thanksgiving weekend.

After the weekend, that would change. I'd be extra busy for a few days consulting on how to get stains out of Sunday-best outfits so folks could wear them for end-of-year holidays, too.

I went down the metal steps, around to the back entry to my laundromat, and let myself in, stomping off my boots on a mat just inside the door as I flipped on the overhead light in my combo office/storage room. I shrugged out of my coat and hung it on the old coatrack, which had been used by my Uncle Horace.

Somehow that coatrack always gives me comfort. It's an antique Uncle Horace bought years ago from Rusty Wilton, who owns the Antique Depot. Rusty'd been trying to buy it back ever since.

I went out into my laundromat, enjoying the morning ritual: flipping the sign in the door over from CLOSED to OPEN, making a pot of coffee at the front table for customers, pouring myself a mugful.

Then I went back to my storeroom/office and settled down at my desk. I fired up my computer—an electronic-age antique in its own right, seeing as how it was seven years old, and I accessed e-mail via my laundromat's telephone line—and brought up the word-processing file for my latest monthly Stain-Busters column.

My stomach curled. My Stain-Buster's column was due to Caleb Loudermilk on Monday and I was so rattled by all that had happened, I didn't know where to begin, which wasn't like me.

And Caleb was going to try to get my column to go weekly, in more newspapers in Ohio. How would I ever keep up with that?

But it sounded like a challenge, I thought, sipping my coffee and staring at the cursor blinking on my blank computer screen. And it might mean a little more money . . . which was usually tight for me. Maybe that meant I could afford to actually do the apartment conversion from two units to one bigger one, something I'd put off not just because of expense, but because at the back of my mind I thought what if Owen and I really became committed to each other, married even, and I moved out . . .

My stomach curled extra hard, and I winced. Until Owen, I'd only dated occasionally and never thought of marriage, but . . .

Hey, hadn't Sally said Caleb was acting sweet on me? Was that possible? He was kind of cute . . .

I shook my head. Owen was my boyfriend. We might have a few problems, but we'd work them out. Right? My stomach curled yet again.

I really needed to get that column done. Thinking about stains, about how to advise people on how to deal with stains . . . that would surely clear my head, if I'd just focus on that . . .

"Vinegar solves an amazing number of life's problems. Just not heartache . . ."

I stared at the opening line to my column and sighed. Column writing and sharing my stain expertise—usually my happy spot—wasn't working for me that morning. Too much on my mind. Owen. Mama and Daddy showing up. Uncle Fenwick murdered. Daddy accused—maybe guilty, for all I knew—and Mama in my apartment upstairs . . .

The bell over the front door chimed and I jumped up, both because I was surprised by the fact that someone would want to come to my laundromat so early on the day after Thanksgiving, and because it was an excuse to get away from my woes.

I went out to the front of my laundromat, expecting to see someone who perhaps had a cranberry-juice or turkey-gravy-stain problem . . . and stopped short at the sight of who actually filled my laundromat.

Paradise's antique shop owners. Practically all of them.

And they didn't look at all happy.

The Antique Depot was in the old train depot that served passengers until the 1950s, when the last passenger train rolled through town. Freight trains still come rumbling through, though, which is why the Antique Depot carries mostly heavy furniture—pie safes and rolltop desks and the like—and very little china, Rusty Wilton, the Antique Depot's owner, once told me with a twinkle in his eye.

Rusty's usual expression of merriment, though, had given way to anxiety. He was, apparently, the designated spokesperson for the group of nine unhappy antique owners—Lorraine McMurphy looking unhappiest of all—who stood behind him and glared at me.

"I think you can guess why we're here," Rusty said.

"You've had an influx of antique linens and need help getting them stain free?" I gave a nervous laugh. "I know how tiresome those rust stains in old linens can be, and of course this isn't the right time of year to use the old salt, lemon juice, and sunshine trick, but I'm sure I can . . ."

"Josie," Rusty said, sounding just a little sad. He was seventy-ish, a small, stout leprechaun of a man, with a pulpy nose, florid face, and hair that had gone from a deep red to white overnight sometime back in the 1970s. I didn't know why. "I think you know why we're here. FleaMart. Your parents. They're the investors in the orphanage, Josie."

I didn't even try to look shocked. I can't ever fake my emotions, even when I want to try. "I only learned that yesterday," I said, "when my parents showed up at a Thanksgiving reunion at my Mamaw Toadfern's house. I didn't know they were coming back to town. I sure had no idea they were behind FleaMart. I'm sorry. There's nothing I can do."

"Oh sure, you didn't know," Lorraine muttered. She's never liked me ever since I pointed out to her that the cleaning technique I'd recommended for linen and cotton tea towels wasn't working on her "vintage" towels because, in fact, they were a polyester blend. She'd been duped by a clever seller. No antique shop owner wants to hear that. "You haven't been in touch with most of the Toadfern clan for years. Everyone knows that. But now, suddenly, you are . . . just when your parents come back with a plan to put us out of business?"

"That May. She always was trouble," someone else said.

"Not that Henry was any better. I remember when he was a young whelp and stuffed potatoes up all the tailpipes at a football game just because he'd gotten thrown off the team and that meant Fenwick was playing instead . . ."

I gulped. Somehow, word had gotten around about my parents being behind FleaMart, but not yet about Fenwick's murder. That would change soon, I knew.

"Hush!" Rusty snapped over his shoulder at the other antique owners. He gave me a sympathetic look, and I felt grateful. "Josie, you know how hard it is to stay in business. These days, people think nothing of abandoning a local store to go to a bigger chain just to save money, no matter if they sacrifice service."

"Yeah! Look what's happening to the Quik Mart!" Lorraine said.

I knew just what was happening. It was a convenient location to pick up last-minute items—emergency chocolate, if your boyfriend was in the process of leaving you, for example—but even long-term customers were willing to abandon it to save some money at Big Sam's Warehouse, even if it meant a half-hour drive up to Masonville. Even if it meant putting business owners they'd known all of their lives out of business. The Quik Mart was in danger of closing. We'd talked about that at the last Chamber of Commerce meeting. I myself knew I was hanging on to my business because of the nature of it—the laundromats up in Masonville couldn't afford to have any more expensive machines than I did—but I knew I'd lost a few dress-shirt customers to the big dry-cleaning chain up in Masonville.

"Josie, if May and Henry go through with this . . . this . . . FleaMart operation, it could easily put us out of business," Rusty said. "We've come to you to appeal to you to talk to them."

"Uh, yeah, Josie," Lorraine said. "Sorry about what I said a minute ago. Everyone liked your parents. Really."

"Look, it's not a matter of me wanting or not wanting to help you," I said. "I don't like the idea of Flea-

Mart any more than the rest of you. But I really had no idea that my parents were behind this." I swallowed. What I was about to say wouldn't be easy, even though everyone already knew it. "Look, you all know I haven't had any contact with my parents since I was a little kid. I've had no idea where they've been all these years. They just . . . showed up. Kinda like bad luck."

Someone twittered appreciatively. Everyone could relate to the sudden, unforeseen appearance of bad luck.

"Josie, can't you think of anything you could say at all to get your parents to rethink this?" Rusty asked.

"No, I'm sorry, I wish I could, but—" and then I stopped, seeing, suddenly, the image of my mama last night, begging me to help her get her beloved husband out of jail.

I did not want to get involved with my parents. I wished they'd never come. I wished they'd just go away. But here they were. Sometimes, reality just changes around you through no choice of your own . . . but you still have to deal with it. So, one way or another I was going to have to deal with my parents.

And in that moment, it seemed to me that the best way to deal with them would be to promise Mama I'd help find out who'd really killed Fenwick—which might mean, I knew, finding out Daddy really was the killer, although I wouldn't point that out to Mama—in exchange for getting Mama to take their FleaMart plan somewhere else. In fact, it seemed a truly inspired idea!

I looked at Rusty. "Someone called you to let you know about my parents being the FleaMart investors?"

"Someone called each of us, late last night."

"Yeah," said Lorraine. "Then we met for breakfast at Sandy's to figure out what to do. Came up with our plan and as soon as your Open sign flipped over, we paid our bills and trooped over."

"Who called you?"

"Anonymous tip," said someone else.

"We all had anonymous messages or calls sometime between eleven o'clock and midnight," Rusty said.

Well after Rachel and I found Uncle Fenwick. Well after I went with Worthy to deliver the bad news to Mamaw Toadfern and Aunt Nora. But well before Chief Worthy and his colleagues had shown up at the Red Horse Motel to bring my daddy in for questioning.

I wondered what time Chief Worthy had received the anonymous tip.

And, already, I had another question. "Anyone have Caller ID?"

Several people looked confused, a few shook their heads or said "no," but Lorraine said she did, and Rusty said, "I do, too. What are you thinking, Josie?"

"I'm thinking I want both of you to look up the number associated with the call and get back to me with that information."

"Why?" Rusty asked.

"Because. I don't know for sure . . . but I think I have a way to solve your problem and get my parents to leave town . . . without going through with Flea-Mart. But I'll need that information from you, and you'll need to trust me."

"They might trust you, but you shouldn't trust them!"

My mama was sitting in my chair at my desk, legs primly crossed at ankles, arms folded across her stomach. She was also wearing my navy blue shirtwaist dress—a 1950s number I'd picked up at the Vintage

Closet, then removed a stain of unknown origin on the three-quarter sleeves (I guessed wine, and I must have guessed right, because the stain is gone), and replaced the missing and chipped buttons with ones from a blouse of the same vintage that refused to release its stains.

On Mama, the dress looked a little loose, but still fantastic. Which made me realize how tightly it fit me. A depressing thought, considering I'd worn it out with Owen on our last date before he left for Kansas City, to Casa Rinalti, a wonderful little Italian place up in Masonville. I'd gotten spaghetti sauce on the sleeve, which I'd removed with white vinegar.

"I'm glad to see you felt at home," I said, a little too sharply.

"You didn't expect me to wear the same clothes I came in, did you?" She wrinkled her nose. "And you don't have much that's stylish in your wardrobe. Except this. This is lovely." She fingered the wide sleeve cuff appreciatively. "I'd say 1950s."

"That's right. Belonged once upon a time to Natalie Boles. I bought it at Lorraine McMurphy's shop, the Vintage Closet, which is just a few stores down from the Antique Depot—"

Mama waved her hand at me. "Oh, I remember Lorraine. She never did like me. She thought I was always flirting with her husband, what's his name?"

"Roy," I said. And here I'd thought Lorraine disliked me because of my truth-telling about her vintage towels. How many people had judged me because of my parents' actions . . . and I had never known it.

Mama rolled her eyes. "Like I'd want to have anything to do with that sad sack of bony—"

I stiffened. "Mama! Lorraine could still be out in

my laundromat," I hissed. "It's not like this room is soundproof."

"Oh, I don't care if she hears me."

"Well, I do," I said firmly. "I still live in this town."

Mama contemplated me sadly. "I always assumed you'd get out, eventually. You were such a smart little girl." She shook her head, as if to rid herself of the sad expression, then glared at the door between my office/storeroom and laundromat. "I'm sure glad I got out of town," she bellowed loudly. "No one here ever cared a bit about little May Foersthoefel Toadfern. Just gossiped meanly about me."

She looked at me and grinned. "You think they heard that? I hope so."

"Look, I don't know why you left—if it was over gossip or something else—and frankly, I'm not sure I care." Mama looked a little taken aback by that. "The fact is, you and Daddy returned because of this Flea-Mart plan."

She grinned. "It's going to be a wonderful store! A model of many future stores! Do you think Lorraine would like to sell us some of her stock for the vintage clothing department?"

"No, I don't. I think the antique shop owners don't like what FleaMart stands for—it takes away the thrill of the hunt for the customers, number one, and—"

"And scares the crap out of the owners that we'll put them out of business," Mama said, narrowing her eyes, looking angry and mean again. "Well, so what? What do I care if the likes of Lorraine goes out of business? Our first FleaMart in Arkansas is a big hit simply because it takes away the effort of finding the just-right antique or vintage item. Everyone is in a hurry these days, Josie, but lots of people want vintage stuff to make their homes look like they've inherited wonderful items or like they know just how to put these pieces together. Our concept is for those who aren't into antiques for the hunt, but for a fast and easy way to get to the hottest version of the shabby chic look. Need a mission-style lamp for the corner of your living room? Don't have time to go to a bunch of old, musty, overpriced places like Antique Depot or Vintage Closet? Then come to FleaMart! You can run in, pick out a lamp, have it delivered.

"Too busy for even that? Well, then, preview our stock on the Internet! Order a lamp, a tablecloth online! We're even working on a book we're going to self-publish and make available on our future Web site—*Vintage Chic in One Week or Less*! With updated links to available items each week."

Mama waved her hand in a gesture that took in my office/storeroom. "You're a businesswoman now, Josie. You should understand this. You have a logo, a motto. So do we. We're in it for the money, sure, but we're offering a service. We even have a motto that says it all: 'Get Historical! Fast!' Like it?"

I stared at her for a long moment. As tempting as it was, there was no point in debating her on the merits of Daddy's and her business scheme. There was no point in throwing in her face that she had no right to lecture me on life, on Paradise, on business, when she'd just up and abandoned me when I was a kid. A fact that made me surprisingly angry, considering all these years I'd told myself—and believed it—that I didn't care.

What I needed to do was lay it on the line for her, and get her and Daddy back out of Paradise—for good—as soon as I could. Then, I hoped, life in Paradise could go back to normal. A sleepy little town struggling to get by thanks to the industries of a pie company, the nearby man-made state lake and state prison, a gravel quarry, a few other businesses, and a dozen or so dusty, sleepy little antique shops, where true antique lovers could come and find a delightful treasure now and again.

"Mama, I'm only saying this once. You asked me last night to help you get Daddy out of jail, to help figure out who really killed his brother Fenwick. And I said no way. Well, I've changed my mind. I'm going to help you."

Mama clapped her hands together, suddenly like a delighted little child. "Oh, thank you, Josie, thank you—"

"On one condition."

She felt silent, clasped her hands in her lap.

"And that is that you and Daddy agree to drop this whole FleaMart deal."

"What? The old orphanage is the perfect property! And believe it or not, this location is great. Folks can drive in from Cincinnati, Dayton, Columbus . . . really think they're going somewhere quaint and old-fashioned, coming here—"

I cringed, knowing that, in fact, folks in big cities did view our town that way—when and if they came for a visit.

"—and you know even if FleaMart puts the antique stores out of business, it will probably generate other support businesses. Maybe another gas station, another restaurant or two . . . although of course we will have a food court . . ."

I held up a hand. "I don't care. Promise to take your FleaMart idea elsewhere, far enough away that it won't impact Paradise's antique shops, and I'll help you."

Mama frowned. "No. I can't do that."

I shrugged. "Fine with me. I doubt you're going to be able to focus on FleaMart, anyway, with Daddy in jail. And apparently—from what the antique owners said and what you've said and what I picked up on at dinner last night—there's no way anyone is going to talk with you and give you the answers you need to help Daddy. So . . . fine. He can rot in jail."

Mama looked at me, annoyed that I'd cornered her. "All right. No FleaMart—if you can help me find the answers we need to help get your Daddy out of jail."

Did I trust her, believe her about that FleaMart promise? No. Not for a moment. Did I even really believe Daddy wasn't guilty of murdering his brother, Fenwick?

Of course, I didn't want to believe he had, but I had to admit the evidence, though circumstantial, sounded pretty damning.

On the other hand, helping my parents was my only chance to find out something, anything that would give me the leverage I needed to make them go away for good with the FleaMart idea. Not that I was curious about my parents for my own sake. Not at all. Just for Paradise's sake. Truly.

"Good," I said. I went over to her, held out my hand. Mama looked confused for a moment, and then took my hand. How odd. Her hands had always seemed so big and strong to me when I was a little girl, when I watched her lift the wash up to hang on the line behind our trailer. Or make biscuits in our tiny kitchen. And now her hand was smaller than mine, thinner . . .

But still strong in her grasp, as we shook hands.

"What's our first step?" Mama said. "I want to go

over to the jail, see your daddy. And I guess I ought to rent a car—"

"Oh, no," I said. "We'll get over to the jail—but first we're going over to the Red Horse to collect your things. And you're going to have to promise to answer any questions I ask. Honestly."

She hesitated a moment, then said, "All right."

I took a deep breath, not quite believing myself what I was about to say next. "And you're staying with me. I don't want you out of my sight."

Mama nodded with a knowing look. "Ah. Safety in numbers. Whoever accused your daddy might come after me . . ."

"Something like that," I said.

Truth be told, I was more concerned at that moment with protecting Paradise from my mama.

10

While Mama went into her and Daddy's Red Horse room—an end unit farthest from the office—I sat in my minivan and started a list.

Mama had whined at me about having to pack and carry out their luggage all by herself. I reckoned that was usually Daddy's job. But I didn't budge. Mama was just in her early fifties and certainly fit enough to carry her own luggage. I didn't want to give her the notion that I was going to be willing to cater to her, like I guessed Daddy did.

Besides, I really did want to make a list. I'd stumbled into murder investigations in the past. But this was the first one I was purposefully deciding to stick my nose into, right at the outset, and I wanted to be organized about it.

Before we left my laundromat, I'd put next to my register a tent card that said, JOSIE'S OUT FOR A BIT, followed by my cell phone number. Normally when I knew I'd be out, such as to the meeting up at Stillwater later that day, I hired Chip Beavy, the Widow Beavy's grandson, to fill in.

But the Friday after Thanksgiving was so slow, I figured I'd only get one or two drop-ins. And I trusted my fellow Paradisites to not pilfer more than one or two sample-sized boxes of laundry soap. Although—after grabbing my column-idea notebook from my desk—I did lock both the door to my office/storeroom and the back door.

Then Mama and I headed over to the Red Horse Motel. The snow had finally stopped, and both the sun and the county salt trucks had come out, so the drive was easy enough.

My van was still warm from the drive over, and my fleece hat and coat were toasty. I took off my gloves so I could write at the top of a page in the middle of my notebook: "Uncle Fenwick's Murder."

Then I started a list of questions and notes:

1. Who would be angry enough to kill Uncle Fenwick?

I chewed on the eraser end of my pencil, sorry to have to make the following notation: *Daddy, of course. But possibly all of his siblings. No one seemed to like him, except Mamaw and Aunt Nora. If his family feels this way, what about colleagues? Employees? Neighbors? See if can get Mamaw and Aunt Nora to talk tonight . . .*

2. Assuming Daddy didn't do it, who would/could pin the murder on Daddy?

First, obvious answer: Another family member who resents Daddy and Mama's return anyway. After all, everyone at the dinner had seen Daddy brandishing the pearl-handled hunting knife.

Then I thought about that morning's visit from Paradise's antique dealers. None had let on that they knew of Uncle Fenwick's murder. Of course, probably by noon everyone in Paradise would know. But what if one of the dealers already knew about the murder and about the hunting knife (I favored Lorraine McMurphy) and made the anonymous phone call, hoping to thwart FleaMart?

So I wrote down: *Anyone against FleaMart.*

Then the uneasy thought sidled through my brain . . . what if pinning the murder on Daddy had something to do with why Daddy left in the first place? There had to be some reason each of my parents took off and then met up again. Maybe it was as simple as restlessness and coincidence, respectively.

Or maybe, I thought, there was some darker reason one or the other, or both, of them left—something to do with someone else in town. And, now, accusing Daddy of his brother's murder was a form of revenge.

So then I had to write down: *Or anyone who had a reason in the past to hate my mama or daddy.*

I shivered. And it had nothing to do with the heat seeping out of my van, and the cold seeping in.

I rubbed my hands together and made a few more notes:

See if Aunt Nora or Mamaw knows about the broken promise that Daddy and Uncle Fenwick shouted about.

Follow up with Rusty and Lorraine about caller ID. Maybe whoever called them also called Chief Worthy.

I sighed and my breath came out in a white puff. What was taking Mama so long? I stared at my list. I'd come to the conclusion that just about anybody—

including my daddy—could have killed Uncle Fenwick, and the only real ideas I had were to look into Mama and Daddy's past and the caller IDs.

Any other angles? Yes! I rubbed my hands together and jotted down: *Winnie's back on Sunday . . . have her check into Mama and Daddy's business, maybe through the real estate company owned by Rachel, and into Uncle Fenwick's company.* Winnie was an awesome researcher. And if I needed the information desperately, I reckoned I could call her at her daughter's in Chicago . . . but how much could happen before Sunday, that being Friday morning?

Looking back, I should have known better.

A tap at my window startled me, and I quickly closed my notebook before looking up. I reckoned I'd see Mama standing at the truck window, surrounded by luggage, glaring at me because I hadn't helped with the packing up and checking out.

But it was Luke Rhinegold, who, along with his wife, Greta, ran the Red Horse Motel. He was heavily bundled up, and hugged an armful of mail to his chest.

I rolled down my window quickly. "Hey. Everything good? How was Thanksgiving? I thought I'd come by next Wednesday instead of Tuesday for the linens if that's okay . . ."

"Everything's fine. Checked out your mama and daddy. Saw her go into their room. As much luggage as your daddy toted in, she's gonna be a while. It's cold out here. Want to come in for some coffee?"

It was getting cold in the van. I could leave the back unlocked so Mama could lift in her luggage.

I hopped out and followed Luke in, slowing my pace to match his careful shuffling across the snowy, icy parking lot, and felt a jolt of concern at his gait.

I loved Luke and Greta like family, like grandparents, really. It hit me that, over the years, I'd put together a makeshift family.

I'd have to ponder that later, I thought. Because it struck me also that Luke and Greta had owned the Red Horse Motel for years before I was even born. And they might be able to tell me something about my parents' pasts.

In the Red Horse Motel's office, just behind the check-in counter in the lobby, Luke made us mugs of hot chocolate from powdered mix in paper packets and hot water from the coffeemaker's carafe. We tossed our coats, hats, and gloves on a spare chair, and sat on a turquoise and chrome couch that looked like it had been ripped from the backseat of someone's 1950s Chevy, but that Greta swore was a 1930s Art Deco couch she'd picked up for a great price at the Antique Depot. The couch was surprisingly comfortable.

I asked Luke about Greta, and he looked sad but made himself smile as he said she was napping more these days and that she'd become a bit more forgetful than usual. They had a doctor's appointment set up for the following month.

I expressed my concern and good wishes and then we fell quiet. That happens, sometimes, when I linger over a cup of coffee or hot chocolate after delivering freshly washed linens, but this time, an uneasiness welled up between us.

We were both, I knew, thinking about my mama and daddy.

"You know," I finally said, "I don't remember much about my parents. I was wondering what you could tell me about them."

Luke swirled his mug, watching the marshmallows, before saying, "Well, why don't we start with what you do remember about them?"

The brief bits of memory—the smell of Daddy's soap, Mama and the wishing well—flashed through my mind. "Not much," I said. "Uncle Horace never said anything that I can recollect about my mama, although she was his only sibling. I asked Aunt Clara once or twice about my parents, and she would just say they were funny-turned." That was her old-fashioned expression for different or odd. Not many people use it nowadays, but I knew Luke would know what I meant.

He smiled. "Sounds like your Aunt Clara. Taciturn."

I nodded. Then, with a jolt, I remembered something else. "She gave me a box—an old hat box—a few months after I moved in with her and Uncle Horace. It held a few of my mama's things, she said. A hair barrette, I think. Some old coins. Photos." I shook my head. "It's somewhere on my bedroom closet shelf. I'd actually forgotten it until now." I shrugged. "Truth be told, after a while I didn't think about my parents much. Uncle Horace and Aunt Clara were my parents, really."

"They were good people," Luke said, sounding a wee bit sad. "And good friends."

I didn't remember him or Greta coming around our house often, but then Uncle Horace and Aunt Clara didn't entertain or go out much. What with the laundromat and Aunt Clara's job at the Breitenstrater Pie Factory, and taking care of Guy, they didn't get much of a chance. What social life they had revolved around the United Methodist Church.

"They were good people," I agreed. "And good parents."

"God rest their souls," Luke said.

We were silent a moment, thinking of them, as we sipped our chocolate.

"What about other things you heard about your mama and daddy?" Luke said. "May and Henry, that is."

"Nothing from the Toadferns, except one night I overheard Aunt Clara ranting and raving that it was wicked of Mamaw Toadfern to cut me off, blaming me in Mama's stead for my daddy running off. And the Toadferns—except for a few cousins—have had nothing to do with me until this Thanksgiving. But even Sally hasn't ever said anything about my daddy—not that she'd remember anything, either, since she's my age—or passed on any comments from other family members."

"What about people in town? I mean, we all ended up thinking of Clara and Horace as your parents, but . . ." he shrugged. I knew what the shrug meant. People talk. People judge. People get bored and stir up trouble where there's no need for any.

I told him about that morning's visit from the antique dealers. Then I went ahead and told him about Thanksgiving dinner at Mamaw Toadfern's and about Uncle Fenwick, leaving out the particularly upsetting details about how he'd been both semi-hung and stabbed.

Luke expressed his shock and then, after he'd had a chance to process the news, he said, "You know, the early days for Greta and me were great at this motel. Families came and stayed so they could go over to Licking Creek Lake, especially when it was newly made. There were more businesses and jobs in the area, too, and people came here to visit their families. You don't remember those days."

I didn't say anything. I'd been born well after those days were over. From the stories of Paradise's old days, by the time I was born, the town had long since peaked.

"We still get families, of course, but . . . well, what I'm saying is Greta and I, to stay in business, we've learned to take seriously 'judge not lest ye be judged.' To not question who's checking in from around here— and with who, if you know what I mean."

I knew. I also knew Luke and Greta had a reputation for never gossiping about their customers. The only dirty laundry I ever got from them was, well, actual dirty laundry. Their tight-lipped-ness helped keep them in business.

"Some folks have judged us harshly for that, though. One was your mama and Uncle Horace's daddy."

I lifted my eyebrows at that. I'd never known my granddaddy on either side of my family—or my ma-maw on my mother's side. These elders had all died before I was born. And, come to think of it, my Uncle Horace never talked about his parents. Uncle Horace was also a man of very few words.

"Your grandfather, Lionel Foersthoefel, was a stern man. Told me many a time at church I should run the sinners out of the rooms. I always just told him it wasn't my place to judge—or to poke my nose into who was meeting who. He was exceptionally stern, and that can have strange effects on children, well after they've grown up. Whenever I saw your Uncle Horace, he seemed quiet and enduring, no matter what was going on around him, and after several encounters with his father, I realized why."

I nodded, understanding that Luke had just given a perfect description of how my uncle had always approached life.

"And for his much younger sister—your mama—it meant, well, a wild, rebellious streak. Your daddy was a wild one, too—mostly because of competing with your Uncle Fenwick and never quite feeling he measured up. When your mama and your daddy got together, everyone thought that would settle them both down. They'd both broken a lot of hearts and sowed a lot of wild oats."

Luke paused and looked away. Finally, he looked back at me. He looked sorrowful about what he was going to say.

"Josie, from my experience one of two things can happen when you put two fiery people together like your parents. They can either help calm each other down. Or . . . they can flare up. Combust."

"And I take it my parents combusted?"

He sighed. "They were so much in love—everyone could see that. But they never quite . . . settled down. There were fights. Things they did to try to hurt one another, to get back at each other. And they ended up hurting a lot of people in the process."

I set the coffee mug on the table. I could feel bile trying to rise up in my throat. I swallowed, my stomach curling. I remembered how flirtatious Mama had been toward Uncle Fenwick, how annoyed my daddy had looked, how red Uncle Fenwick had turned, how scared Aunt Nora had looked, how angry Mamaw had been. And I remembered Mama's references to C. J. Worthy, Chief John Worthy's daddy and to Lorraine's husband, Roy.

Had Mama had an affair with Uncle Fenwick? Or with other men?

Had Daddy had affairs, too, maybe to get back at her for her infidelity?

Or had she had affairs to get back at him for his infidelity?

Was any of that connected with Uncle Fenwick's murder . . . or why someone had called in a tip that pointed to Daddy as his killer?

"Who all did they hurt?" I asked, trying to keep my voice steady. And failing.

But Luke shook his head. "You'll have to ask your mama and daddy about that. Don't know that they'll tell you. I don't know the whole truth, anyway. I just know I heard lots of talk, and saw each of them around here a few times not with each other. After all these years, I'm truly not sure I remember who they were with.

"I'm just telling you, as someone who cares a lot about you, that your mama and daddy can turn on the charm. But together, they can be like fire and oil—one makes the other burn higher and brighter, and people around them get burned. Be careful, Josie. I don't want to put your parents down—they are who they are—but fire doesn't know—or care—who or what it's burning. And I just—"

Suddenly, Luke stopped, his eyes wide. I turned around. There stood Mama, in the doorway, looking angry. How much had she overheard?

But I was suddenly angry, too. "Mama, why didn't you ring the bell?"

She ignored me, glaring at Luke. "Did you know you left the door between the check-in desk in that pathetic excuse for a lobby and your office wide open? And that your voice carries, Mr. Gettlehorn?"

Primly, she added, "I've left the key to our stuffy little room on your counter. Believe me, I won't be recommending this place in the future FleaMart brochures!"

11

Mama did not speak to me all the way from the Red Horse Motel to the tiny Paradise jail, where she visited with Daddy and made sure he was okay. Other than being rattled and whiny, he was. I'd taken the opportunity to go out in the hallway and call Cherry and leave a message asking if she could possibly keep an eye on Mama after we were back from Stillwater.

Mama didn't speak to me all the way up to Stillwater.

In the parking lot, I said, "I have to go to this meeting. You'll just have to come in with me . . ."

"I don't want to. Why didn't you just leave me at your apartment?"

"I told you, I think you'll be, um, safer if you're not alone."

"I'll wait here." She crossed her arms.

Right. Like I would leave her alone here at Stillwater, where my cousin Guy and other autistic adults lived. If she got out and wandered into the general meeting room where group activities took place, who knows what she might do? She could upset lots of people . . .

But she looked at me, her eyes wide. "Please, Josie, I'm just really tired. And I need a break from people. I'll take a nap."

"It's starting to snow," I said impatiently, gesturing at the windshield to the lazily drifting flurries outside. "You'll be cold. Come on."

"I have this thick coat," she said, wrapping her mink more tightly around her. "And there's a quilt in the backseat, I noticed." Her eyes got even wider. I felt my heart soften.

"I bet you carry it for emergencies," she said. It was true. My van was, thankfully, reliable, but before it I had a car that broke down often, so I got in the habit of keeping an old quilt in my vehicle. If my vehicle broke down while it was cold, I'd stay warm. If it was hot, I could sit outside on the grass while waiting for AAA without my thighs getting itchy. "You always were a smart girl, Josie. Very smart," she said.

I know, I know. And yet, I felt myself falling for it. What kid—even a twenty-nine-year-old kid who was abandoned years ago by both parents—doesn't love compliments?

She picked up a book from the stack at her feet—returns I meant to take to the bookmobile the next week when Winnie was back and making her appointed stops.

"Oh, look! An Anne George mystery! Ooh, I just love that series, too," Mama gushed.

Did she? Or had she just read the author's name off the most recent title I'd checked out—*Murder Boogies with Elvis*?

But then she said, "I just loved the one where Mouse and Sister went down to the condo in Destin, Florida, didn't you?" That did it. My resistance was mostly down. Here was my fifty-something mama, looking like a little girl in her fur, having complimented my intelligence, gushing over one of the most beloved aspects of my life—books—practically begging to be tucked in with a quilt so she could read.

Then she said, in a hushed voice, "And I haven't read this one yet."

That did it. I trusted her to stay in the van, snug in her fur and quilt, reading.

"What do you suppose the meeting is going to be about?" asked Nellie Kaiser, who was sitting next to me at one of the tables in the cafeteria. We each had Styrofoam cups of coffee.

I didn't really want any coffee, but I'd gotten some anyway, mostly just to have something warm to hold on to, something to do with my nervousness. Nellie, whose son was also one of the full-time residents, had already drunk her coffee, and was tearing off bits of the rim of the cup, and making a tidy pile of the Styrofoam shards.

Our nervousness had nothing to do with the caffeine in our cups. Meetings like this at Stillwater were rare. We knew the announcement had to be something important, but we didn't know what.

Stillwater was so important to us and our loved ones. When people hear the phrase—a residential home for adults with autism—the reactions vary. How sad, many say. Can't they be mainstreamed? others say, a little outraged, having read reports of the progress made with children with autism.

But the fact is, the adults at Stillwater have severe cases of autism. Many, like my cousin Guy, who is in his midforties, were children in an era that didn't understand autism nearly as well as it is understood now—not that it is currently a fully understood condition. Living at home with one or two caretakers would be difficult for all concerned—sure, it was possible to do, but would the adults with autism really blossom as they did here?

The answer was no. Stillwater is a special place. It is anything but depressing—in fact, it's one of the most uplifting places I know. The adults who live there are nurtured to be the best individuals they can be, not in spite of their autism, but simply because the leaders of Stillwater understand the residents in their care are, first and foremost, individuals. The autism is never ignored, but it's not the sole focus of how Stillwater's residents' lives are organized.

It's kind of like going with the current, instead of against it, in a journey down a river.

And that's important, because autism doesn't have just one face. In fact, in the United States alone, as many as one and a half million children and adults are thought to have autism. And autism is unique to each person because it's a neurological disorder that presents as a developmental disability on a whole spectrum from mild, moderate to severe. So autism manifests itself as uniquely as fingerprints. Of course, just as all fingerprints have certain characteristics, so does autism—difficulties with speech, with interrelationships, with repetitive behaviors, with eye contact, with change, with motor skills. It's a complex disease, but just like with fingerprints, the loops and whorls of autism are unique to each individual.

For example, my cousin Guy loves to grow things, especially pumpkins. No one knows why. Does it really matter? He is encouraged, with guidance, to work in the greenhouse and gardens of Stillwater.

But he hates the color red. No one knows why. It doesn't really matter. And since no one at Stillwater in particular loves red, the color is kept to a minimum, and he's been taught techniques to follow when he sees red—such as focusing on his breathing. He also has minimal speech, so we communicate with him in other ways, in drawing.

Nellie's son, Stuart, on the other hand, has fairly good speaking skills, although a stilted, repetitive style. So during activities that bring the public to Stillwater—and Stillwater is lucky to be surrounded by a supportive, loving bunch of tiny communities and farms—he's usually the greeter at the annual harvest festival, etc., etc.

And he loves to calculate distances. Somehow he knows just how far it is from anywhere—no one has yet to stump him—to Stillwater or anywhere else. He's fascinated with maps. So he's allowed to study them, only not to be so obsessed with them that he doesn't do anything else.

But he seems to have no comprehension of time. The staff at Stillwater works with him on that.

Although Guy is a much older cousin, he is really emotionally like a younger brother to me. And for Nellie and me and the other parents or caregivers streaming in, Stillwater is like a big old extended family. We come from all walks of life, from nearby and far away, to this place to make sure our loved ones with autism find the shelter and support they need to function as fully as they can—more fully than they would in a traditional institution or even in our homes—and we support each other, calling and e-mailing and sharing laughter and tears. Just like a big old family.

"Have you been following the state budget-cut news?" Nellie asked.

I nodded. "I have. Scary."

She nodded. We both knew quite well that Stillwater—though funded through private donations and trust funds from families of residents—also needed state funding. Yet, the state was cutting funding to any number of programs for the disabled, elderly, and poor.

"I'll do anything I can if that is what this is about—fund-raisers, a fund drive, organizing a march in Columbus, even if it means leaving my job . . ." Nellie's eyes watered. She lived up in Detroit, working as an insurance agent, supporting two young grandchildren, whose parents—Nellie's daughter and son-in-law—had died in a car crash. That meant visits for her were rarer and harder to organize. And, like me with Guy, she was the sole guardian of Stuart. Her husband had passed away several years ago and Stuart was their only child besides her daughter. I guessed she'd missed Thanksgiving with her grandchildren, who visited their dad's parents in Chicago on some holidays, to come down to Stillwater just for that meeting.

I smiled, trying to look comforting. "I know you would, and I'll be with you. But let's wait and see. I haven't heard anything about budget concerns."

I visited Guy at Stillwater regularly on Sunday afternoons, and sometimes in between, and often stayed after dinner Sunday nights to help the laundry staff with particularly difficult laundry issues. Sometimes from Edna, one of the laundry room workers, I picked up tidbits of gossip. Stillwater always welcomed donations, of course, but I didn't think that this particular meeting was about budgets.

The room quieted as Don Richmond entered and went up to a podium that had been moved into the cafeteria for the occasion. My stomach and my throat both tightened.

"Thank you all for taking time out of your Thanksgiving holiday to come here," Don said. He sounded both sad and nervous. I tensed some more. "I wanted to make my announcement to as many people here in person as I could, rather than just by letter, and I knew many of you would be here for the holidays, especially people from farther away.

"I'm not sure how to say what I need to say, except . . . I've loved every minute of my past ten years here."

Oh no, I thought. Surely Don couldn't be about to announce what it sounded like he was going to announce. Nellie and I looked at each other. I could see in her eyes that she sensed, too, what was coming.

"As some of you already know, I have long been interested in studying neuropsychiatry. I have an opportunity to go to Pennsylvania to study, and this would place me closer to my parents as well." There were murmurs and nods of understanding throughout the cafeteria. We all knew Don's dad had suffered a debilitating stroke a year before, and that Don's mom could use some help, and that Don was close to both of his parents.

"So, it is with both sadness and joy that I announce my resignation as director, effective the end of this year," Don said. There was a collective murmuring and I felt tears prick my eyes. "But Assistant Director Mary Rossbergen will take over at that point. We've already started working on the transition. The board of directors and a search committee that will include guardians of residents and our psychiatric and medical consultants will be formed early in December."

As he said this, he looked toward me. His gaze crossed the room and our eyes met briefly.

Me? He thought I should be on the search committee? Nah—that had to be wishful thinking on my part.
I was sure the Stillwater board would want more educated guardians on the committee—people like Nellie.

I reached over and patted her arm. She had pulled a
tissue out of her purse and was dabbing at her eyes.
Don was taking questions, and I would have loved to
stay, but I wanted to get back to Mama. I felt uneasy
that I'd left her alone in my van—and not for her sake.

"It'll be okay," I whispered to Nellie.

"I know," she whispered back. "It's just that . . ." she
stopped, her voice catching. I knew just how she felt. I
gave her another pat, and stood up, working my way
quietly out of the room. I'd find out more the following
week, when I'd go up for another visit.

I slipped out of the cafeteria and into the lobby—
really just the front parlor of the old, big rambling
farmhouse that had been converted over and added on
to, to create Stillwater Farms. I was just about to the
front door when the door to the activity room opened.
Mary Rossbergen came out.

"Josie! You're leaving the meeting already?" she
looked confused, knowing that wasn't like me.

"I have . . . out-of-town guests," I said, stretching the
truth just a little. "I know you'll do a great job, but—"

Mary patted my arm, as my voice caught, just as I'd
patted Nellie's only moments before. Maybe I wasn't
taking this as well as I thought.

"Things will work out just fine," she said, glancing
at the door to the cafeteria. "How did everyone seem to
take Don's announcement?"

"Definitely surprised. I'm sure everyone is sad to
see him go, but understands. This move sounds like the
right one for him and his family." Who among us

couldn't understand the call to take care of a loved one? "Is everything okay? I was surprised that you weren't in there."

"I meant to be. We had a surprise visitor show up." She looked at me curiously. "But of course, you knew that."

My heart clenched. I glanced at the exit door. Oh no . . .

"Your mother is really quite charming. I can understand her eagerness to see her nephew after all of these years. But I'm a little surprised you didn't call ahead—"

There was just the faintest bit of admonition in her voice. Of course I knew not to spring surprise guests on the Stillwater staff or residents.

I put a smile on my face and said carefully, "My mother was a surprise guest this weekend. I told her to wait in my van. I'm sorry she didn't listen to me. Where is she?"

Mary smiled reassuringly, mollified that I'd at least tried to keep my mother in control, but she still looked a bit confused. No wonder. Everyone knew my parents hadn't been part of my life since my early childhood and just accepted my Uncle Horace and Aunt Clara as my parents, as I had.

"She's in the activity room—and don't look so worried. Stephanie and Robert are in there, too, and they have her working alongside Guy on a project." Mary looked thoughtful for a moment. "She's actually quite good with him."

We said our good-byes. I took a long, deep breath to steady myself. As much as I might want to dash into the activity room and yell at Mama for ignoring my plea to just wait in the van, I knew how upsetting that would be to Guy and the other residents.

So I entered the room, quietly.

Stephanie and Robert had Guy and several residents working on a craft—in this case, mosaic trays. The trays would be sold at the craft fair in a few months.

For Guy, this was a perfect wintertime activity. One of the things he liked about the greenhouse work was the careful handling of small seeds.

For the mosaics, I knew, there wasn't a set pattern or design. The residents who liked working on the mosaics were given a collection of tiny tiles and the trays and the glue, and created their own patterns or just glued them down abstractly.

For Guy, of course, there were no red tiles. He seemed to like working in pale blue and green and cream. And he always placed the tiles one right next to another, starting in the upper right hand corner, working row by row, never working out a design ahead of time. And yet, his trays always ended up looking like an enlargement of a wave or swirl.

Guy stood at the work table—he liked to stand and found sitting often uncomfortable, and the staff didn't force him to sit if he didn't want to—rocking from foot to foot. He liked rocking, too. A rocking chair was one of the only ways he would sit. He wasn't very verbal— just talked in brief phrases, usually repeating what he said several times, sometimes reversing the words of the phrase.

Mama sat on the chair that was for Guy, if he had wanted to use it.

Carmine, one of the few female residents of Stillwater (autism occurs more often in men than in women), was brushing my mother's hair. Mama didn't seem to mind, and I knew this was a treat for Carmine, who would brush hair all the time if she could. It was one of the few ways she would relate to others. Usually, she was aloof and preferred to be alone.

In fact, Mama didn't even seem to notice Carmine's brushing of her hair. She just stared up at Guy, fascinated with him, her eyes filled with wonder. He didn't seem to even be aware of her presence.

And I saw two things in Mama's face. One was wonder. And the other was sadness.

As much as I wanted to hang on to it, I felt my anger draining away—at least, most of it.

"You're mad at me," Mama said for the third time on our drive from Stillwater Farms back to Paradise.

"No, I'm not," I answered for the third time—this time through gritted teeth. "Just annoyed."

Then we lapsed into silence—well, our own silence. I had the radio on the Masonville country station—WHEE. Dolly Parton was singing about love, loss, and hope. Mama started humming along and stared out her window, taking in the stubbled, snow-draped fields and farmhouses and grain silos and patches of trees as if she were visiting a foreign land, all new to her.

I tried to take pleasure in the swirl of snow as I drove—and couldn't. I was fuming.

"Damn it, Mama, why didn't you listen to me and sit in the van and read, like I told you to?" I burst out, and then winced. I sounded like I was berating a small child. Which, in attitude at least, was how she was acting.

"See, I knew you were mad at me."

I groaned. "You don't understand. You can't just walk into a home like that the way you walk into, say, a restaurant or hotel lobby. Adults with autism . . ."

"No one seemed upset, at least, after that nice Mary

Rossbergen and I chatted. And I had a nice time seeing Guy again . . ."

"Yes, it worked out okay this time, but . . ."

". . . he looks just like Horace did at that age," Mama said. She wasn't listening to me. Her voice had taken on a different quality—a little wistful, a little distant. "Same beefy build. Square jawline. I remember how excited Horace and Clara were when they found out they were finally going to have a child—they'd had a hard time trying, just like Mama did. I was eight when Guy was born. And about eleven or twelve when they realized something was really, really wrong—that Guy didn't relate to other people the way other kids did, that he rarely talked and when he did, he repeated phrases over and over or mimicked what other people said.

"My parents—especially Daddy—wanted Horace and Clara to put Guy in a home far away, an institution. The doctor . . . Daddy . . . all said it was because Clara was a bad mama that Guy had autism. People believed stuff like that then. But Clara didn't let them get to her. And Horace stopped talking to our parents, rather than letting his wife hear such nonsense.

"I was proud of them, but I missed Horace. They knew that, and one day, when Guy was eight, I went over to visit, anyway. I told them our parents said it was okay, which was a lie, but I knew Horace would send me back home if he knew I wasn't supposed to be there.

"And I could tell they needed a little time to themselves. I told them, hey, why not go get a cup of coffee and pie, over at Sandy's? Guy had finally settled down for a nap."

My stomach clenched. I grasped the steering wheel

harder. I had a feeling that I wasn't going to like what was coming, that something terrible—from the lilt in Mama's voice—was about to happen in her story.

"But he woke up when some friends of mine came by. They saw me hanging out on the porch. I heard Guy inside, starting to cry and scream. I reckon that was how he always woke up. I ran in and my friends followed me.

"I guess his behavior made them nervous—and they started laughing and making jokes. That made him cry and scream more and start banging his head against the wall.

"I should have held him. Or called over to Sandy's, which is what Horace and Clara told me to do if there was a problem. But I panicked. And I didn't want my friends to drop me. So . . . I ran off with them."

I gasped. "You left Guy all alone?"

"Yes, Josie, I did," Mama said. "Horace and Clara didn't talk to me after that." Her voice was thick with anger—whether at me, Aunt Clara and Uncle Horace, herself, or even Guy, I wasn't sure. "I never saw Guy again until today."

Our silence again. Dolly was done with her song. A truck commercial—with a man screaming "deals for wheels!"—came on. I turned the radio down.

"I always admired Horace and Clara for how they took care of Guy," Mama said. The anger was suddenly gone from her voice. She just sounded weary. "And I admire what you're doing for Guy. Some folks, Josie . . . some folks just aren't cut out for taking care of kids." Her voice got a little softer. "Not just challenging kids like Guy, but . . . ."

Go on, say it, I thought. Say you weren't cut out for staying around, that it wasn't anything I did, that I could have been as easygoing as Guy was challenging and you still would have taken off . . .

"When you had me take those coins to the wishing well, what were you wishing for, Mama?"

All the questions I had, and that's what popped out? But it was the same question that had haunted me the night before, too.

"Coins? I don't remember any coins." I could tell she was lying.

"I know you must," I said. "Whenever you'd get mad about Papa leaving, you'd say, that damned man, ran off and left us with a bag of worthless coins, can't even use them at the laundromat, and then you'd . . ."

My cell phone rang. "Oops, there's your phone," Mama chirped brightly.

"It's in my purse by your feet. Just fish it out and hand it to me—"

"No, too dangerous to drive and talk," she said, pulling my cell phone out of my purse. She flipped it open. "Hello. Josie's cell phone, Josie's mama speaking."

"Mama! Give me my phone—"

She shushed me and swatted my hand away. "Sorry. Josie was babbling and driving dangerously, but she has both hands back on the steering wheel now. Who did you say this was?"

I stared at the snow and road, fuming, while Mama said oh, and mmm hmm, and oh yes, of course I remember!, and we'll be there as soon as we can.

"Well, how refreshing. That was Cherry Feinster. She says she still remembers the joy it brought her and her family when she came home from our Ranger Girls meeting with all those glittery pinecone turkeys."

Cherry taunted me once at school that her mama had

thrown those away since my mama was a tart. Not that I knew what that meant at the time.

"And she remembers my yummy oatmeal cinnamon cookies."

Cherry hated those, I recalled. We all did. Mama always put in too much cinnamon.

"And she wanted to welcome me back with a complimentary facial and manicure."

I glanced over in time to see Mama stretch out her hands and admire her nails. "Well, I just had my nails done before we came. Maybe she'll throw in a pedicure. I do love foot massages. Wasn't that nice of her?"

"Very," I said. I'd thank her later for taking my mama off my hands—and making it seem like it was something she really wanted to do for her old Ranger Girl leader.

"Do you think we'd have time to pick up the ingredients for those cinnamon oatmeal cookies . . ."

"No! Now, listen, while I'm glad—"

"You're mad at me, aren't you?"

"No," I said through gritted teeth. "It's just that when my cell phone rings, I'd rather . . ."

"Oh, listen, a newer song!"

Mama turned up the radio. It was the country singer, Sara Evans, singing "Suds in the Bucket." Mama sang with the chorus: "Now she's gone in the blink of an eye, she left the suds in the bucket and the clothes hangin' out on the line . . ."

Yeah, she sure did, I thought. And then I reminded myself to resist the temptation of bitterness. It helped to remember all the times I'd hung out the wash with Aunt Clara, or helped Uncle Horace at the laundromat—even if I had to awkwardly wipe my eyes with the back of my gloved hand.

12

"No, this is your mama, here," Mrs. Beavy said, pointing to a picture on a page opposite the one I'd been gazing at.

I looked at the black-and-white photo, just above the tip of her slightly trembling index finger.

It was a junior-year picture—a young, fresh face, an early 1970s long shag haircut, wide hopeful eyes, loop earrings, and a mischievous curve to the smile.

I double-checked the name. Sure enough. May Foersthoefel.

This was the last face I'd have picked from the pages as my mama, even though I saw in it where I got my nose, where I got the curve to my chin and eyebrows. It was just so hopeful, confident, eager.

I looked up at Mrs. Beavy. She's one of my regular customers—at least for rugs and throws and bedspreads, which I do for her in the big drum washers. She's eighty-something, and it's her grandson, Chip, who works for me on a semiregular basis.

In fact, about a half hour after I dropped Mama off at Cherry's, and went back to my laundromat to stew over my column—there were, as I'd known would be the case, no customers—Chip came by the laundromat and said his grandma would like to see me. I didn't ask questions; I just left my laundromat, still open, and customerless, except for Chip, who had a load of jeans to do. I walked through the snow one street over to Plum Street and Mrs. Beavy's little Cape Cod–style house.

Mrs. Beavy—who I think of as being like a great-grandmother to me—is the head of the Paradise Historical Society. She used to store much of the society's holdings in her second story and in the converted garage out back and even throughout her house, but now the historical society had inherited the old Breitenstrater mansion and was in the process of converting it over to a local museum. The grand opening would be not that Christmas, but the following one.

Getting the society's holdings out of Mrs. Beavy's house had made it more spacious and comfortable to be in. In fact, if for reasons as yet unknown to me I hadn't been looking at the old high school yearbook from when my mama and daddy had attended East Mason County High School, I'd probably have enjoyed sitting next to Mrs. Beavy on her doily-covered settee and drinking hot chocolate. (She was sipping ginseng tea.) As it was, my drink had gone cold and mostly untouched.

"It took Chip all morning to find the right box with the old yearbooks—which of course will be shelved in the library at the Paradise Historical Society's new home, but he finally did it."

That, I thought, explained the dusty jeans and shirt on top of Chip's load.

My gaze strayed back to the photo of Mama. There was nothing angry or penetrating about those eyes. The photo, I thought suddenly, must have been taken before the awful incident with her friends at my Aunt Clara and Uncle Horace's house . . . or had it? Did I just want to believe that?

"Why are you showing me this?" I asked. I knew there had to be a pretty good reason. Showing me the photo seemed, somehow . . . cruel. And I knew Mrs. Beavy was anything but cruel.

"Luke Rhinegold called this morning," Mrs. Beavy said lightly. "He suggested it might help you to, well, get to know your parents better if you knew something about their past."

I raised my eyebrows. "Why do I get the feeling that there are lots of people in this town who know things about my parents that I should have known all along? Why doesn't someone just tell me whatever it is?"

Mrs. Beavy's smile was that of someone who has learned patience over time, but didn't really expect younger people to understand. "It's not that simple," she said. "I don't know of any one thing you need to know about your parents. I don't think anyone else does, either. But twenty-some years ago, they were quite the talk of the town. Maybe that matters, with all that's happened since their surprise return to town. Maybe not."

Since Uncle Fenwick's bizarre murder, I thought, with a shudder.

I glanced down at the picture of Mama, did some quick mental calculating. "This is from when Mama was a junior in high school?"

"She's sixteen in the picture," Mrs. Beavy said. "One of my children was a grade above her and your papa's grade. The school pictures were taken in early fall, and I remember your mama. She was such a pretty, sweet thing. Not a close friend of my daughter's, but sometimes she'd drop by on the way home for a glass of lemonade or cocoa." Mrs. Beavy paused. "Your mama always seemed a little reluctant to go home," she added quietly.

I thought about that. With the estrangement between her brother and her parents, and the apparent heavy-handed judgmental attitude of her parents, that wasn't too surprising.

"Do you have the yearbook from her senior year?" I asked. "I'd like to see her senior-year picture, too, after I look at Daddy's senior-year picture in this one."

Mrs. Beavy looked at me evenly. "Your mama didn't have a senior-year picture, Josie. She dropped out of school before graduating. She . . . had to."

I sucked in a breath. I understood what the euphemism meant. But Mama had been in her early twenties when she had me. So that meant I had a brother or a sister. Oh my God.

My breath went out of me with a sudden heaviness. Surely Mrs. Beavy had to be wrong. I studied her face.

Mrs. Beavy was right. I swallowed, wondering how her parents—my grandparents—must have reacted. And I knew right away. Given how they'd reacted to Horace's son, they would not have been very loving about their only other child, their only daughter, getting pregnant out of wedlock.

Mrs. Beavy gently turned pages and pointed out other pictures to me. My daddy and Uncle Fenwick, side by side in their senior-year pictures. Both of them looking handsome and full of promise, too, both of them looking proud and tough in the East Mason

County High School football photograph—never mind
that West Mason County always managed to beat our
high school.

And then the homecoming court photo. There was
Mama and Daddy. But they weren't with each other.

"Who are they with?" I asked. "Mama always said
she and Daddy were high school sweethearts."

"And they were. But not in the fall of that year," Mrs.
Beavy said. "Your daddy is with my daughter, Sue
Ellen."

I looked up at Mrs. Beavy, startled. But Mrs. Beavy
was smiling pleasantly. If my daddy had broken her
daughter's heart, Sue Ellen must have recovered
quickly. Mrs. Beavy didn't look troubled by the memory of my daddy and her daughter at all.

"And your mama is with Lenny Burkette," Mrs.
Beavy said.

"They dated," I said flatly. Effie Burkette had been
insistent that Lenny and my mama had been just
friends.

"They didn't just date. Lenny worshiped your
mama. I think he thought they would get married
someday."

I swallowed. No wonder it had seemed awkward to
Effie when Rachel had me over a few times to their
house . . . and when I went over there on Thanksgiving. That explained why Lenny looked at me so oddly,
commented about how I looked like my mother, kept
staring. Lenny had never married. I wondered if he'd
ever gotten over his broken heart.

Next Mrs. Beavy pointed to a picture from a Christmas dance that showed the East Mason County High
School gym festooned with tinsel and garlands.

"Turn about dance," she said. I looked at the picture

of my mama and daddy dancing, their eyes locked, clearly oblivious to the photographer and the other kids.

"Your parents started dating just after homecoming," Mrs. Beavy said. "My Sue Ellen cried for a whole night after she and your daddy broke up—and promptly started dating Tommy Groves." She chuckled. "Lenny took it a lot harder. Probably that was in part because his grandpa died that year, and his daddy took off. His parents were already divorced, but I think it bothered him a whole lot that his dad didn't stay in touch.

"Of course, it wasn't unusual for Lenny's dad to take off. Everyone in Paradise knew Junior Hedberg to be a mean drunk who abused Effie and Lenny," Mrs. Beavy said, sounding scornful—a rare attitude for her. "But when he was gone long enough that fall that it appeared he was never coming back, and word got around that Lenny had gotten a letter from him to that effect, we were all relieved." She shook her head. "Lenny took it hard, though. But a few years later, of course, his mama remarried Rich Burkette, and . . ."

"My parents," I said, trying to refocus Mrs. Beavy on them. Otherwise, she'd go off in a tangent about the Burkettes—and I already knew all about how hunky-dory everything had gone with them. I'd spent months lying on the roof of that storage shed hearing about it from Rachel Burkette.

"Oh, yes, I'm sorry," Mrs. Beavy said. "Well, you see, later that school year, your parents had to get married. Your mama dropped out of school. After high school, both your Uncle Fenwick and your daddy got jobs as helpers in the C. J. Worthy Plumbing Company. Your parents tried to make a go of it, but it was hard. Your daddy, especially, just couldn't seem to settle down. And your mama would try to get back at him by flirting with Fenwick. This was before he married Nora, by the way.

"Fenwick loved the attention from your mama because he knew it drove your daddy nuts. Those two just couldn't get past their competitiveness.

"And then, your mama lost the baby. She was so torn up. I still remember seeing her around town, her face all swollen from crying. Henry tried to be a good husband. But they were still young and didn't have a clue how to handle grief, and no support from their families, who didn't want them to get married in the first place. Henry would have an affair, May would get mad and flirt, they'd break up, get back together, and the whole cycle would start again.

"Until May got pregnant again. This time, with you. After that, they stayed settled down again, but then Henry just up and disappeared, and well . . ."

I nodded. "I know the rest of the story." Well, I didn't know the real why's of Daddy and Mama's disappearances, or how they'd reconnected. But Mrs. Beavy couldn't tell me any of that.

But there was something else she could tell me.

"You said Daddy had affairs and Mama flirted and maybe had affairs. Do you know with who?"

"Does it matter?" Mrs. Beavy asked.

"It must. You wanted me to come here, to tell me all of this. My daddy's in jail for murdering his brother. Maybe he did it. Or maybe someone else did, and it has nothing to do with him, but they want to blame him. Or maybe someone else did and it has everything to do with him."

Mrs. Beavy sighed, rubbed her eyes little-kid fashion. She was getting tired. "I don't know if it matters or not. It might. It's just . . . I know they both supposedly broke a lot of hearts."

I thought about what Luke Rhinegold had told me at the Red Horse.

"I don't recollect now all the details. But a lot of folks would resent them coming back—even if they weren't the ones behind FleaMart. I'm not sure how your Uncle Fenwick is mixed up in their past—or if he is. But I just wanted you to be aware, honey. Your parents were in over their heads and had very little support from their families. They did the best they could at the time—maybe not the best you could have hoped for, or that I would have hoped for for you—but their best. And when it got to be too much for them . . . they were at their worst. A lot of folks saw it as a blessing when they each left . . . and a blessing for you, too, considering that your Aunt and Uncle Foersthoefel took you in.

"Now that your parents are back . . . who knows. There may be a lot of folks who don't want old secrets revealed—folks who thought their secrets went with them when your folks left town, and who were relieved to see those secrets go.

"I'm not saying your uncle's murder has anything to do with those secrets or with your parents' return. I don't know. I'm just saying . . ." Mrs. Beavy paused, and gave me a long, hard look. "I'm just saying I'm always suspicious of the easy explanation of coincidence."

I took in what she was saying. The solution to my uncle's murder—not just the fact someone wanted my daddy blamed for it—might rest in my parents' past. And the only way to find out was to dig into their past. I shifted uncomfortably. Was I really ready to do that?

Mrs. Beavy's serious look suddenly disappeared, and she gave me her usual sunny, childlike smile. "More hot chocolate, dear?"

13

I stood just inside the doorway of Cherry's Chat N Curl and stared at the scene before me, unable to believe what I saw.

Was that really Mama, in Cherry's styling chair, preening as she gazed into a hand-held mirror, admiring her new ash-blond do—shorter, but spiffier?

Was that really Cherry and her assistants, Carson and Darlene, gathered around Mama, extolling her beauty? Telling her that her new makeup and hair really brought out the angles in her face? Which, by the way, round-faced me hadn't inherited?

And there was Mrs. Arrowood, who still manages the Happy Trails Motor Home Court, where Sally and her boys live. Mrs. Arrowood was laughing, too, something I'd never seen her do. Yet here she was, in one of her shapeless, baggy housedresses, and her thin graying hair pulled back in a stringy ponytail, telling my mama that the Sassy Salmon nail color she'd chosen for her manicure looked just perfect with her skin tones.

And Mama was smiling and laughing as though no one had ever complimented her beauty, and telling Mrs. Arrowood that she still had the fantastic cheekbones she'd always envied, and perhaps a cropped hairdo would bring them out, while Cherry said, yes, yes, she'd love to give Mrs. Arrowood a free makeover.

Somehow, my mama had managed to turn Cherry keeping an eye on her into a chick party at which she was the ruling chick. More amazingly, Cherry didn't seem to mind stepping out of the limelight for once.

Finally, Cherry noticed me standing in her doorway.

"Hey, Josie!" she called. "Don't stand there pouting. Come on over here. See what wonders I've wrought with your mama's hair—although she already was beautiful."

"I'm not pouting," I said, through gritted teeth. And I wasn't jealous, either, I told myself. Really. I was just in a bit of a hurry. I'd stayed longer than I'd planned at Mrs. Beavy's, then went back to my laundromat and struggled through a draft of my vinegar Stain-Busters column, and now we were going to be late to Mamaw Toadfern's.

I looked pointedly at my watch. "We're going to be late to Mamaw Toadfern's," I said.

"Aw, why don't we just skip it?" said Mama. "Mother Toadfern always was such an old crow. Who wants to eat leftovers while the men are supposedly out hunting? They're out drinking, truth be told. Besides, after the turkey incinerated, what fun are the leftovers?"

Everyone but me laughed appreciatively, clearly understanding what Mama was referring to. I winced, realizing Mama must have told the story of the awful ending to the Toadfern Thanksgiving dinner. Irrationally, illogically . . . I wished she hadn't because I felt a sudden surge of protectiveness toward the Toadfern clan.

"Never once," Mama went on, "in those first few years when I tried to go along with the Toadfern traditions, did the men come home with more than a bunch of empty six-packs."

Again, everyone—besides me—giggled. Mama actually rolled her eyes, as if she were a teenager. I tried to remember that when she was actually a teenager, she suffered a great deal. Early marriage and pregnancy, the rejection of her own parents, the loss of a baby, a husband who acted out his anger and fear and immaturity with multiple affairs.

"What a dumb tradition, anyway," Mama went on. "The women gathering round to pick over each other while picking over the leftovers." She folded her arms. "The only Toadfern that turned out to be worth a lick— besides you and Henry, of course—is Sally. I say, let's skip the Toadferns and go with Cherry."

Cherry looked sheepish. "I mentioned to your mama that Dean and I were going over to Sally's bar later tonight for a little dancing—"

"Which sounds like a lot more fun than going to the Toadferns'," Mama said. She waggled her finger at me. "And, really, you need to stop giving Cherry such a hard time about Dean. She showed me his picture. He's really cute."

I wasn't sure who to glare at first, Cherry—for complaining about me to my mama—or my mama—for encouraging Cherry in romance over something as shallow as looks (although Dean really was cute), especially when she didn't know Cherry's heartbroken past like I did. So I glared in general.

"Maybe you should run along with Josie, Mrs. Toadfern," Cherry said, eyeing me nervously. "It may be a while before Dean and I show up at Sally's, anyway. After all, I have to give Mrs. Arrowood her makeover."

Mrs. Arrowood rubbed her cheeks with her hands. "This old saggy baggy face . . . do you really think it's worth the cost?"

"This is on me," Cherry said. "And with the right haircut and the judicious use of blusher . . ."

"Bone structure," Mama intoned somberly. "You have magnificent bone structure. In the end, even death doesn't take that away, if you think about it."

Mrs. Arrowood looked thrilled. I had to keep from blanching. Basically, Mama had just told Mrs. Arrowood she'd look great as a skeleton.

And Mrs. Arrowood was absolutely charmed.

Somehow, the charm gene had been obliterated in me by the blunt gene, which burst forth. "Mama, remember our deal? Well, we need to go to Mamaw Toadfern's. Now."

Everyone else looked confused, but I could tell Mama understood. I needed to talk to Mamaw and Aunt Nora. Find out what happened after I left the flaming turkey carcass scenario. See if I could learn anything that would help me remove suspicion from Daddy as Uncle Fenwick's murderer. Assuming, of course, Daddy was innocent.

Mama sighed. "Oh, all right. But after that, we're going to Sally's." She grinned at Cherry. "I want to meet this cute hunk in person." Cherry giggled.

Dingbats of a feather flock together, I thought. "Fine," I ground out through clenched teeth.

"Well, let's get started with Mrs. Arrowood," Cherry said to Carson and Darlene.

Mrs. Arrowood looked terrified. But Mama hopped out of her chair and suddenly hugged Mrs. Arrowood, who hugged her back, fiercely. They didn't look all that different in that moment. In fact, I suddenly realized, they had a shared past, a friendship that was more like sisterhood. Maybe Mrs. Arrowood had seemed like family to Mama, when her own family and Daddy's family had deserted her.

They slowly released each other, although they held each other's arms.

"Now, you promise me you'll go on through with Cherry's beautifying makeover. Trust her, okay?" Mama sounded choked up, and I knew it was over something far more important than Mrs. Arrowood's lovely bone structure.

"I'll promise that . . . if you'll come see the results before you leave town."

"I will."

"You promise, this time?"

Mama let go of Mrs. Arrowood's arms and wiped a tear from her cheek. "I promise."

What the hell was that all about? I wondered. I'd just witnessed a reality version of a Hallmark made-for-cable-movie moment, and I had no clue what it signified—context being everything for such moments.

Although it sounded like Mama had made a similar promise once, long ago, and not kept it.

Mama looked at me and sighed. "Let's go," she said.

* * *

So once again, over the river and through the woods to Grandmother's house I went, this time with my mama.

For the most part, we were quiet. Mama huddled down in her fur and stared out at the darkening twilight. I concentrated on driving. The snow had stopped and the county had done a nice job of salting the roads, but I was wary of black ice—slick spots so thin the black-topped road showed through, so it looked like there was no ice at all. You didn't want to go too fast over such spots. Worse yet would be braking suddenly on one.

But after a little bit, both the quiet and my curiosity got to me.

"I remember Mrs. Arrowood," I said. "The wishing well in her front yard, where you had me drop coins." And there was something odd about those coins, I remembered. They weren't coins that would work in laundromat or gumball machines. "Little bits like that. I guess you two were close friends."

Mama didn't answer right off. Then at last she said, "We were like sisters, Josie. You make a family where you can. I know it hurt her that I left without telling her good-bye, but—"

That's when I saw it—the deer plunging across the field toward the road. I swerved and floored the accelerator, praying I wasn't coming up on black ice.

Mama screamed.

The deer dashed behind us.

Why do deer cross the road? Truly, I think it's just to get to the other side.

By the time we got to Mamaw's, Mama had stopped screaming, I had started breathing again, but by then the time had passed for Mama to tell me more about Mrs. Arrowood.

* * *

Supper was so quiet and somber, I found myself nostalgic for the flaming turkey carcass.

Of course, there were no turkey sandwiches, and that's the best part of Thanksgiving: turkey with extra salt between white bread slathered with mayo. I wasn't going to get that at Mamaw's or at my home. My apartment would smell like burned turkey until Christmas.

And in fact, there were no Thanksgiving dinner leftovers. Mamaw said that without turkey, there was no point to the leftovers, so she'd frozen everything to use with a roasted chicken some Sunday. And to have room in her freezer to store everything, she'd made a meal of frozen pizzas (still cold in the center), lima beans, chicken dumplings, and coconut ice cream (freezer burned).

Ugh.

I couldn't catch a Thanksgiving meal, even from leftovers.

After we ate, the women were supposed to keep the meal warm for the men, whenever they got back from hunting.

Mama, I realized, was right. This was not only boring, but annoying. Couldn't the men reheat their own damned dinners when they returned from hunting? Wasn't that what microwaves were for? I realized some of my grumpiness about our pointless servitude came from my hurt and anger at Owen.

Mamaw, Aunt Suzy, cousin Fern, and Sally's sisters-in-law stayed in the kitchen to tend the food, in denial about the microwave right there on the counter. Sally was already at the Bar-None, getting ready for the Friday-night rush, while her sons spent the night at Mamaw's with their cousins, aunts, and uncles. Aunt

Nora had never joined us. She was resting in the trailer, Mamaw had said.

Mama and I sat in the living room. Mama pointedly read a *Hunting Today* magazine, which featured on the cover a deer that greatly resembled the one who had tried to commit suicide-by-vehicle with my minivan. Of course, if you've seen one deer, you've seen them all. Maybe Mama was plotting revenge.

I occupied myself with the kids, playing an impromptu game of charades.

They were all gathered around me, while I stood in front of the fireplace with my hands behind my head, my fingers above my head, antler-like. I had my eyes bugged out and I stood very still.

"A tree!" hollered Larry. Creative answer, I thought.

"A mohawk haircut!" That was one of Sally's brother's kids.

"Rudolph!" shouted Barry. My heart warmed. I couldn't help it. I really did feel like a doting aunt to Sally's kids, even though they were cousins-once-removed. And like any good, doting aunt, I knew without doubt that my darling "nephews" were smarter—not to mention handsomer and more talented in all ways—than other kids.

I bugged out my eyes to help my nephews-of-the-heart along.

"Ooh, ooh, I know!" shouted Harry. "It's a—"

"Deer in the headlights," said Mamaw Toadfern from the door.

Harry looked disappointed, because Mamaw was right, and he'd almost had it. Mama gave me a look that said, "See. Spoilsport. Old crow."

I put my hands down and rubbed my eyes, which were a wee bit strained from all that bugging-out.

"Actually, I was charading a grasshopper having a bad-hair day," I said.

Mama smiled and went back to *Hunting Today*. Harry giggled, forgetting his earlier disappointment.

"Grasshoppers don't have hair, silly Josie," he said.

I looked perplexed and crossed my eyes at him. "They don't? Well, the ones I hang out with must wear wigs, then."

All the kids giggled.

Mamaw sighed loudly. "Josie, I have to talk to you. Privately."

Well, there were a few things I wanted to ask her, too. Privately.

Still, as I followed her out of the room and up the stairs, I thought . . . spoilsport.

14

Mamaw and I sat on the end of her bed and contemplated the quilt she had shown me the day before. She stroked the square that had come from Uncle Fenwick's jersey. At least on the day after—perhaps as part of her mourning ritual—she'd laid off the Youth Dew perfume. She was also dressed in black pants and a black turtleneck.

"Poor Fenwick," she said. "And poor Henry. I always knew it would come to this—one of them killing the other. They fought so horribly all the time as kids. They were always so competitive. You always hear about twins being close. Well, if that's the case, then they were the exception that proved the rule."

"You really think Daddy killed Uncle Fenwick?" I knew that was a possibility—the circumstantial evidence certainly pointed to him—but I didn't want it to be true.

"It surely looks that way," said Mamaw.

"Someone called the police and told Chief Worthy about the fight and the knives. It had to be one of us from dinner. Who do you think it was?"

Mamaw looked surprised. "What? I didn't know that."

"Then why do you think it looks like Daddy's the killer? Just because he and Uncle Fenwick always fought as kids?"

Mamaw looked away. "Sure. That's it."

"Mamaw, what happened after the turkey carcass fire? After I left?"

Suddenly, she looked at me sharply. "Same thing that always happened to them—at least after they were seniors in high school. Before that, they competed in sports and school. Fenwick always managed to best your daddy. Until suddenly the most popular and beautiful girl in school fell—hard—for Henry. Then Fenwick decided he wanted May Foersthoefel, too. He kept trying to get her away, but she only wanted Henry."

Mamaw shook her head. "Fenwick was always a rule follower. Always tried to be the best at everything. Henry couldn't keep up. Even at birth he was the smaller, weaker baby. Almost didn't make it. So Henry made up for it by being more lovable, funnier, fun loving. And May liked that. I don't think Fenwick ever quite got over that."

"What happened last night?" I asked. The history was interesting, but I suddenly wished I hadn't left so hastily. Whatever happened after I left might help me solve Uncle Fenwick's murder.

"Like I said . . . as always, May happened. She told them both they were big babies. Told them to act like men, go take a walk or drive or something, work things out. That seemed to get their attention. Neither one's ever liked it when May was unhappy with them.

"So off they went to take a walk on the old towpath. Well, as soon as they left the house—and I have to say, they were at least trying to act like real brothers—Nora started crying and blubbering like a baby about how Fenwick had really always loved May and not her. I'm afraid Nora always was jealous of your mama.

"Then May got mad and said she wasn't going to sit around and listen to Nora whine when everyone knew that of course Fenwick loved her. May took off on a drive in that red sports car. Said she wanted to make sure it worked okay, that it just had some scratches from the run-in with Fenwick's RV. Nora stomped off to the RV and none of us saw her until, of course, Chief Worthy and you came to the house."

Mamaw's eyes watered and she sniffled at the thought of that. "Poor Fenwick."

I felt a surge of sympathy for her, but while she was in the mood to talk, I wanted to get all the information from her that I could. "After Mama and Aunt Nora left, what happened? How long was everyone gone?"

Mamaw snorted. "Well, of course, the women who'd stayed here cleaned up from dinner while the men watched football. I swear, I wished I'd have paid more attention to them women libbers. Every Thanksgiving, when my hands are chapping and my back's hurting, I rue the fact I used to make fun of 'em. Why, I'd just love to go into the living room and whop those lazy sons of mine upside the head, and—"

"Mamaw."

"Oh. Right. Well, your daddy came back first. After about an hour or so. He was mad. Said of course he and Fenwick had gotten into a fight again because Fenwick was a stubborn ass."

I lifted my eyebrows at that.

"That was a quote," Mamaw said. She sighed. "But I'm sorry to say, though he was my son and I'm all tore up about his murder, that it's the truth. Anyway, then Henry went into the living room and watched football, too. I think he fell asleep in the easy chair.

"May came back maybe an hour after that. She and Henry left immediately, said they were tired and going to the Red Horse. We never saw Fenwick after that. Of course, we all assumed he was back with Nora in the trailer." She sniffled, then grabbed a tissue from the box on her bedside table, and blew her nose loudly.

So after Daddy and Uncle Fenwick left, Daddy was gone an hour, Mama was gone two hours, and Aunt Nora was basically unaccounted for. Daddy could have killed him out of anger. Aunt Nora could have killed him out of jealousy, over some renewed hurt that Uncle Fenwick could have loved Mama instead of her. And Mama . . . could she have killed Uncle Fenwick, maybe over unwanted attention? Maybe while she was out driving, she saw him walking, stopped to pick him up, and killed in self-defense?

The image of Uncle Fenwick, hung up on the telegraph pole, came to me. I shuddered. Uncle Fenwick was a big man and hanging someone from a telegraph pole was no easy task. He would surely have struggled, fought back. It was hard to imagine one of the women managing to kill him—and display him—in such a way.

Come to think of it, it was hard to imagine Daddy or anyone all alone being able to do what had been done to Uncle Fenwick. But if two people had worked together . . .

"Josie, are you okay?"

"What? Oh, sure."

"You were looking a little pale, there."

"This has been a shock to everyone. Even to me, although I didn't know Uncle Fenwick, really."

Mamaw smiled sadly. "My fault. I made everyone turn against you. And there's a reason for that. You see . . . May and Henry had to get married."

"I've heard about the baby who didn't make it."

Mamaw lifted her eyebrows, but didn't ask who had told me. "That was real hard on May and Henry. And I'm sorry to say, Henry went back to his wild ways after that. Trying to escape the pain, I guess, taking up with any floozy he could pick up at any countryside bar he stumbled into.

"May decided to get back at him by having her own affairs. They'd split up, have affairs, get back together. It tore your mama up and it made me so mad at both her and Henry. And then, May finally decided to get back at Henry in the worst way possible. By flirting with Fenwick."

I gasped. "Oh, Lord. Don't tell me she and Uncle Fenwick . . ."

Mamaw shook her head. "It never came to that. But for a time both Fenwick and May let everyone think that they had . . . been a couple. To hurt Henry."

"How could Uncle Fenwick do that to Aunt Nora?" I didn't like that my mama had done that to Daddy, but given the circumstances, her motives were understandable, even if her actions were not morally acceptable.

Mamaw shook her head. "His competition with his brother meant more to him than his affection for his wife. It really tore up the family. And of course, the easiest thing to do was blame May, hate her for it."

"It's always the women who get blamed," I said stiffly, "when it takes two. It's not like she forced Uncle Fenwick to go along with this terrible lie."

"I know that. But I wanted to believe what I wanted to believe," Mamaw said. "As you get older, though, it gets harder to keep up delusions like that. Anyway, for a time, we all thought when May was pregnant the second time, that it was by Fenwick."

"When she was pregnant with me?"

Mamaw nodded. "That's what both of them wanted Henry to believe. To hurt him. But then Nora surprised everyone and showed some backbone. She left Fenwick. He was brokenhearted and begged her back and made sure everyone knew he had never really slept with May. Nora took Fenwick back. Not long after that, they discovered they couldn't have kids because Fenwick was sterile. Then Henry and May got back together—again. You know, I don't think even they know how many times they've broken up and gotten back together."

Mamaw put her hand to my face. "You're Henry's all right. I can see him—and May—in you."

"So Mama had me, and?"

Mamaw dropped her hand. "And she and Henry tried again, but it just didn't work. Henry disappeared all of a sudden. I blamed May. When May took off, she wasn't around for me to blame for the problems between my sons. So I took it out on you."

Mamaw's jaw trembled. I didn't want to feel a bit sorry for her. I made my voice stiff as I asked, "So what changed your mind all of a sudden?"

"The phone call from Henry that he and May were coming back to town and wanted to join us for Thanksgiving. It was so casual. Like no one had missed them or worried about them all these years."

"You hadn't been in touch with Daddy after he left?"

Mamaw shook her head. "Nope. And after I got off the phone with him, I suddenly realized I've been an ass, too." She smiled at my expression. "I'm just quoting what I was thinking."

"You wanted to blame everyone but your son for his actions."

She sighed. "That's right. And I wanted to tell you this and . . . and apologize. And I thought you should see your parents again, and they should see you, and maybe understand how selfish they've been . . ."

I laughed, but not bitterly. My parents were a reality I had to finally deal with, but in the most important sense, they hadn't been my parents. Uncle and Aunt Foersthoefel had been.

"I don't think they've figured that out."

Mamaw put her face to her hands. "If I had known what would happen, I'd have never let them come back—"

I sighed. I'd never be close to this woman as my grandmother. The time for that had come and gone. But, as a human being, I couldn't help but feel sorry for her. "They'd have come back, anyway. They had something to prove."

"With FleaMart," she said, dropping her hands, and leaning into me.

"Exactly."

We sat quietly for a few minutes. Then Mamaw said, "You should know that Sally's been nagging me for years to get in touch with you. She's told me all along I've been an ass."

"Another direct quote?"

Mamaw nodded. I laughed. "That sounds like Sally."

Mamaw got another tissue and blew her nose. "She's the only one I'd take that from, you know."

"She's a good person," I said. "Straight shooter."

Mamaw patted the quilt on her lap. "I wanted to tell

you all this before your parents got here. That was the secret—about your parents' past—I thought you should know. And I wanted to give you this quilt. Can I give it to you now?"

I stared at the quilt in her lap. Did I want it? I had a quilt that Mamaw's mama had made for me when I was born. It had been a baby gift. Aunt Clara had told me that my paternal great-grandmother had made quilts for all her grandchildren and great-grandchildren as baby gifts. And I cherished that quilt, given as it was with a pure heart.

But did I want this other quilt? This quilt made with a sentimentality I could never share, given with guilt? I wasn't sure. It seemed rude to say no. But it didn't seem quite right to say yes, either.

"I'm not . . . can I think about . . ." I started, and Mamaw said at the same time, "If the time's ever right for you to want it . . ."

I stopped, and let her finish.

"Just let me know if you're ever ready for it," she said. "I'll keep it here for you."

She stood up, crossed to the closet with the quilt, and tried to put it on the top shelf, which was too high for her. I stood up and helped her get it on the shelf.

Then I tried to think about what to say to fill the suddenly awkward silence, and was saved from having to say anything by a knock on the bedroom door.

Mamaw rushed to the door and opened it, obviously also relieved to have the awkward moment broken.

In the doorway stood Aunt Nora. She looked past Mamaw to me. "I heard you were here. I'd like to talk with you, Josie."

15

"This was Fenwick's favorite shirt," Aunt Nora said, sniffling. "I know he'd want to be buried in it. But the cranberry stain . . ."

"I got the stain on the shirt," I said. "I can get it out. Do you have any white vinegar?"

We were standing at the sink in her and Uncle Fenwick's kitchen. Their trailer was a thing of beauty. Top-of-the-line cabinets and counters and appliances in the kitchenette, stainless-steel fixtures, real wood paneling polished to a high sheen, leather upholstered seats and chairs. This was no run-of-the-mill trailer you'd find parked on any old Kampgrounds of America. Why, this beauty would be envied by some of the finest country and western bands.

"Vinegar?" Aunt Nora asked.

"I usually do a column about recent stains I've helped customers with," I said. "But I thought I'd try something different. This time, my column is on all the uses of white vinegar. Two-thirds water, one-third vinegar, applied to the cranberry stain with a spray bottle or eyedropper . . . let it soak ten minutes, and then spritz with your favorite laundry enzymatic pretreatment, and the shirt should be fine."

Aunt Nora looked skeptical, but found a small bottle of white vinegar in the kitchenette cabinet and an eyedropper in the bathroom. I treated Uncle Fenwick's shirt over the kitchen sink, and Aunt Nora watched in amazement as the stain started to disappear.

"There," I said. "I can take it to my laundromat, wash it for you—"

Aunt Nora waved her hand toward the back of the trailer. "We have a custom-made, built-in mini washer and dryer in a special cabinet next to the bathroom. I'll just wash it here." Her eyes teared up again. "Thank you so much for helping me. It may seem silly, but he really liked that shirt. I want him to be buried in it. If there's anything I can do to repay you . . ."

Suddenly, she sat down on the leather built-in couch, and put her hands to her face. I sat down next to her. She looked so pathetically tiny, in her dark brown pants and sweater, which was appliquéd, again, with turkeys. But these didn't flash. I guessed she'd picked more demure seasonal wear out of respect for Uncle Fenwick. Somehow, the lack of flash in these appliquéd turkeys made me sad.

There was something she could do to repay me— answer some questions. But I thought I should try to be more subtle than just start peppering her with questions. So I sat down next to her and said, "This is so lovely. Uncle Fenwick spared no expense."

At that, Aunt Nora looked up and beamed. "Fenwick was so good to me. Top-of-the-line everything. He knew how much I loved camping."

I've been camping. Camping is a tent, raccoons getting into your food, a sleepless night brought on by needing to pee but refusing to leave the tent to take care of business out of fear of rabid raccoons and because the storm of the century just decided to pitch a fit right where you pitched camp, and your limbs being used as an all-you-can-eat buffet by mosquitos. This trailer was more like a luxury suite on wheels.

"Well, he must have been quite successful in his plumbing business to afford something this nice," I said. "Even though he didn't like plumbing."

Aunt Nora's face suddenly became guarded. "He liked it well enough."

Uh huh, I thought. Uncle Fenwick had said the afternoon before, at the disastrous Toadfern Thanksgiving dinner, that he'd hated plumbing. True, plumbing business owners could make a nice profit. But most entrepreneurs don't make a lot of money unless they like the trade they're in. And even if he had made a lot of money, this decked-out trailer probably cost more than a lot of the stationary homes in Paradise. Certainly more than double wides permanently double parked in the Happy Trails Motor Home Park, just outside Paradise. Definitely more than my laundromat/apartment combo.

How, I wondered, had Uncle Fenwick afforded this?

It was just one of several things that didn't make sense to me about the Toadfern family. But I couldn't ask about Uncle Fenwick's fortune directly. Aunt Nora's expression told me she'd just shut down. And although I was curious about his fortune, there was no real reason to think it pertained to his murder.

I decided to try a different approach. "You know, Aunt Nora, there are so many secrets in this family. I just found out today that my parents had a child before they had me."

Aunt Nora startled. "Who told you about that?"

"A friend here in Paradise. And Mamaw Toadfern. She told me also about how wild my parents were. That they hurt a lot of people. Including you," I said as gently as possible.

Aunt Nora looked away. "Yes. Your mother and Fenwick hurt me. I admit I wasn't sorry to see Henry leave town, or your mother's pain after that." She looked back at me, anger flashing in her eyes. "Does that make me awful?"

"I think it makes you human," I said.

"Well, I wasn't sorry to see your mother go, either. All I know is that after they left, Fenwick seemed happier. Freer. He started making a lot more money."

"In his plumbing business, of course?"

Aunt Nora looked away again. "Of course."

She was hiding something.

"You're good at keeping secrets," I said. "Like your cranberry sauce recipe."

She whipped her head back around and glared at me. "What's that supposed to mean?"

"Your husband's been murdered. My daddy's been accused. Maybe it really was something as simple and awful as sibling rivalry. But I don't know. It doesn't quite feel right to me. After all, Daddy wanted to show his brother that he could be just as successful. Kind of hard to do, with Uncle Fenwick dead."

Aunt Nora gasped, realizing the truth of what I said. And the minute I said it, I realized it, too. Daddy hadn't killed Uncle Fenwick. Maybe he was capable of it. Sure, I could see him reacting in anger to Uncle Fenwick, and maybe hitting him hard enough to kill him.

But only after FleaMart was a big success and Fenwick had finally—grudgingly—given him the recognition he wanted.

"If not your daddy, then . . . who?" Aunt Nora's question was nearly a whisper.

"I don't know," I admitted. Maybe you? I thought. Jealousy over Mama? I eyed the trailer door. I was just a few feet away in case I needed to make a dash for it. "But anything you can tell me about their quarrel yesterday might help. Daddy was only gone an hour. Mamaw said Uncle Fenwick never came back to the house. Did he come back here? Talk with you?"

"He came here to take off his shirt before going on the walk with your daddy. Didn't want the cranberry sauce to get into the inside of his jacket, plus he didn't want to wear a messy shirt." She half smiled. "He was always like that after plumbing jobs. Wanting to clean up as soon as possible. Didn't like being messy. But he seemed in a hurry to go on the walk, so he just put his jacket back on. I worried he'd be too cold, and he told me not to be silly."

"So then he went on a walk with Daddy. And didn't come back. And you didn't miss him or worry about him?"

Aunt Nora cut her eyes away from me. "I found the argument at supper yesterday afternoon to be emotionally exhausting. I came back here and took a nap."

I considered the timing. I'd left Mamaw Toadfern's at about 2:30. Shortly after that, by all accounts, Aunt Nora had come back to the trailer. Uncle Fenwick had come back long enough to change shirts, then went on a walk with Daddy. Mama had left for a drive. Daddy came back at 3:00. Mama came back at 4:00. About a half hour later, I arrived at the Burkettes'. An hour or so later, Rachel and I discovered Uncle Fenwick's body, stabbed and hung from the telegraph pole. By the time the police came and Chief Worthy and I came to Mamaw Toadfern's, it was nearly 7:00.

I looked at Aunt Nora. "You took a five-hour nap?"

She shrugged. "Like I said, I was emotionally exhausted from the scene at dinner. I told Chief Worthy that yesterday. He didn't question it."

That, I thought, was because Chief Worthy was more than happy to pin this murder on my daddy—both because of our rocky past and maybe because my mama and John Worthy's daddy had flirted with one another, at the very best.

In any case, I knew Aunt Nora was lying. She was a little, high-strung bird of a woman. A scene like that would have had her too keyed up to sleep. She would have paced the floor, fuming, turning the events over in her mind, wondering if Fenwick maybe really had had feelings for Mama all those years, after all.

"Aunt Nora," I said gently, "you said you appreciated how I'd helped with Uncle Fenwick's shirt, and that you would like to repay me. Well, someone murdered Uncle Fenwick. And I think you know something that could help us figure out who. I wish you'd tell me—or the police."

Suddenly Aunt Nora stood up. "Look out that window, Josie."

I stood, looked, gazed across the yard in the space between two trees.

"What do you see?" she demanded.

"Uh . . . a yard?"

"What's missing?" she asked.

I stared and pondered. And then it hit me. The clothesline that had been strung between the two trees was missing.

I looked at her. "Clothesline," I whispered.

"That's right," she said. "And I know who took it. Fenwick. He came back. Got it. I asked him why? And he just snapped at me. Said he had to check on his treasure. But I didn't tell John Worthy that. Worthy didn't say how Fenwick died, just that he was murdered. But every now and then, Fenwick would threaten to kill himself. 'Just go hang myself from some tree,' he'd say. 'I'd be worth more dead to you than alive—if the insurance would pay.' I thought maybe somehow Fenwick had killed himself and tried to make it look like he'd been murdered. I didn't want Worthy to know that."

"Because of the insurance."

"Yes, but also, I didn't want him to not investigate Fenwick's death. And if he thought Fenwick had a hand in his own death, he might not."

"Aunt Nora," I said, "were you the one who called the police, left the anonymous message about Daddy and Fenwick's fight?"

Aunt Nora looked away. "That's one nice thing about a behind-the-times-town like Paradise," she said. "It's not hard to find a pay phone."

I imagined her wrestling that RV down the road to the pay phone outside Elroy's gas station, making the call, driving back in the previous night's snow. She was tougher than I thought.

Tough enough to take the news that, even if he had threatened suicide in the past, he had actually been stabbed?

I decided I'd let the police tell her that.

"Aunt Nora, when Uncle Fenwick came back here to change out of his dinner shirt before his walk with Daddy," I said. "Did he say anything then, about how he felt about Daddy and Mama coming back?"

"Just that he had some old business to settle with Henry and he hoped they could work it out on the walk," Aunt Nora said. "Then he left. And I took a nap. A long nap, until he came back and took down the clothesline. He seemed excited, more than depressed, so I didn't worry."

She dropped her head. "I guess I should have. Are you going to tell the police?"

"I think you should," I said. "This information will help the investigation, not stop it."

She nodded. "All right Josie. I'll call."

16

"What you got there, good-lookin'? A laundry list?"

I clapped my hand over the paper that was, in fact, a list of questions based on what I'd learned so far about the circumstances surrounding Uncle Fenwick's murder.

Then I looked up at the source of the question—and it was one of the hunkiest, dreamiest men I'd ever set eyes on. He had just enough wrinkles to save his blond crew cut, baby face, blue eyes, and deep dimples from being overly cute. The dimples punctuated perfectly kissable lips, which were arced in a smile that revealed straight, white teeth. The blue eyes were focused on me, but I was having a hard time focusing on the blue eyes, considering that this gorgeous face was just the icing on the beefcake, so to speak. I didn't even mind the muscle shirt or tight jeans, accentuating as they did a perfectly muscled and fit body. Even the damned boots looked good on this guy.

I made myself focus on the blue eyes. I made myself

remember Owen. I made myself say: "That has to be the cheesiest pick-up line I've ever heard."

The blue eyes flashed confusion, the perfect smile faded. The lips still looked kissable, though, even as they uttered, "Huh? I was serious. Sally there—" he gestured with his thumb, and I looked behind him to the bar, behind which stood Sally, smiling and nodding encouragingly at me while she wiped glasses, "told me you own the laundromat in Paradise. Then she sent me over here. So I thought, you know, maybe you was working on a laundry list."

I sighed, staring up at the proverbial gorgeous dumb blond, male version. "I am," I said, folding the list, and tucking it into my jeans pocket. "But I can't show it to you. Trade secret, you know."

"Oooh," gorgeous said, nodding his understanding. Then he stared at me, waiting for me to take the conversation from there.

Owen, my virtuous side thought, was a great conversationalist.

Owen, my not-so-virtuous side reminded me, was also not there. He was with his ex-wife and son in Kansas City, interviewing for a job that would require him to move there.

Owen, my virtuous side thought, is still your boyfriend and even if he weren't, you know it's stupid to take up with men just because they're gorgeous. Wait, make that, really gorgeous. Just take Cherry, for example . . .

My virtuous self made me look out on the dance floor, where Cherry was dancing away happily with her own gorgeous hunk, Deputy Sheriff Dean. She didn't look in any danger of being miserable.

And there on the dance floor near her was my mama, dancing happily with some man I didn't even recog-

nize. Mama had had several bourbons. I, being the designated driver, was nursing a Big Fizz Diet Cola, on
the rocks, and sitting by myself in a booth. Well, not
entirely alone. I had both my coat and Mama's fur
wedged between me and the wall.

Which is why, my virtuous self reminded me, you
are smart enough not to ask this man to sit down with
you at this booth . . .

Shut up, my nonvirtuous self said.

"Have a seat," I said aloud.

"Okay," the man said, sitting across from me. He put
his bottle of beer on the table. Then he smiled and
stared at me. "You know, you're awfully cute. For a
laundry lady."

I tried to ignore the warm feeling that suddenly
surged in me. "Oh? What did you think a laundry lady
would look like?"

He frowned, thinking it over. Then he smiled. "Very
clean?"

I lifted an eyebrow and smiled back. "You think I'm
dirty?"

The minute I said it, I moaned inwardly. Oh Lord,
I'd just topped his cheesy pick-up line with an even
cheesier one.

But he didn't get it. "Oh, no, ma'am, you look clean.
Well groomed, in fact. I just meant, um, well, I'm not
sure what I meant . . ."

Ma'am? This man had called me ma'am? Then I realized that, despite the few wrinkles around his eyes,
he was probably at least five years younger than me.
Maybe six or seven. Which meant he was in his early
twenties, and I was just a few months shy of thirty . . .
I felt like I'd just been dumped in a cold rinse cycle.

"Look, why don't you tell me why my dear

cousin—" I glanced over at Sally, glaring, but the bar was too dark and smoky for her to see me glare, and besides, she was paying attention to a customer now "—why Sally sent you over here."

"Well, see, I help her out on some of her carpentry work on the weekends. I live up in Masonville and work in apartment maintenance and repair during the week. But I like to come to her place and hang out on the weekends. She said that you have two apartments over your laundromat, and you're thinking about converting them to one. So she sent me over to talk to you."

He took a swig of beer, then went back to staring at me.

"You want to talk to me about a job."

"Yeah." He looked worried. "Hope I didn't jinx it by calling you cute. I mean you are cute and all and—"

I held my hand up. "Stop talking." He stopped. "Thank you," I said. He took another swig of beer. I sipped my diet cola. We stared at each other a little longer. I ignored the new wave of heat. He was just interested in work, after all. And I had Owen to think about.

"Let's start over, by exchanging names. I'm Josie Toadfern."

He smiled. "Nice to meet you, Josie!"

I waited. Then I said, "And you are . . ."

"Oh. I'm Randy. Randy Woodford."

"Randy. It's nice to meet you, too. But the truth is, I'm not quite ready to start converting my apartments over. I'm really just in the planning stages. However, if you'd like to drop by my laundromat sometime during the work week, I could take you upstairs and show you my apartment—"

I stuttered to a stop. Oh Lord. That hadn't come out

right. I was turning red. But Randy didn't seem to notice that. Or the implications of my phrasing.

"I mean, I could review with you what the project would entail," I finished lamely.

Randy nodded. "Okay. Next Wednesday should be slow. I'll come by then. We'll have lunch, my treat, and talk over your plans. Thanks."

He started to stand up, but then he sat back down, and grinned. It was a smile a girl—even a nearly thirty girl—could fall right into. As dumb as that would be . . . "'Course, that will be strictly business. But that's then. And this is a Friday night. Feel like a little two-steppin'?" He held out his hand toward me.

I looked at it. What a nice, well-formed hand. A little calloused, but a little roughness could be . . . I shook my head.

I pulled my list back out of my pocket. "Sorry," I said. "I'm behind on my laundry list. I really need to catch up."

Randy didn't take my rejection too hard. He just nodded. "Okay. I understand. But if you change your mind, just let me know." Then he stood up, took his beer, and walked off.

I only let my eyes linger on his cute behind for a few seconds. Truly.

I unfolded my list and looked at it. It was a laundry list—of questions I had about the events surrounding Uncle Fenwick's murder:

1. Did Aunt Nora tell the whole truth? Or did she do anything else besides worry and fret in the trailer for the five hours between Uncle Fenwick's walk with Daddy, and Worthy and I bringing the bad news?

2. Where did Mama go on her ride after dinner? Did she see anyone? Was she alone the whole time?

3. What about Uncle Fenwick's business? Find out about that.

4. Who called Chief Worthy about the antique hunting knives?

5. Could just one person have killed Uncle Fenwick? How do you get someone to hang themselves? Wouldn't he have fought back?

I'd called Rusty Wilton, the Antique Depot owner, and he'd told me that Caller ID had shown the calls about FleaMart traced to the phone booth out at Elroy's Filling Station.

Aunt Nora, I thought. But just because she'd called the antique store owners and Chief Worthy and was jealous of my mama, did that make her a killer? I thought it at least made her a suspect.

What else? I looked at the list, and thought about the scene when Rachel and I had found Uncle Fenwick. There hadn't been any footprints on the towpath, except ours. Yet Mamaw had clearly said that Uncle Fenwick and Daddy had planned to walk the towpath. That led to the next question:

6. Could the snow have filled in Uncle Fenwick and Daddy's footprints that fast? Or did they walk somewhere else—in the woods, off the towpath? Why?

"Laundry list?"

I startled, clapped my hand over my notebook protectively, and looked up at Caleb Loudermilk, who was grinning down at me.

"Oh, for pity's sake. What's with that line tonight?"

Caleb's smile faded. "Don't tell me blondie over there used that line on you, too," he said. He gestured to Randy, who was dancing with a thin brunette with painted-on jeans. Go away, I told my sudden surge of envy.

"He did," I said. "But he really thought I was making a laundry list."

"Ah," Caleb said, sitting down across from me, obviously not caring he wasn't invited. "He's dumb. Thus, not your type."

I lifted an eyebrow. "That's right. My boyfriend . . ."

"Has multiple PhDs. So I've heard. But he's not here. I just have a lowly BA in journalism. But I'm actually here. Which should make up for all those degrees of separation."

I actually laughed at Caleb's lame line. "Caleb, I appreciate the interest but as I told Randy . . ."

"I know. You're taken. All alone, but still, taken."

I frowned at him. "Do you know you have an annoying habit of interrupting? As well as stating the obvious?"

Caleb sighed, and took a drink from his glass, which looked like a gin and tonic with lime. "Two character flaws that have kept me from rising in the world of journalism, beyond the regional weekly." He leaned forward. "But I'm counting on you, Josie. I plan to ride your coattails of cleaning-column fame—"

I tapped the side of his glass. "I hope you have a designated driver."

Caleb thumped back into his seat. "Now you're interrupting, and also—"

"Sorry."

He arched an eyebrow at me. I grinned.

"And also insulting me. This is tonic and lime, nothing more. I just came out to observe the wild life. And when I saw you all alone, I came over here to ask you something."

Protectively, I put the list back in my pocket. "If you want to know about my Uncle Fenwick's murder, please talk to Chief Worthy. All I can say is that I'm sorry for this tragedy and that I'm sure the officials will soon find out the truth behind this horrible event."

Caleb pulled his face into a hurt look. "You really think I was going to ask you about your uncle's murder?"

I rolled my eyes. "Please. My daddy is in jail for his brother's murder. You're a reporter. You're not going to ask me about this?"

"Okay. I was. But I was hoping to buy you a drink first, you know, comfort the grieved."

I picked up my drink glass, rattled the cubes, took a long drink. "It's just cola. So don't count on me having loose lips."

Caleb lifted his eyebrows. "I wasn't, but that's an intriguing image."

I rolled my eyes again.

"Didn't your mama tell you your eyes could get stuck like that? Mine did."

"My mama left when I was a little girl, my daddy when I was two. I consider my parents to be my dear, deceased Aunt Clara and Uncle Horace Foersthoefel. And you can quote me on that."

Caleb followed my gaze to the dance floor, where my mama was now dancing with Deputy Dean, while Cherry watched and laughed and clapped happily. But there was nothing untoward about Mama's dancing. Just a look of innocent fun.

"Your mother?"

I nodded.

"She seems to be taking the fact that her husband is

in jail for his brother's murder quite well," Caleb said.

"She's confident he's innocent."

"And you?"

I looked at Caleb. I was confident Daddy was innocent, for the reason I'd figured out while visiting with Aunt Nora. But I wasn't about to share that with Caleb.

"I think the officials will do a fine job investigating Uncle Fenwick's murder."

Caleb laughed. "You're a tough interview. But thanks for the quotes."

"You didn't write them down."

He lifted an eyebrow. "I've heard those bland statements plenty of times before. It's kinda like the baseball rookie saying he just wants to help the team or the politician saying he believes in the little guy. Reporters don't need to write those things down."

I smiled. "Touché."

He leaned forward. "So why don't you tell me what you really think. Strictly off the record."

"If it's going to be off the record, why do you want to know?"

"I'm curious." He smiled. "You should understand that."

Caleb had heard of my nickname, of course. I matched his gaze evenly.

"Okay, no comments off the record then," Caleb said. "I have another question—"

"I will have my column in by Monday, as promised," I said. "In fact, I completed a perfectly wonderful draft of the column today. It's about vinegar, which has many stain-busting properties . . ."

"Fascinating, I'm sure, but that wasn't my question. I have complete confidence in your professionalism, Josie," Caleb said. "My question was . . . would you go as my guest to Rich Burkette's retirement party tomorrow night?"

I gaped at him. "Let me get this straight. You're asking me out ... even though you know I'm serious about someone—"

"Who's not here," he said, grinning.

"Whatever. Look, I can't go with you tomorrow night."

"Plans?"

"No—"

He interrupted me with a grin this time. "I understood the 'no,'" he said. "But let me tell you why I want you to go with me. I'm doing this piece on Rich Burkette, right? Well, I went out to their place, to do the interview. Which went smoothly, except I was getting those canned answers. You know—"

"Yeah. Here to help the team. Belief in little guy. Trust the officials to investigate."

"Right. Until I say, 'so how did you and Mrs. Burkette meet?'"

"That's easy. They met when she filed for divorce from her jerk first husband. Junior Hedberg. Everyone knows that."

"Right again. Except I did my homework before I went out to the Burkette's. Researched every angle I could about Rich Burkette's law practice. And the truth is, his specialty has always been real estate and corporate law. His partner does all the domestic work. Like wills, divorces, so forth. And when I asked his partner, well, didn't Mr. Burkette write up the divorce papers for Mrs. Burkette—back when she was Mrs. Hedberg—he got all flustered and said, well, yes, but that was an exception."

"So?" I said.

"Come on, Josie, you're more curious than that. Why the exception? Why did the then Mrs. Hedberg go to Rich Burkette for the divorce papers? Why didn't he just direct her to his partner?"

Those were all questions I would have wanted to know, too, but I was still smarting from his taunting grin when I said I didn't have any plans for the next night.

So instead I said, "Aren't you just supposed to be writing a fluff piece about Rich Burkette's career? In honor of his retirement?"

Caleb pounded the table with his fist, making the lime jump out of his glass. He picked up the lime, squeezed it very hard over his glass, and plopped the now-extinguished lime back into his glass.

"That's just it, Josie. I don't want to always just write fluff pieces. I'm trying to make something of this chance. I've failed too many times before—"

My curiosity radar went ding, ding. I didn't know much about Caleb's past, what he'd done before he came to Paradise. Why had he taken a job as the *Paradise Advertiser-Gazette* editor? He seemed too smart for the job.

Caleb shook his head, as if trying to clear it. "Okay, look, now I'm going to tell you something off the record. There's something odd about how the whole divorce played out. So I decided to look up old Junior Hedberg, and ask him about it. But no one seems to know where Junior Hedberg took off to."

"So?" I asked. "He was, by all accounts, not someone anyone would miss."

"But I can't find a trace of him anywhere. Where he went off to. No one disappears without a trace."

"My parents did," I said. I looked out at the dance

floor. Mama was dancing with yet another man, this one slightly overweight. Mama didn't look like she'd broken a sweat. But the man was having a hard time keeping up. I hoped she wouldn't give the poor man a coronary.

Caleb shook his head. "No. Not without a trace. You just didn't want to find them."

His comment struck me. Oh, my Lord. He was right. I'd never tried to track them. Never asked Aunt Clara or Uncle Horace to help me find them. I would probably have gone my whole life without tracking them down.

"Josie? You okay?" Caleb was asking worriedly. "Sorry if that was too harsh."

I shook my head. "No. That's fine. So no trace of Junior Hedberg."

"That's right. And I know there's something about that divorce—about Junior—that Rich and Effie are trying to hide. I can just sense it. But the second I asked why Effie had asked Rich to handle the divorce for her, the interview was over."

"They actually kicked you out of their house?"

"No. But it was clear I wasn't going to get any information out of them. That's when I thought of asking you to the party tomorrow night."

"So I can say, congratulations Mr. Burkette, and by the way, 'why did you handle your wife's divorce from her first husband and where is he anyway so Caleb here can ask embarrassing questions about your wife's past?' Somehow, I don't think Mr. Burkette will be in the mood to answer that one in front of his peers."

Caleb laughed. "I know that. But when I arrived at the Burkette house, Rachel answered the door. And do you know what the first thing she said to me was?"

"Um, 'come in'?"

"She said, 'oh, I remember you. I met you at the restaurant. You're Josie's editor. I'm so glad you're going to help her with her career. We've always thought the world of her.' And then Lenny passed through the foyer, stopped and said, 'That's right. She and Rachel were such good friends. In fact, Josie was here yesterday, and we had such a good time.' So now, I'm thinking, how about you come to this party with me, and somewhere along in the evening, see what you can get Lenny and Rachel to spill about Effie's divorce and marriage to Rich. Surely they know something—or can at least tell you something that I can work with. People like to talk with you, Josie. You know you can get them to open up to you."

"And I would want to do this . . . why?"

Caleb leaned across the table, and peered intently into my eyes. "Because I know you. You've got to have some questions about your Uncle Fenwick's murder and your father's involvement. Questions I could help you research. Off the record, of course. And if you go with me to this party and see if you can find anything out for me, then I will help you."

I thought about the list of questions in my pocket. "And if I can't find anything out for you, then?"

"Then I'll still help you. Off the record." Caleb took another sip of his drink. "Of course, I may want to see if I can interview you on the record again later, but—"

"It's a deal."

Caleb looked surprised at his success. "Really?"

"Yes. I'm curious about the party, curious about if there's anything to your sense that something's not quite right about Effie's divorce—although I doubt it . . ."

"I don't know. Here's my theory. I think Rich and

Effie were having an affair before her divorce. Rich took care of the divorce for Effie, but somehow messed it up, and Effie wasn't really divorced. So, she's really been married to two men all this time. Junior figured it out, and has been blackmailing them from some exotic island ever since, which is why they live in such a modest house when—admit it—you know Rich is much more the type to be living in an elegantly renovated Victorian-era house in town, rather than in a modestly updated house in the countryside, a house that's really his wife's."

I'd wondered about that, too, but Caleb's theory seemed far-fetched, and I said so. "I think you're just trying to create a story where there isn't one. But I'll go with you. Now, off the record, here's what I want you to find out for me."

I hesitated. Should I trust this man? But Winnie was out of town and I couldn't ask her to do this research for me. And in fact, I wasn't sure she could do it for me, anyway.

"I'm listening," Caleb said.

"My Uncle Fenwick appears to have made a lot of money, and yet he swore before he died that he hated the plumbing business. Usually people who hate their work are not wildly successful at it."

Caleb looked thoughtful and then nodded. "You think he might have had some shady deals going, something like that, and his murder was business-related—nothing to do with family issues?"

"It's an angle that I think bears looking into," I said.

Caleb grinned. "I like the way you think." He stood up. "I'll pick you up tomorrow night at six o'clock, if that's okay."

"That's fine," I said.

He gestured at his glass. "Mind if I leave this here? I'm heading home."

"Sure. You're not going to stay and dance the night away?"

Caleb grinned. "Josie, I only came because I wanted to talk with you. You weren't at your apartment—and there weren't many other places you could be."

He walked away. I stared into what was left of my cola. Had I really just agreed to two dates? But they were both business, I told myself. And neither man was my type. One was too dim . . . although gorgeous. Very gorgeous. The other was too bitter. But funny and smart . . .

I shook my head, looked at my watch. It was just after nine o'clock. Owen should be back in his hotel room by now. I picked up my purse, fished around in it for my cell phone. It wasn't too late to call him, to say I understood about the job—I did, didn't I?—to . . .

"Whew. Aren't you the belle of the ball—and you've never even danced one two-step. I never thought I was going to get a chance to sit down." I looked up as Mama sat down across from me. I dropped my cell phone back into my purse. "Why didn't you come out and dance with one of those boys? Especially that first hunky one."

"I was guarding your fur," I said.

"Nonsense," Mama said. "Everyone here is so nice."

"Yes. You especially seem to be having a good time."

Mama gave me a look. "Nothing wrong with that," she said.

"That's right—that's what the Bar-None is all about," said Sally. Mama scooched over for her. Sally put drinks on the table, then sat down next to Mama. "This is on the house."

Mama took a long drink of her bourbon and water. I sipped my fresh cola. Sally had a beer.

"So, what did you think of Randy."

"You sure he knows a wrench from a hammer?"

Sally laughed. "He's actually a good contractor."

"And cute, too. Why didn't you dance with him?" Mama asked.

"Mama, drop it. He wasn't interested in me."

"Yes, he was," Mama said.

"No, he wasn't."

"Yes, he *was*."

"*No*—"

"Actually," Sally broke in, "for the record, he was interested. And Caleb is interested in you, too, I mean from the way he was looking at you. Kinda like the way he did the other day at Sandy's Restaurant. Even across the bar I could tell—"

"Doesn't matter," I said stiffly. "I'm spoken for."

"Oh good Lord," Mama said, chugging some more of her bourbon and water. "How prim. And where is the Owen I've heard so much about?"

"He's away . . . on business." Well, technically that was true, what with the job interview and all. "And I haven't told you a thing about him—"

"I've been hearing about him from Cherry, at the salon, and between dances, from Sally. Doesn't sound like he's good enough for you, dear."

I glared at Sally. Sorry, she mouthed. I kicked her under the table, anyway. For once, she didn't kick back.

"Look, Mama, my personal life is really none of your business, especially since, since . . . since . . ."

I broke off lamely, letting the unspoken hang in the air.

"Especially since I haven't been much of a mother to you? Abandoned you when you were little? Well, that's true. I wouldn't blame you if you didn't speak to me at all."

I looked down into my fresh glass of cola, my eyes misting. Damn it. I kept vacillating between not caring—being the young woman who knew her parents were really, emotionally and spiritually speaking, Aunt Clara and Uncle Horace—and being the young girl from before Mama had left.

"But I'm speaking from experience, Josie," Mama said. "It's fine to follow your heart—but be sure you know where it's leading you. And that you really want to go there."

I looked up at Mama. She was talking about Daddy, I knew.

"Hello, May."

We all looked up, startled. Lenny Burkette was standing by our booth. None of us had heard him walk up.

Sally and I exchanged a look. I thought of what Caleb had said about finding me here—he'd come here because I wasn't home, and where else could I go on a Friday night in Paradise. Apparently, Lenny had figured out the same thing about Mama. I didn't think he'd come to the Bar-None just to hang out. He didn't seem the type. In fact, he was wearing a suit and tie, looking uncomfortable and uncertain.

The bar had quieted, I realized. The music had switched over from the rollicking two-stepping music and hilarious country ditties such as "Prop Me Up Beside the Juke Box When I Die," to something slower, more mournful. I recognized the classic ballad, "Your Cheatin' Heart."

"I picked a song just for us, May," Lenny said.

I gasped. Sally frowned. But Mama just smiled sweetly. "What about our song?" Mama asked.

"Our song's not on the juke box anymore," Lenny said, his voice thick. "But when I was putting in the coins for the juke box, this one seemed—"

Mama sighed. "Just ask me to dance, Lenny."

Lenny swallowed hard. "May, would you dance with me?"

She smiled and suddenly looked younger. "I'd be glad to."

Sally stood up and let Mama out of the booth. Then Lenny led Mama onto the dance floor, and they danced together, a simple one-two-three. They didn't dance close, keeping their bodies just from touching, but their eyes were locked.

Sally sat back down. We looked at each other. "Oh, my," she said. Then we looked back at Lenny and Mama on the dance floor.

"I'm ready for a break. How about you, hon?" Cherry plopped down next to me. "Skooh," she said.

Dean remained standing, staring out at the dance floor.

"What?" Cherry asked, looking at Sally and me. But we ignored her. By now, it was just Mama and Lenny on the dance floor. Everyone—even the hunky, dim Randy—was watching them, somehow captivated. They seemed to have landed there, on the dance floor, out of a different time, Lenny in his suit, Mama in her full-skirted soft dress, both of them staring into each other's eyes.

Even Cherry finally looked and understood and said "oh," and then was silent and watched.

17

"You're mad at me again, aren't you?"

Mama and Lenny had shared only the one dance, and then he'd left—wisely, it turned out, before the latest round of snowstorm hit. I'd been ready to go then, too, but Mama insisted on staying another hour or so. I'd even ended up dancing—just one dance, mind you, and not slow or close—with Randy, which was way more fun than I'd wanted to admit to myself.

And now Mama and I were back at my apartment, curled up on the couch in pajamas. My ensemble was a T-shirt that said WAKE ME LATE FOR BREAKFAST and PJ pants dotted with miniature Tweety-Birds. Mama was wearing elegant burgundy pajamas.

After we got home, changed into pajamas, I'd wanted to go to bed, but Mama insisted on making hot chocolate and talking. We hadn't said much in the process—she'd asked if it was okay if she left her cell phone charging on my counter, and I said sure, but mostly we'd been quiet up until the moment we curled up on the couch with our mugs of hot chocolate. Which should have made a cozy scene. Except I was grumpy and quiet and instead of letting it go, Mama was insisting on talking about it.

"I'm not mad," I said.

"Yes, you are. You've been fuming ever since we left the Bar-None."

"The drive home made me tense. Creeping along at twenty miles an hour in a snowstorm is not my idea of fun," I said.

Mama tsk-tsked. "You drove just fine. I'd have insisted we leave earlier, but you were finally having a good time, and I get the feeling that doesn't happen as often as it should."

Okay, now I was mad. "I like my life, thank you," I said.

We sipped our hot chocolate in silence. Then Mama said, "I know you were bothered, seeing Lenny and me dance. We dated back in high school. It was just a childhood sweetheart, first-crush kind of thing. Lenny's just a sweet memory to me, that's all."

"Didn't look back at the Bar-None like Lenny's reached that same kind of resolution. Did you go see him yesterday?"

"What?" Mama snapped.

"I know you disappeared for a while, while Daddy and Uncle Fenwick went for a walk. That's what Aunt Nora said, anyway."

Mama glared at me. "I went for a drive—that's all. I just needed to get away."

"But you stripped the gears later that night?"

"I was pretty shaken up about Henry being in jail, Josie. Why does everyone read too much into my actions?"

Maybe because your actions can be pretty out-landish, I thought, but didn't say.

Mama shook her head. "I really, simply went for a drive. Tonight's the first time I've seen Lenny since I left this sorry little town. Look, I feel sorry for Lenny because he had a hard time after his father disappeared, even though his parents were already divorced, and his mama had been taking up with Rich Burkette for a while. A long while."

"Before the divorce was final?"

"Long before, from what Lenny said. And of course his grandpa—who was really like a daddy to him—died. It all happened at once, and so Lenny was a little sensitive already when I broke up with him to go with Henry."

"You couldn't have waited a little while?"

"What?"

I tightened my grasp on my mug. I feared if my hand was too loose, I might be tempted to whop my own mama upside the head. Not a good impulse. "Why didn't you put off breaking up with Lenny to go with Henry—I mean, Daddy—if Lenny was already having a hard time dealing with his grandpa's death and his daddy running off? Wouldn't that have been the kinder way to break off?"

More silence. "I . . . I just didn't think of that." Mama's voice sounded perplexed, and I knew that she really hadn't thought of that. I could kind of understand that as a teenager she might have been that self-absorbed. But even as a fifty-something woman, she sounded perplexed by the idea. Maybe, I thought, some folks just never develop the capacity to think beyond their own immediate needs. And maybe my mama was one of them. Which meant, I thought, that her leaving really didn't have anything to do with me, and everything to do with . . .

"Henry just wasn't the kind to wait around, anyway," Mama said. "And sometimes waiting to break off doesn't work. There would never have been a good time, not from Lenny's point of view."

The comment stung. Would there ever be a good time for Owen to break off with me, from my point of view? Even with him in Kansas City, interviewing for a new job, I was still telling myself we had a chance together, but truth be told . . .

I took another sip of hot chocolate, pushing away thoughts of Owen, focusing on the hot chocolate. Yum. Mama had used cocoa, milk, sugar, and a dollop of vanilla, not the instant packets I kept handy. Maybe I'd stop using the instant. The from-scratch hot chocolate was worth it.

I looked at Mama, about to tell her how great her hot chocolate was—after all, her dancing with Lenny had been innocent, and it was really none of my business—but she was staring off in the distance. "Mama?"

She looked back at me abruptly. "Sorry. I was just thinking."

"What?"

"Nothing," she said.

Something, I thought.

"Mama. You look like you've suddenly figured something out. About Uncle Fenwick's murder?"

"No, I haven't," she said, giving me a look of pure innocence. I saw right through it.

"Mama," I said, warningly. "If you've thought of something, you'd better tell me and the police."

Mama narrowed her eyes. Her look of innocence

transformed to stubbornness, and I knew I wasn't going to get anything out of her. "I know that."

I sighed. "Fine," I said.

"Fine," she snapped right back, and stood up abruptly—immediately sloshing hot chocolate down the front of her silk pajamas.

"Damn it!" she exclaimed. "These PJs were expensive! Now they're ruined!"

"No, they're not," I said. "Come on, let me help you."

Who knew. I'd bonded enough with Aunt Nora over the cranberry stain that she'd told me about Uncle Fenwick coming back for the clothesline from his mama's front yard.

Maybe I'd bond enough with Mama over the hot chocolate stain that she'd tell me whatever she'd just realized.

I loaned Mama a pajama top—this one in blue that proclaimed, TELL ME WHEN THE COFFEE'S READY. It didn't really go with her pajama bottoms and mules, but she didn't care after I assured her the hot chocolate would come out of her pajama top.

"Hot chocolate is a combination stain," I told Mama. "A protein stain—from the milk—and an oily stain— from the chocolate. You want to treat the protein element first, soaking in cold water. Not hot—that will set the protein in the fibers. Then, for the oily part, we'll soak in a bucket of a quart of warm water, with about a teaspoon each of cloudy ammonia and dishwashing soap for about fifteen minutes. Then we'll wash as usual. If there's still some stain left, we'll soak in an enzyme product and wash again."

"Wow," Mama said. "You really have developed an expertise."

I couldn't help but feel a twinge of pleasure at the admiration in her voice, and it stayed with me through the soakings and then hand-washing and rinsing the top—I feared it was too delicate for a machine wash, and I didn't really want to brave the cold night again to go down to my laundromat.

I left the now clean pajama top on a padded hanger on the shower rod so it could dry overnight and went back into my bedroom. Mama was sitting on my bed, looking at a framed photo I keep of Guy on my nightstand. I sat down next to her, looked at the photo of Guy she held in her hand. I'd taken it a few autumns earlier, at the Stillwater harvest festival. In the photo, Guy was holding a big pumpkin and smiling broadly.

Mama set the photo back on the nightstand. Her hand trembled a bit.

"He looks so much like Horace did, the last time I saw him," she said.

"It must have been hard," I said gently, "being so disconnected from your family."

Mama looked at me sharply. "Who told you that?"

I smiled. "It's a small town."

"And everyone knows everyone, and everyone's business. Or they think they do," she said bitterly.

"There are good parts to living in a small town," I said.

"Good and bad to everything, I guess. I didn't see it that way when I was young. I just wanted to get out of here. Away from all the gossip. Most of what was said about me wasn't true, you know."

Which meant part of it was. Which part, I wondered? I'd probably never really know.

"That was the plan all along, you know," Mama went on. "Henry and I were going to graduate and leave town. But . . ."

She stopped.

"The first baby," I said gently.

"Yes," Mama said. She wiped a tear from her eyes. "I was so torn up after that. Henry, too. We couldn't seem to get our act together to leave. We acted . . . badly. And then we had you. We decided we'd try to make a life with you here. But Henry never liked it here. He always felt like a failure compared to Fenwick, and he always compared himself to Fenwick, no matter how often I told him not to.

"And then one day, when I thought things were starting to go well, Henry just didn't come home. He left me nothing but a note that said, 'I've found our treasure,' and a small pile of weird coins."

"The coins you used to have me take to the wishing well," I said. "I remembered I still have them in a hat box." I hopped up.

"Don't—" Mama started.

But I'd already hopped up. Eagerly, I trotted to my closet and stood on tiptoe and shoved aside some summer T-shirts and shorts and pulled down a box from the corner. I went back over to the bed and sat down again. I opened the box and pulled off the lid.

"Look," I said, suddenly compelled to find the coins.

"No—" Mama said, but she stared into the box as if she were compelled, too.

"I think they're at the bottom," I said. I scooted a little away from Mama to make space, and started pulling out items—little swatches of hair, tied up in pink ribbons, from my various haircuts, with tags labeled with my age at each haircut. I put those out along with a rubberbanded bunch of report cards and some handmade Christmas cards and a few pictures and my school pictures. My volleyball medals and my high school tassel.

All of it, saved by Aunt Clara, from third grade forward. The only thing from before then was the small leather bag, lumpy with coins.

I picked it up. "See!" I said. "This is the bag of coins Daddy left."

I looked at Mama, eagerly. She was pale, her eyes glistening. "Oh," I said. I reckon a lot of folks would say I had every right to be angry with her, but I felt suddenly sorry for her. She'd missed watching me grow up and I could see in her face that at least part of her regretted that.

Mama smiled sadly. "I guess I don't have any right to suddenly feel jealous of all your Uncle Horace and Aunt Clara got to experience with you."

"You could have had that with me. Why did you choose to go away?"

My voice was steady, clear, almost nonemotional. I was simply . . . curious.

Mama shook her head. "That was just it. I couldn't have experienced it. I'd have never done all of—" she waved her hands over the spread of mementos—"of this. See, I loved your daddy. I've always loved him. It's a crazy love. Every time I think how he and I would be better off apart, I know we can't be apart. Not for long. I thought, for those years after he left, that I was over him.

"I tried to be a good mama to you. But I wasn't good at it. As much as I mourned the loss of the first baby, I knew even then that I wasn't really cut out to be a mother. That made me feel guilty, so I tried to make it up with you—but I still wasn't cut out to be a parent.

Some folks just aren't, Josie. Henry and I are among them."

I took in what she had just said. Mama realized she and Daddy just weren't cut out to be parents. Well, I couldn't argue with that.

But while she was in the mood to talk like a reasonable human being, I had another question. "How did you connect up with Daddy again?"

"Very simple," Mama said, with a rueful laugh. "I got a call one day. From Effie Burkette. Just after the trailer burned. Did you know that that was because I fell asleep with a cigarette?"

I shook my head. "I don't remember you smoking."

"Well, I did. I've long quit, but I did. Usually I smoked outside, both to keep the smell out, and out of concern for you. But it was my fault the trailer burned. It's amazing we got out alive, and managed to save anything at all. Anyway, what was I saying?"

"Effie Burkette." Amazing, I thought, how much more connected to that family we'd been than I realized.

"Oh, yeah. Well. Effie and I stayed in touch through all the years. She kept it secret from Rich and Lenny, because she knew Lenny still felt something for me, and she didn't want him nagging her about me. And she kept it secret from Rich because he was always telling her who she needed to associate with to make him look good—and believe me, I didn't make that list.

"But Effie had been kind of like a mother figure to me when Lenny and I went together, so we stayed in touch off and on. Anyway, Effie and Rich had been on vacation at some fancy hotel in North Carolina, and what do you know—they saw Henry working as a bus-boy in the hotel restaurant."

"Coincidence," I said.

"Fate," Mama said firmly. "Some folks say there's no difference. Anyway. We were staying with Chief Hilbrink and his wife. I knew they'd dote on you if I left. So I took off, thinking I'd find Henry and give him a piece of my mind and demand some money from him. But instead . . ."

She shifted her gaze back to the collection on my bed. "Instead . . . what?"

She looked up at me. "I saw him and I couldn't be angry. I wanted to believe his pretty stories about how he was finally going to hit it big with this or that scheme. Then we'd come back and show Fenwick. One thing led to another, time passed, and . . ."

"And you just decided not to come back."

Mama sighed. "I heard from Lottie Arrowood, too, now and again—she promised not to tell where I was. When she told me you were at the orphanage, we started making plans to come back up here, but then Clara and Horace took you in. And then I heard how well you were doing with them, and I realized, well, that you'd be better off with them than with us.

"That's not meant to sound selfless, Josie. Like I said, some folks aren't cut out to be parents, and that includes me and your daddy. We loved you, but I guess we're just too selfish."

She picked up the picture of Guy again, stared at it. "I never could do what Clara and Horace did. What you're doing." She looked up at me. "I can't envy you, but I don't know if I should pity you."

I took Guy's picture from her, held it to my chest. "Don't you dare pity me," I said. "I love Guy like a brother and I wouldn't trade my love—or responsibility—for him for anything."

Mama stared at me, clearly not understanding.

I sighed. She was right. It was sad to say, but she and Daddy had done me a favor by leaving me with Uncle Horace and Aunt Clara. I just wished they'd come back, explained it to me years ago. But then, if they had thought of doing that, would they be the sort to have been unfaithful to each other, to have dropped their responsibilities in the first place?

I put Guy's picture back, picked up the bag of coins, opened it, and shook out the contents into my hand. I fingered a few of the coins.

"They're so . . . odd," I said. "Old-looking." I looked up at her. "Are these antiques?"

Mama shrugged. "I guess so."

I frowned. "You're planning to open FleaMart, and you don't know if these are antiques?"

She shrugged again. "Your daddy is the one who knows something about antiques. Not me. I take care of the business end of our ventures—financing, book-keeping, marketing."

"So . . . what kind of ventures have you two had all these years, besides FleaMart?"

Mama looked away. "Oh . . . this and that."

Uh huh, I thought. They'd tried various get-rich-quick schemes, half-baked business ideas like Flea-Mart, and hadn't succeeded at a single one. Otherwise, they'd have been back by now so Daddy could brag to Fenwick. But they'd made a hit with one FleaMart, down in Arkansas, much to their surprise.

I looked at the coins. "I remember you grabbing me from my room in the trailer. And I wiggled free so I could grab this bag of coins. You kept it in the kitchen drawer with the spatulas and such."

Mama nodded. "That's right. And I was angry, because you could have gotten hurt, straggling in the trailer." She smiled. "I may not have been much of a mama, but I didn't want you to get hurt." She patted my cheek. "I still don't."

I was still staring at the coins, though. "I thought these meant so much to you. That's why you wanted me to make a wish with them."

"Oh, Josie. Every time I got angry at Henry running off, I sent you to toss one of his precious coins down the wishing well. It felt like a little bit of revenge." I looked up at her. "Besides," she added, smiling ruefully. "They wouldn't work in the Masonville laundromat machines."

18

Coins spun around my head, annoyingly, like gnats. Even worse, clothespins were chasing the coins, snapping at them. The dizzying race they made around my head looked like some mutant variation of the vintage Pac-Man arcade game Sally kept in the back room of the Bar-None.

Of course, I knew I was dreaming, and that the clothespins weren't really going to snap my nose, or the coins dash into my eyes. Still, as I stood in the middle of my dream fog, I swatted at the coins and clothespins, all the while hollering, "Mrs. Oglevee, enough! Make it stop! I don't know what your point is, and this is getting tiresome. Mrs. Oglevee!"

Finally my former junior high teacher appeared. She was dressed in a cowgirl get-up and holding a length of clothesline. And she was grinning, amused at my discomfort.

I crossed my arms and resolutely ignored the cicada-like clothespins and coins, which had just started buzzing. Just a dream, I reminded myself. Although in the past, my Mrs. Oglevee dreams had helped me sort out problems. Just my subconscious, I told myself, perversely taking the form of my most feared teacher. At least, that's what I preferred to believe.

"Just what do you think you're going to do with that?" I said. "Have some laundry to hang out to dry?"

Mrs. Oglevee shook her head and clucked. "Josie, Josie. Didn't I always try to tell you to use your imagination, to see things from more than one angle?"

Actually, once I tried to explain on a multiple choice test why two of the four options could be the right choice, and even though one of them was the right choice according to the teacher's guide book, Mrs. Oglevee had not only counted the answer wrong, but gave me an F because I hadn't followed the directions to simply circle a., b., c., or d. But I didn't think this was the time to bring up this fine memory.

Suddenly, Mrs. Oglevee turned the clothesline into a lasso, and snapped it toward my head.

I admit it. I ducked, squeezing my eyes shut. When I opened them again, Mrs. Oglevee was once more smiling. She was circling the lasso in front of her, and somehow the coins and clothespins floated in the middle.

"See? The clothesline can be used as a clothesline, or as a lasso." She snapped the lasso suddenly, and it went flying into the air. She caught the ends and the coins and clothespins fell at her feet, no longer possessed.

Mrs. Oglevee started jump-roping with the clothesline. She'd never been that spry in life.

"Cut that out!" I snapped. "You're not making sense. Lassos and jump-roping have nothing to do with Uncle Fenwick's murder! Or the rest of this mess!"

"You still don't get it, do you," Mrs. Oglevee said,

chortling, and not losing a bit of breath while she kept jump-roping. If she suddenly doubled and did double-Dutch with herself, I was going to close my eyes and poke my fingers in my ears until I woke up.

"When is a clothesline not a clothesline?" Mrs. Oglevee asked.

"Don't you dare turn that thing into a snake," I hollered, eyes narrowing, fingers ready.

But Mrs. Oglevee laughed, while still jump-roping. "Ah! Now you're getting it! One thing can have many uses. But sometimes, a clothesline is not a clothesline because—"

She stopped suddenly, and held half of the clothesline in each hand.

"How did you break that in half in midair?" I know, I know. It was just a dream, and anything is possible in dreams, but it was still a remarkable image.

But Mrs. Oglevee ignored my question and finished, "—because it's two clotheslines."

I stared at the clotheslines in each of her hands. "Two . . . two clotheslines?"

"And sometimes," Mrs. Oglevee went on, "a clothesline is not a clothesline, but a noose."

The clothesline in her right hand suddenly flew from her hand, snapped itself into a noose, hovered over her head for a brief moment, like a perverse halo, and then dropped down over her head and tightened itself around her neck. Her face turned purple immediately, her tongue stuck out, and suddenly she was dangling and kicking and gagging.

I squeezed my eyes shut and stuck my fingers in my ears. "Stop it!" I cried. I knew she was already dead, of course, and couldn't really hurt herself, but the image still bothered me. "I know someone tried to hang poor Uncle Fenwick before stabbing him—"

"Answer A *and* answer B, Josie," Mrs. Oglevee said, her voice quite normal—though a little distant-sounding, since my ears were plugged.

The comment frustrated me enough that I unplugged my ears and opened my eyes. "You gave me an F for that," I hollered. Then I stared at Mrs. Oglevee. She was back to normal—well, as normal as she could be for an apparition of my subconscious . . . or of wherever (I'd never quite decided where I thought Mrs. Oglevee ended up in the afterlife), except that she had the clothesline(s) back into a lasso, which she was spinning with the coins and clothespins.

"Wait," I said. "Answer A and answer B . . . you mean Uncle Fenwick tried to kill himself . . . *and* someone killed him? Finished him off instead of trying to stop him?" I shuddered. The idea was horrendous. But still. Answer A and answer B, both right . . .

Mrs. Oglevee just shrugged. Suddenly, the clothesline lasso, coins, and clothespins all disappeared. I thought maybe that meant she was going to disappear, too, but instead, she suddenly made another coin appear out of her cowgirl blouse sleeve, just like the clichéd magic trick.

"Is this something only Josie can figure out . . . or does she need the help of others?" Mrs. Oglevee said, staring at the coin. "Heads, only Josie; tails, help of others." She flipped the coin, and I watched as it spun impossibly high up into the whiteness of my dream. Then she caught it perfectly in her right hand, and slapped it on her left forearm.

She moved her hand away, and stared at the coin on her forearm. "Hmmm," she said.

"Well, which is it?" I asked anxiously. "Heads or tails?"

But Mrs. Oglevee just smiled, and did her usual Chesire-cat-like disappearing act, all the while saying, "Answer A and answer B, Josie. Heads and tails. A and B . . ."

". . . heads and tails, A and B, heads and tails . . ." I woke up mumbling—and then sat bolt upright in my bed. I jerked open the drawer in my nightstand, grabbed my dream journal, and quickly began jotting notes. I'd started the dream journal after Halloween, when I realized that Mrs. Oglevee probably wasn't going to go away and that even without her, I often had vivid dreams.

So, in this dream, what had Mrs. Oglevee been trying to tell me?

Uncle Fenwick had committed suicide . . . and been murdered.

Only I could figure this mystery out . . . and I had to solve this with other people.

I tapped the pencil against my teeth—a habit that had annoyed Mrs. Oglevee in school, but she wasn't here to stop me—and tried to think.

It was possible that Uncle Fenwick had started to commit suicide, and then had his deadly work finished for him.

But how could only I solve this mystery, yet solve it with other people?

Apparently there was something only I could know, or find out, but I'd also need others' help. I'd already, in fact, enlisted others' help. All I'd really learned was the whole sad saga of my parents' past. Everyone else seemed to know them far better than I did. What could I know about that no one else did?

And there was something else, too, in the dream . . . two clotheslines, just like two answers to a question . . .

I shifted in bed. Something plunked out and onto the floor. I peered over the edge of my bed.

The bag of coins.

I was distracted from thinking about two clotheslines. There was something only I knew about the bag of coins? Or maybe something only I could find out about the coins. Something only I could ask my parents . . .

I listened for my mama stirring, but didn't hear anything. I looked at my nightstand clock, which said it was just after six in the morning. I frowned. I realized I'd been writing in my dream journal—but I hadn't turned on a light. There was enough light seeping through my bedroom curtains for me to write by, which meant it had to be fairly late in the morning.

I threw back the covers on my bed, horrified that I'd overslept, and then felt the chill. I looked at the clock again. Its digital second hand wasn't ticking along as usual.

And suddenly I was shivering.

Damn. I hopped out of bed.

The electricity in my building was off.

Electricity and heat out in the middle of a cold spell is no fun for anyone, but it can be downright disastrous for someone whose business is water based. I'd already dealt with water damage at the end of October from burst pipes in the street outside my laundromat. I sure didn't need to deal with pipes bursting inside my laundromat because the heat was off. I'd have to turn off the water to the whole building.

I pulled on socks, stuffed my feet into boots, pulled

on my coat, dashed through the living room, hollering, "Mama, don't start a shower or coffee! I'm going to turn off the water!"

Then I hurried down the exterior stairs, as best I could considering the steps were still icy, let myself into the back of my laundromat, went to the water shut-off, and turned off the water to the whole building. Then I heaved a huge sigh of relief. I'd woken up in time to turn off the water and keep the pipes from freezing and bursting.

I went to my desk, and wrote CLOSED DUE TO POWER OUTAGE with laundry marker on a spare manila file folder, and then trotted into the main part of my laundromat. I taped up the sign, right under the smiling toad, which I'd painted on the plate glass front window along with my slogan, ALWAYS A LEAP AHEAD OF DIRT!

Then I started back up to my apartment. It would soon be too cold to stay in the apartment. Maybe, I thought, Mama and I could go to Mamaw Toadfern's house. Or better yet, Mrs. Beavy's. Or Sally's, or Cherry's.

I smiled, pleased that I could come up with a list of places to go on such short notice. I'd have included Winnie on the list if she was in town. I started to think of Owen, and then told myself to stop.

"Mama, get up," I said to the lump on the couch. Mama was, I figured, nestled deeply under the comforter on the couch. She didn't respond. "Get up," I said again, and poked where I thought her shoulder would be.

Mama wasn't there. I whipped back the jumbled-up comforter. No Mama.

I looked around my living room. Her suitcase was still next to the couch, but her fur and purse were gone. I opened her suitcase. Her clothes, Daddy's clothes.

I went into the kitchen. Her cell phone was gone, but her connector was still plugged into the outlet.

I went into the bathroom. Her satin pajama bottoms and my night shirt were dropped on the floor. Her makeup and hair-styling supplies were piled up on the metal shelf over the sink.

Mama had left sometime in the middle of the night, and apparently in a hurry. It was also apparent that she'd planned on coming back because most of her things were still in my apartment.

But where could she have gone? She couldn't have driven anywhere. I couldn't imagine her walking very far in the snow—not in her stilettos.

I trotted back out to the exterior landing and gazed down at the small parking lot next to my building. I hadn't noticed before, because I'd been in such a hurry to shut off the water, but now I stared at the two sets of footprints, in the night's new snow, leading around to the front of my building. One set with a pointy toe and a dot for a heel—Mama's trademark stilettos. Another set looked like hiking boots. They stopped by the street. Tire tracks in the road were indistinguishable.

Who had she left with?

Daddy . . .

Oh, Lord, I thought. Somehow, Daddy had broken out of the jail, stolen a car, picked up Mama, and they'd taken off again. Then he'd come by here, told her, don't worry, May, just leave this stuff, we'll replace it later, and they took off.

I paused before going inside. How would I feel if they really had taken off again?

A little relieved, I had to admit.

There was one way, I suddenly realized, that I could be sure if Mama had left for good, on her own volition.

I got out the area phone book—thinner, in my neck of the woods, than the weekly cable guide—and looked up Mrs. Arrowood's phone number.

"Um, I'm sorry, did I wake you?" I asked—then immediately felt foolish. I knew from her voice I had. It was still early.

"Who is this? What do you want?"

"Mrs. Arrowood, it's Josie Toadfern."

Silence on the other end.

"May's daughter."

"Oh, yes. Would you tell May that Cherry did a wonderful job! I look—and feel—ten years younger, and of course I'd never have had the courage without May . . ."

"Mrs. Arrowood, I was hoping that maybe Mama had called you or dropped by to see you—maybe sometime in the night? Or very early this morning."

Silence again.

"She's left again," Mrs. Arrowood said, her voice deflated with disappointment.

"Yes. But she said she wouldn't leave without coming by to tell you good-bye this time," I said. "She sounded sincere." I took a deep breath. "Mrs. Arrowood—do you think she was sincere?"

More silence. Then, "Yes." Mrs. Arrowood's voice was suddenly firm with conviction. "Yes, I know she wouldn't have left this time without coming by—not of her own free will."

I finished the conversation with Mrs. Arrowood. Mama hadn't gone by to see Mrs. Arrowood. Which meant either she was still in the area or hadn't left of her own free will.

I picked up the phone again and called the Paradise Police Department.

A few minutes later, Jeanette, the dispatcher on duty, sounded amused as she said, "Of course Henry Toadfern is still here. I just served him breakfast. He asked for cappuccino—again. I explained we have the standard coffee. His tastes sure have gone upscale since I knew him back in high school. Back then—"

I tuned out Jeannette's rambling. If Daddy hadn't broken out to take Mama, then who had picked her up?

Lenny Burkette immediately came to mind. Mama had protested that she didn't have any feelings for Lenny, but I didn't completely believe her. I'd seen how they'd looked at each other the night before at the Bar-None.

And where had Mama gone after the disastrous Thanksgiving dinner, while Daddy and Uncle Fenwick were out walking? My guess, to see Lenny.

So, if Mama had left voluntarily with Lenny, that wasn't a matter for the police. But I didn't know for sure that that's where she was.

And I still needed to talk to Chief Worthy. I thought I'd figured out who'd killed Uncle Fenwick.

"Look, I still need to talk to Chief Worthy," I said, interrupting Jeanette's chatter. My request didn't come out as smoothly as I would have liked. I was shivering, even though I had on my coat, because I'd had to do without a hat or mittens to use my cell phone.

"He's busy," Jeanette snapped, clearly displeased that I'd interrupted her trip down memory lane.

"Then I need to talk to whoever else is in charge!"

"Everyone's out on patrol, checking on the elderly to make sure they're okay. There's been a power outage in about half the town—ice on the lines—"

"I know that! My power is out, too! I just need to talk to someone in charge!"

"That would be the power company, but they're well aware—"

"Not about the power!" I shrieked. "I need to talk to someone in charge at the police station!"

"Well, Chief Worthy is busy, and that means I'm in charge, I guess. How can I help you?"

I pressed my eyes shut. "You can tell Chief Worthy I'm coming down there, now, because I've figured out who really killed Fenwick Toadfern."

I hung up. I looked over my dream journal notes, thought through again the conclusions I'd come to. I'd only glanced at the dream journal when I came into my bedroom to get my cell phone from my purse, but that glance was enough to trigger an important realization about the two clotheslines.

I left the journal on my nightstand, and pulled on my hat and gloves. I gave Rocky—my pothos ivy—a sympathetic look as I passed through the living room. Rocky was already looking droopy in the cold room. "Good luck," I said.

I'd need it, too, I thought. Then I locked up my apartment and walked the three blocks to the police station.

19

"Let me see if I have this straight," Chief Worthy said, staring at me over the tops of his fingertips.

I glared back at him across his desk. We were sitting in his office. At least I wasn't cold any longer. For one thing, the power outage hadn't hit the police building. Plus, I was angry because John Worthy was again treating my ideas dismissively. And anger always sent heat rushing to my face and hands.

"You think Rich Burkette killed Junior Hedberg years ago," Chief Worthy said. "And that your Uncle Fenwick somehow knew this and was blackmailing him this whole time, and so Rich killed your Uncle Fenwick—or, at least, finished him off after your uncle tried to commit suicide, which he did, because somehow he figured the blackmail gig was up because your parents returned to town."

All right. It did sound a little over the top, the way he described it.

"Okay, I know there are some holes in my theory—"

"Yeah. Starting with the leap that Junior Hedberg is dead, instead of just living somewhere else."

"Why is that such a leap? I already told you, Caleb Loudermilk tried to track the man down and came up with nothing. And Caleb is a—"

"Second-rate reporter who thinks he can come up with a hot story."

"He's a good researcher," I said. "Anyway, what about the rest of my theory?"

Chief Worthy glared at me. "You really expect me to go arrest Rich Burkette on suspicion of murder because a clothesline is missing from his yard?"

Without mentioning my dream as the trigger for the memory, I'd told Worthy that when I'd visited the Burkettes on Thanksgiving afternoon, I'd seen Rachel duck where the clothesline should have been. She was used to it being out, to ducking under it whenever she walked across the back yard.

"There were two clotheslines, weren't there? There had to be. One that Uncle Fenwick tried to hang himself with." I had already filled him in on Aunt Nora's confession to me that Uncle Fenwick had suicidal tendencies and had come back and taken the clothesline from Mamaw Toadfern's yard. "And one that someone tied him up with, before stabbing him."

"Or, there's one clothesline cut in half," Chief Worthy said. "And someone—and in my mind, your father is still the top suspect, based on the fact that your father and Fenwick had a fight in which they threatened each other—someone stabbed Fenwick, then tried to make it look like a hanging and really botched the job. That's the original theory, and the one that makes the most sense to me. Your uncle was a successful man and had everything to live for."

"Unless he was successful only because he was blackmailing Rich Burkette," I said. "And that wealth threatened to disappear for some reason when my parents showed up."

"Why do you think he was blackmailing Rich Burkette?" Chief Worthy asked.

I'd thought he'd never ask. "Because. Uncle Fenwick made it very clear at Thanksgiving dinner that he'd never enjoyed the plumbing business. It's hard enough to succeed in business if you love it. It's nearly impossible if you hate it. And yet he made enough money to buy things like that superfancy trailer."

Chief Worthy shrugged. "Fenwick and his wife didn't have any kids. Maybe they saved a lot of money."

I shook my head. "Maybe. But not that much. And on the other hand, Rich Burkette, who should have a lot of money after his years as an attorney, could be living much more extravagantly than he does. But he lives modestly in what was his wife's daddy's farmhouse. Does that fit the personality of someone like Rich Burkette?"

Chief Worthy's eyebrows went up a second, and he seemed to actually be considering my theory. But then he shook his head. "It's possible that Rich and Effie just like to save their money. Maybe they're planning to move to Europe or the Caribbean after his retirement. In any case, you don't need to come up with scenarios to get your daddy off the hook for killing your uncle. Henry Toadfern is all yours."

"What? What do you mean?"

"I mean there isn't enough evidence to hold him. Oh, I still think he killed his brother, and we'll find evidence soon enough, but for now we have to let him go. So . . . he's all yours." Chief Worthy stood up.

"But what about my mama taking off? I mean, my guess is that she's with Lenny Burkette—" I'd given Chief Worthy a brief description of their past and their dancing at the Bar-None—"and if Rich really killed Junior and Uncle Fenwick, maybe she's in danger if he thinks she knows something . . ."

"Or maybe she just took off again," Chief Worthy said. "It's what your parents do, isn't it?"

"That's not fair!" I snapped. "Look, I've heard about how my mama flirted with your daddy years ago, and I reckon it caused resentment in your family against mine, and maybe that's why your parents didn't want you to date me years ago, but as an officer of the law, you have an obligation—"

"I have no idea what you're talking about," Chief Worthy said. His face had gone even stonier than usual—which, considering his jaw line usually looked like it had all the flexibility of a retaining wall, was quite a feat. "My daddy was always faithful to my mama. You and I broke up because . . ."

His voice trailed off. I grinned, rather unkindly. "Because you were unfaithful to me."

He snorted. "We were kids back in high school."

"It still counts," I said. "And considering you were the one who was in the wrong, I don't understand . . ."

"You embarrassed me by putting in your high school newspaper gossip column that I'd been seen holding hands under the bleachers with one of the cheerleaders after the big game, when you knew I was dating the coach's daughter!"

"Of course I knew that. You fooled around with her behind my back. And yet she was so surprised when you fooled around behind her back," I said.

"What does this have to do with anything?" He

yelled. "That was years ago! In high school! Move on! I have!"

Had he? John Worthy had never settled down. He just enjoyed a series of love affairs that left a lot of women unhappy.

I slapped the desk. "You know, I'm so tired of men who think they can just get away with whatever they want. You. Sally's ex."

"Your daddy. Owen." Chief Worthy interjected and grinned at me.

I didn't know what to say. So I slapped the desk again.

"Maybe you'd better start hanging out with a better class of man, then," Chief Worthy said. "Meanwhile, if your mama is not back in forty-eight hours, you can file a report. In the meantime, don't let your father run off, too. We can't hold him for now, but he's still a suspect."

He motioned to the door. "Now let's go fetch your daddy for you."

"Start from the beginning and tell us everything," I said.

Daddy looked from me to Caleb.

We were at the *Paradise Advertiser-Gazette* office. After Daddy and I left the Paradise Police Department, we walked back to my apartment. My plan was to pack a few things, then call Sally and see if she could take us in, at least until the power was back on.

But Caleb was waiting for us outside my laundromat. He had, he said, the information I'd asked about. I explained about the power, and he said we could go back to the newspaper office, which happened to be in the half of the town where the power was still on.

So there we were, in the *Paradise Advertiser-Gazette* office, which was really just a big room with Caleb's desk, a few computers, and bookshelves. There was a desk for his assistant, too, who worked part-time, but she wasn't in on this Saturday morning.

Daddy, despite the neat suit—complete with silk pocket hanky—he'd insisted on changing into in my cold apartment, and despite the lined, leathery texture of his face, looked much more like a lost little boy than the businessman he affected.

"I—I don't know," he finally said.

"It's all off the record, just like I promised Josie," said Caleb. "For now, at least."

"This is pretty simple, Daddy," I said. "Mama left this morning with someone. I think it was with Lenny Burkette."

Daddy frowned. "She wouldn't do that. She knows I dislike him. Whenever there was a problem, even a little problem in our marriage, back when we still lived here, he'd always call or write or even come to town—"

"Look, she was talking with him last night," I said. "I think there's a reason she might have left with him, but before I tell you, you're going to have to answer some questions."

Daddy must have been thinking along the same lines, because suddenly he dropped his head to his hands. "I want to find her," he said miserably. "Of course I do. Nothing matters, not even FleaMart, without her." He looked up at me, his eyes glistening. "But I'm not sure what you want me to tell you."

"I'm not sure, either, at least not specifically," I said. "Let's start with the coins. We were looking at them last night, and I could tell from Mama's face that seeing them triggered something. A memory, maybe."

"The coins," Daddy said flatly.

"When you took off from Mama and me," I said, "you left Mama a note and a bag of coins. When our trailer caught fire, just before she left, I grabbed the bag of coins. I got the coins out last night and we looked at them."

"Oh." Daddy looked embarrassed. "When I was working for Fenwick, we were called out to the Bur-kette place to take care of a plumbing problem. They'd switched over to county water and a sewer system years before, but there was a problem with standing water out near the old septic tanks and cistern."

"Cistern?" Caleb said.

I grinned. "City boy. A cistern is just a big holding tank in the ground to hold water. Most old farms have them."

"That's right," Daddy said. "Farms around here, most of the cisterns date back to the early 1900s. Ce-ment floor, dirt walls coated in plaster, cement lid over the opening. And most have been plugged up."

"So they're just sitting empty?" Caleb said. "Isn't that dangerous?"

Daddy shook his head. "Not so long as the lid's in place. Anyway, Fenwick took a look at the cistern. I was supposed to check out the old septic tank." Daddy wrinkled his nose and shuddered. "I hated plumbing." Well, at least he and Fenwick had had something in common besides an attraction to Mama and a bitter ri-valry. "I can't remember what the problem was, al-though I reckon we fixed it. Anyway, I found an old metal box that had been tied shut. I was curious, of course, so I pulled it out and pried it open.

"It was filled with old coins—antique ones. I'd heard about Duke Ross, Effie's daddy, collecting them and about Junior Hedberg selling them from time to time at the antique shops in town. Then, suddenly, he stopped selling them. Shortly after that, he and Effie divorced."

"With Rich Burkette representing Effie," Caleb said.

"Yeah. And after that Junior took off—or, if Josie's right, was killed. Anyway, at the time, I figured that Duke must have hidden his coins away from Junior, then never told anyone where he'd hidden them. He died kind of suddenly, from a heart attack," Daddy said. "Fenwick came up behind me while I was looking at the coins. About startled the daylights out of me. I told him I'd share the coins with him, after I found out what they were worth."

"You stole the coins," I said, appalled.

"Well, now, Josie honey, Effie and Rich were doing fine, about to sell the house and build a big house in town. At least, that's what Effie said when we came to do the job. She was really bragging about it. She wanted the house all ready when Rich came back to town—he was out of town on business, and of course by then Lenny had grown and moved out of town, so she was home alone with just little Rachel.

"Anyway, it wasn't like they needed the money. But your mama and I did. But I knew I couldn't get them appraised here in Paradise. I was afraid the antique dealers would recognize the coins. Since I'd followed the antique business for a while—always wanted an antique shop of my own—I knew of some good shops down in North Carolina. I figured it was safe to get them appraised there.

"I told Fenwick that's what I'd do, and amazingly, he didn't argue with me. He just had this stunned look on his face. Anyway, I left a note and a few of the coins with your mama. I knew if I told her my plan, she'd say no, we should do the right thing and return the coins to Effie. She'd said once or twice that Effie had been kind of a mother figure to her, back in high school. So I took off, and . . ."

"And never came back," I said, somewhat bitterly.

"Now, honey, I had good intentions. I sold the coins. Got a good deal of money for them, but then . . ." Daddy's voice trailed off and he looked embarrassed again.

"Then what?" I prodded. "Come on, just tell us."

"Well, then I got into a poker game and, well, I lost it all," he said miserably. "After that, I was too embarrassed to come back. I took odd jobs here and there until your mama came and found me. We tried various ventures and finally hit on FleaMart. It was your mama's idea. After we connected up again, she started reading everything she could about business. And now she's great with business."

"She told me she found you because Rich and Effie Burkette saw you bussing tables at a restaurant while they were on vacation in North Carolina," I said. "Then Effie gave her a call."

"Interesting coincidence," Caleb said.

"Fate," Daddy said, echoing Mama. I rolled my eyes. Daddy didn't notice. Caleb did, grinned, and winked at me. I looked away, back to Daddy.

"I don't remember seeing them," Daddy went on. "But I know your mama has stayed in touch with Effie all these years, even though she knows it bothers me because Lenny still has feelings for May. But like I said, Effie was kind of a mother figure to May, when her own parents . . ." his voice trailed off in bitterness. "Never mind that. Anyway. That's how Rachel, after she became a real estate broker, ended up helping us.

We finally scraped together some money, invested in real estate, made a killing, and started the idea of Flea-Mart. After the first one succeeded in Arkansas, I wanted to come back here. May wanted to stay away, said we'd be better letting things be, but I wanted to show Fenwick." He looked bitter and angry again for a moment, then suddenly looked scared. "But May might have been right. How are we going to find her?"

"Let's talk about the walk you took with Uncle Fenwick," I said. "By all accounts you came back mad. Aunt Nora said he came back mad, too, then took the clothesline from the yard, and left again. Why did you get mad at each other this time—or was it the usual rivalry?"

"Well, believe it or not he was still sore that I cut him out of the coin deal," Daddy said.

"That's what he meant by you were supposed to share, when you were fighting at dinner?" I asked.

"That's right." Daddy shook his head. "I can't believe he's held a grudge all these years, considering how well he's done in plumbing, at least from the looks of things. Anyway, I told him on the walk that we were working with Rachel Burkette to buy the old orphanage and that two weeks ago, she'd contacted Rich and asked him if he wanted to be a partner with May and me after his retirement. He's off the county commissioners, so it wouldn't be a conflict of interest, and with him involved in the deal, it's more likely to go through. That was your mama's idea, too.

"And from what Rachel said, he was really surprised, but then he liked the idea. He wants to talk with us next week. We're pretty excited. He's got to have a lot of money squirreled away. On our walk, I told Fenwick about it, told him I'd write him a check after this deal went through to cover more than his share of the coins. I just didn't want him to mention the coins to anyone, botch up the deal we seem to have going with Rich. But Fenwick got really upset at me, told me I'd ruined everything as usual, and then took off running. Thought the blubber-butt would have a heart attack." Daddy stopped, looked chagrined. "Oh. Sorry."

"And you have no idea why Uncle Fenwick got that upset?" I asked.

Daddy shook his head. "I thought he'd be glad to get the money, and then some, for the coins. As well off as he is."

Caleb cleared his throat. "Josie's right, though. He's probably not well off from his plumbing business. It's privately held, so I don't have specific numbers, but it was easy enough to check into business listings online. He employs himself, three full-time plumbers, a few part-timers, and a secretary, and has his building in a not so great part of Masonville. Hard to see how he makes the kind of money to buy the kind of toys and jewels he and his wife apparently like to flaunt.

"On the other hand, Rich should be, well, rich. Again, I don't have specific numbers, because the firm is privately held. But I checked out his partner's address. He lives in a half-million-dollar house on multiple acres north of Masonville, and has registered several expensive automobiles and a new houseboat," Caleb said. "I suppose it's possible that Rich decided to save all his money, but it doesn't seem to fit his personality."

Daddy frowned. "But from what Rachel was saying, he had plenty of money to invest in FleaMart."

Caleb shrugged. "Maybe so. Or maybe he was just curious about your plans."

Daddy balled his hands into fists and hit his knees. "I don't understand what this has to do with finding May!"

I took a deep breath. "I have a theory that Rich Burkette killed Junior Hedberg, Fenwick was blackmailing Rich, and Rich finally snapped and killed Fenwick to end it, and somehow that was motivated by your and Mama's return."

Both men looked at me. Caleb gave a long whistle. "Wow," he said, wonderingly. "Were you thinking that last night, when you asked me to look into your uncle's business?"

"No," I said. "I was just curious about Uncle Fenwick and Aunt Nora's wealth. It didn't fit his comments about hating plumbing. People usually don't get rich doing something they hate."

"Hell, I love journalism," said Caleb, giving me an appreciative look, "and I'll never get rich doing it. Ever thought of being a journalist?"

"No," I said, grinning, glad he was taking my theory much more seriously than Worthy had. Of course, if I was right, Caleb would end up with a wonderful story, especially since he'd gotten me to wondering about Junior in the first place. "I love being a stain expert, although I'll never get rich doing that, either. Plus, really, Caleb, you started me thinking last night, when you brought up how odd it was that Rich and Effie live so modestly, and how you couldn't find Junior."

"If you two lovebirds would knock off the mutual admiration," Daddy shouted, making us jump and look at him, "maybe you could tell me how this fits my wife's apparent disappearance?"

I wanted to take exception to the description of Caleb and me as lovebirds. We were colleagues of a sort, I thought, and there was Owen, and—oh, never mind, I told myself. "Well, I'm thinking, last night at the Bar-None, Mama and Lenny—chatted."

Daddy frowned.

"Perfectly innocent," I said hastily. "But what if something he said made Mama come to the same conclusion? She got this look last night, like she'd suddenly realized something. Maybe something Lenny said drove her to the same conclusion about Rich and Uncle Fenwick. So what if Mama called Lenny, thinking they could confront Rich? From what I've learned and observed, Rich has a habit of subtly putting down Lenny and Effie, and Lenny adores his mother," I said. "Both Mama and Lenny could be in danger if they've confronted Rich." I looked at my watch. It was just after eleven in the morning. "Mama's been gone at least four hours, now."

Daddy stood up. "Let's go to the Burkettes now!"

"Wait," I said. "We can't just barge in. It is possible, after all, that, well—"

"That what?" Daddy said, glaring.

"That Mama just took off again," I said, although I didn't believe it. Deep down, I wanted to believe Mrs. Arrowood—that Mama wouldn't have taken off without keeping her promise to this time come by and say good-bye. Daddy glared at me even harder. I glared back. "You two have been known to do that, you know."

Caleb winced audibly, embarrassed, I think, to observe this particular bout of family fun.

Daddy sank back to his chair.

"We have to think, put our heads together. Something about those coins . . ." my voice trailed off. I pressed my eyes shut. What did Mama know about those coins? She'd kept them, studied them, left them behind with me. Knew, as I now did, that Daddy had found them in the septic tank on the Burkette property, that Fenwick had surprised Daddy looking at the coins, had seemed oddly disinterested although years later he was resentful Daddy hadn't shared the wealth . . .

My eyes popped open. "Oh, my Lord," I said. "Tell me again, what did Uncle Fenwick seem like, after he came from the cistern?"

Daddy shrugged. "A little rattled. But then, as he said, he never really liked plumbing. Smells always got to him."

I looked at Caleb and I knew he knew exactly what I was thinking. He said it for both of us. "I have a feeling we both know where old Junior Hedberg's been all these years."

"What?" said Daddy. "Well, let's call Worthy." He reached for the phone. I put my hand on his arm. I looked at him and then at Caleb.

"I have a—" I hesitated to call it better. "—a different idea."

20

"Are you sure we should be doing this?" I asked.

"Josie, it was your idea," Caleb said.

We were sitting in my van at the back of the parking lot at the Run Deer Run lodge. The lot was packed with cars and trucks. Rich Burkette's retirement party was under way, and it was a popular destination.

"I say we go in there, grab the son of a bitch by the throat, and demand he tell us where May is!" Daddy growled. We'd tried Mama's cell phone several times, and always got an out-of-service message, which, considering I knew she'd charged it overnight, had us all concerned.

"Daddy, we've already discussed why that's not going to work," I said. "All Rich has to do is say he has no idea what you're talking about, and everyone will believe him. Then you're back in jail, and we have no idea where Mama is. Or proof that my theory—"

"Our theory," Caleb interjected.

"Okay, that our theory is right," I finished.

Daddy balled his gloved hands and pounded his fists on his knees. "Damn, I wish I knew exactly where that cistern was!"

Of course, we'd eliminated calling Chief Worthy and asking him to check the cistern for Junior Hedberg's remains. He would have laughed us off the phone. Even if a miracle had occurred and he took our theory seriously, law enforcement can't just go searching private property without a warrant, and our guess wasn't enough of a reason to get a warrant.

So, it seemed obvious that the simple thing to do was trespass onto the Burkette property while the Burkette clan was all at Rich's retirement party, find the cistern, open it up, and check for Junior Hedberg's remains, then call the police, and then deal later with trespassing charges.

But that's not as simple as it sounds. Daddy had never seen the cistern, just the septic tank, which would be located a distance from the cistern for obvious reasons. After twenty-seven years, he wasn't sure where the septic tank had been, so he couldn't take an educated guess about the location of the cistern based on that.

Plus, snow covered the ground, making spotting a cistern lid simply by walking the grounds around the house impossible.

Taking Daddy to the Burkette property and hoping his memory of the septic tank's location would return didn't seem like a good idea, either. After all, the trees around the property would have grown considerably in twenty-seven years.

Which led us all back to my original idea.

Kidnap Rich Burkette from his own retirement party.

Here's what I figured. If my theory was right—that

Rich had killed Junior Hedberg, dumped him in the cistern, been found out by Uncle Fenwick and then blackmailed—then Rich would definitely know exactly where that cistern was. And chances were he'd left that body exactly where it was because, after all, what better place to hide a body than in an old, empty cistern?

Of course, if my theory was wrong, we'd all be liable for a lot worse charges than trespassing . . .

But I seemed to be the only one with any doubts.

"This is going to make a great story," Caleb said.

"Yeah, if you don't get fired. How many ethics violations are you making?" I asked. My voice was shaking.

"I don't know. I'll add them up later." He sounded excited, up for the adventure. So different than Owen, who would have tried to talk me out of this. Which suddenly seemed like a good idea . . .

"Either get going, or I'm going to go in there and—" Daddy started.

"Fine," I said. "We're going. You know what to do?"

He nodded. I handed him the keys to my van. Caleb and I got out. Daddy moved over to the driver's side of my van.

Here was the plan. Daddy would wait in my van; after all, he hadn't been invited to the party. And we didn't want Rich to see him—or him to see Rich—anyway.

Caleb and I would go inside. Caleb would pull Rich aside, tell him he'd uncovered some interesting facts that they might want to discuss privately—outside.

As they were leaving, I would go outside, too. I'd wait for Caleb to give me the signal—a single flick of a cigarette lighter—and then from behind I'd quickly loop a scarf around Rich's mouth. Then Caleb and I would force him to my van, and Daddy would take off with all of us.

Then we'd lie and tell Rich we'd found proof in Uncle Fenwick's possessions that Rich had killed Junior years ago, but that if he'd tell us where the cistern and Mama were, we'd destroy the proof.

Of course, we planned on instead going to the cistern, checking for Junior's body, and calling the police.

Funny how plans don't always work out.

"You really do look lovely," Caleb said. "Too bad this isn't a real date."

I was just about to stuff a stuffed mushroom into my mouth when he said that.

"I can't look lovely. I'm too nervous," I said, and stuffed the stuffed mushroom into my mouth.

He grinned, focusing on my chewing, which annoyed me, so I frowned, which made him grin more. The power had finally come back on at my laundromat/apartment building, and so I'd been able to shower and change into a black knit skirt, black boots, a bright green sweater, and loopy earrings. Perfect attire for a retirement party. Or a kidnapping.

I swallowed and licked my teeth. "Yum. You won't find that at Sandy's."

"Ah. So the laundromat lady likes upscale munchies."

I lifted my eyebrows. "You thought I wouldn't?"

"You've never turned in a column about how to get out caviar stains."

We'd stationed ourselves in the crowded lodge by the hors d'oeuvres table. I had to admit, the fancy eats and candelabras and elegant flower arrangements of lilies and roses seemed at odds with the down-home, woodsy interior of the lodge, which was decorated in dark paneling and moose and deer heads.

Still, I didn't especially like Caleb's implication that

my hometown and I weren't capable of some upscale partying. I picked up a cracker topped with black caviar, popped it into my mouth, and munched.

When I finished, I said, "Notice I didn't get a dollop on my sweater. If I had, the way to handle a caviar stain is to first realize that it's oil based. So, rinse from behind with warm water, and treat with cloudy ammonia and dishwashing liquid diluted in water. Use distilled water for fine fabrics, as distilled water won't leave a ring, but tap water can, with all the minerals in it, especially around here. Then, use a solution of one-third vinegar and two-thirds water to get rid of the black stain. Or try hydrogen peroxide—similarly diluted—depending on the fabric."

"Well, I'm impressed," Caleb said. "Will all that be in your column . . . due Monday?"

"I'm focusing on uses of vinegar," I said. And then I gave in to the cough that had been building in my throat. "Actually, that was my first experience eating caviar." I coughed again. "Salty."

Caleb laughed. "I prefer stuffed mushrooms, too." He picked one up and ate it.

We scanned the crowded room.

I moved closer to Caleb so no one would overhear me, and said softly, "Do you see Rich anywhere?"

Caleb shook his head. "He's got to be here somewhere, working the crowd. I thought I spotted Effie, earlier."

"And I saw Lenny and Rachel at different times, chatting with people." So, Mama wasn't with Lenny.

We'd been at the party for about fifteen minutes. If we didn't act soon, it would be time for Rich to get up on the small stage and make a toast. Then it would be nearly impossible to get to him before the crowd started thinning out. And we sure couldn't kidnap him while people were going to their cars.

"Let's split up," Caleb said. "Look for him separately."

"How will we reconnect in this crowd?"

Caleb thought. "All right—whichever one of us finds him first, get him over to the side door and keep him there somehow. We'll meet there in ten minutes."

I was worried. "This plan doesn't seem like such a good idea after all," I said.

He smiled reassuringly. "It'll work," he whispered. "Mama for you, Pulitzer for me."

I started to work my way through the crowd, to where I'd last seen Rachel. Caleb tapped my arm. I turned and looked at him.

"How about a real date sometime," he said. "When we're through with, you know."

"I have a boyfriend, remember?"

"Question still stands," Caleb said.

"Don't you have a girlfriend?" I asked.

A pained look crossed Caleb's face, and I regretted the question. "Not any longer," he said.

I patted his arm. "We'll see."

He nodded. "Good enough." Then he turned and started working his way through the crowd. I did the same, trying to ignore the nervous flutter in the pit of my gut.

Then I felt someone tap my shoulder again. I turned around. This time it was Lenny.

"Josie, I am so glad to see you," he said, sounding relieved.

"Lenny! Well, it's nice to see you. I wanted to congratulate your daddy—"

Lenny grabbed me by the elbow and pulled me closer to him. "Listen, I need your help! Rich and Mama went back to the kitchen to pour special glasses of champagne to bring out to toast each other in a few minutes," he whispered. "But Mama spilled the champagne on her dress! I told her not to worry about it, but she's frantic. She says she won't come out with her big obvious splotch, and rubbing at it to try to dry it has flattened the velvet and made it worse, and Rich is getting annoyed, as usual. I thought maybe you could help."

I looked around. I didn't see Rich or Effie anywhere, although I did catch a glimpse of Rachel, who waved. I waved back. I looked at Lenny. He looked really concerned, as usual, about his mama.

Well, this was a way to get to Rich and get him over to Caleb. I swallowed hard. Was I really prepared to kidnap one of Paradise's most prominent citizens?

You bet I was.

And my stain expertise was going to help me do it!

I was nearly preening as I followed Lenny back to the kitchen.

I stopped preening the minute I stepped into the kitchen and Lenny grabbed my arm, and pulled a gun on me.

Rich and Effie weren't back there. Just me, Lenny, and a gun in my back.

I glanced around . . . where were the caterers? Some knives I could grab? An iron skillet to whop Lenny upside his crazy head?

Lenny said into my ear, "I paid the caterers to leave early. Told them to come back in the morning to clean up."

"I feel a scream coming on." I widened my mouth.

Lenny shoved the gun harder into my back. "Ah, but then you'll never get to save your mama."

I shut my mouth. Then I opened it again, and said, "well, you won't shoot me here. Everyone would hear."

"You sure about that?" Lenny said. "Try me. Of course, that way, you still won't get to save your mama. Or your daddy."

"Who says I want to save them? I don't care. They took off when I was a kid. My real parents are Aunt Clara and Uncle Horace."

"Oh, but Josie, I think you can't help but try to help your parents, because you'd do the same for anyone."

I sighed. He had me there.

"Now, let's go get your daddy and take him and you to see your mama . . . and my daddy."

My stomach convulsed. "What . . . what do you mean . . ."

"You'll see," Lenny said. "Out to my car."

"But . . . my coat . . . I checked it out front . . ." I started lamely.

Lenny shoved me forward. "Oh, please. Do you think I care if you freeze to death? That's the idea, after all."

"I d-d-don't k-k-know why you think you're going to g-g-g-et away with this," I said. For the record, my teeth were chattering because it was cold in Lenny's car. And I didn't have my coat.

Lenny, who sat in the passenger's seat, had his coat and seemed perfectly cozy, sitting there pointing the gun at me as I drove.

"Very simple," he said cheerfully. "No one will miss me at the party. I'm not Rich and Effie's kid, after all. Rachel has always been the belle of the Burkette ball. It's not like anyone's going to say, where's Lenny? Meanwhile, your daddy is knocked out cold. It was so easy. I saw you and that reporter—what's his name?"

"Caleb," I said.

"You and Caleb came in, and I thought, why wait? I knew I would have to take care of you and Henry sooner or later. I went outside to unlock my car—no fumbling for keys while forcing you inside—and saw your daddy sitting in your van. I went over, said, Mr. Toadfern, can I have a word with you, and he eagerly hopped out, started to say something about wanting a word with Rich, and I whacked him with the handle of my gun. Dragged him to my car, gagged him with an old rag, and tied his hands and legs with more old rags. Have a lot of those, to keep this old car running. Not that I think he's going to come around for a while."

That was true. I'd caught a glimpse of Daddy, knocked out, bound and gagged in the backseat. Exactly what, more or less, Caleb and I had planned for Rich.

"I'm taking you and Henry to the cistern," Lenny went on, "where you'll join my daddy and your mama. Daddy's been dead for years, of course. Not much left of his remains. And your mama may well already be dead, of course, since she's been in there since this morning. Your daddy and you may freeze to death tonight. Not sure."

"People will notice that we're missing," I said, stuttering half the words.

"Of course they will," Lenny said. "Well, they'll notice you're missing. Why would Josie run off and leave her business? Her dear cousin?"

I clenched the steering wheel and told myself staying calm was my best bet.

"But as for your mama and daddy—well, they've run off before. No one will think much about that. For you, there will be a search. But your disappearance will remain an unsolved mystery. Who knows? Maybe people will think you ran off with your parents. Anyway, no one found my daddy for years, of course, except your damned Uncle Fenwick. And for years, he black-mailed Rich . . . in Henry's name."

"What?!" I exclaimed, so shocked that for just a microsecond I forgot the danger Daddy and I were in.

"Oh, you want to hear the whole story, Nosey Josie?" There was a grin in Lenny's voice. I clenched my teeth and didn't say anything. Of course I wanted to know. "Well, it's pretty simple. Let me start at the beginning. Let's see . . . oh yes. Daddy's routine beat-ings of me and Mama. She never stood up to him, of course. And neither did I.

"Until somewhere in my junior year in high school. See, I was dating your mama then. And she kept telling me, Lenny, you don't need to take that. Lenny, stand up for yourself! And one night, not long after Grandpa died, and Mama was in town working in one of the an-tique shops, Daddy came by.

"By then, he and Mama were divorced. But he'd heard that Rich and Mama had had an affair. Had been, for a long time. He decided to take it out on me, for not telling him, he said. He pulled me outside, started to take off his belt to beat me again, and I heard your mama's voice in my head. Lenny, you don't have to take this. So I grabbed a rock, threw it at him. It shocked him so much, the bastard dropped his belt. So I jumped him. Hit him hard. Knocked him out.

"And then I had an idea. It was a great idea, too. Whoever looks in old cisterns? And with the lid on, I wouldn't have to worry about smell. So I drug his body to the cistern. It was a long trek, but he was skinny and I was young and strong and angry, and we were far enough from view of the road that I didn't worry about being seen. He stayed out of it. I pulled back the lid, shoved him in.

"Don't even know if he was dead or alive when he hit the bottom. And didn't care."

I swallowed hard at the image. The car skidded a little.

"Oh no, you don't," said Lenny, poking the gun in my ribs. "Don't think you can get us into a wreck and somehow get out of this."

"Okay," I said, forcing myself to focus despite the fact my eyes were watering. "But you never let me get my coat and it's kinda hard to drive steadily when I'm shivering."

Lenny turned up the heat.

"Thanks," I said. Maybe if I kept him talking, like I was a friend, I could think of something. "So you got rid of your daddy. But the plan went wrong, somehow, when Uncle Fenwick found his body in the cistern."

"That's right. I'd moved by then, or I'd have stopped Mama from calling the C. J. Worthy Plumbing Company. A few weeks later, Rich got a blackmail letter—and a photo of what was left in the cistern of Daddy. It was signed Henry Toadfern. And there was a P.O. box to send payment to—somewhere in Michigan. Of course, Rich knew he hadn't killed Daddy. And it wasn't hard for him to figure out I had.

"He confronted me. Rich was worried about his career if the truth came out about his stepson. And I didn't want to go to jail. I'd already lost years of my life to my daddy's cruelty. I wasn't about to go to jail for what I'd done. So Rich and I agreed we'd each pay half the blackmail. Of course, it didn't end there. Every few months, another blackmail note. A different P.O. box, from a different place. Mama had no idea, of course. She would have immediately gone to the police, so we simply didn't tell her."

I took in what Lenny was saying. Effie had stayed in touch with my mama, not knowing about the blackmail that allegedly came from Daddy. And Uncle Fenwick, with his fancy RVs . . . why, he could go somewhere, set up a P.O. box, and then have the mail forwarded to another P.O. box. All in his brother's name. The ultimate revenge for not sharing the initial wealth—the antique coins in the septic tank. I'd never know for sure, but that was my guess.

"How did you figure out it was Uncle Fenwick, not Daddy, who was blackmailing you all along?"

"Simple. Rachel doesn't know about any of this, of course. When she came to Rich and told him Henry and May Toadfern had contacted her, wanting him to buy into their FleaMart idea, Rich realized that Henry must not have been the blackmailer all along. Otherwise, he wouldn't have exposed himself to Rich, let him know how to find him so easily. Rich told me about it, and I realized that was right.

"Thanksgiving afternoon, I went out to take a walk on the towpath, to think over what to do. Someone knew about Junior and had been using Henry's name as blackmailer out of convenience. We thought of everyone—but the obvious choice. And then I saw your uncle, hanging from the telegraph pole.

"He was still alive, Josie. Struggling. Kicking. Looking like he wished he hadn't made the choice to kill himself, wishing he could undo it. Our eyes met. He couldn't say anything of course—but I knew. He was the one who'd found Daddy years ago. I ran back, grabbed the clothesline, tied him up to keep him still. I didn't want to risk him somehow managing to undo what he'd started. And then I stabbed him. Repeatedly."

I gagged. "I know that," I said, swallowing to try to keep my stomach and throat under control. "I found him. Actually . . . Rachel and I . . ."

"Ah yes, poor little Rachel," Lenny said. "She was so traumatized. But it worked out well, didn't it? Your daddy accused of the murder. The blackmailer out of the way."

"But why take Mama? And Daddy and me?"

"May knew that Henry and Fenwick had fought on their walk on Thanksgiving. That Fenwick had been horrified to learn Henry was going to work with Rich on FleaMart. She told me about it at the Bar-None because it seemed so strange to her. She was like that, you know. If something didn't seem right, she'd get curious about it, pursue it."

Like me, I thought. Or, rather, I was like her.

"It was like old times, when we'd share our thoughts, whatever was on our minds," Lenny said. His voice got a little dreamy. "Like when I'd tell her about Daddy. Or she'd tell me about her family problems. I don't think she could talk like that with Henry. He's too shallow. I never did figure out why she went with him."

Love bears no explanations, I thought.

"Then that night, she saw the coins you had kept. And she finally figured it out. She called me up this morning, told me to come get her. Of course, I did. She told me about the coins Henry had found in the septic, how seeing them reminded her of him telling her years ago about finding them, not sharing with his brother, who'd been working on the cistern.

"She'd wondered why Fenwick would be so upset about Henry working with Rich, and made the same leap I'm sure you did. That Fenwick had been black-mailing Rich over Dad.

"But, of course, she'd also made the same mistake you did. You should have seen the look on her face when I told her, 'no, sweetheart. You told me to stand up to my daddy. And I did.' Then I took her into Rich's office at the house—Mama and Rachel were already at Run Deer Run taking care of details—and I told him she'd figured it out. He told me to just dump her like I'd dumped my daddy."

"And you did that. To the woman you love."

"Loved! In the past! And she dumped me," Lenny said, sounding agitated, "for a no-good bum. She got what she deserved. I wouldn't have killed Daddy if it weren't for her."

"I saw the way you looked at her at the Bar-None. You still love her. And I'm sure when she said stand up to him, she didn't mean kill him," I said angrily, forgetting that part about staying calm being my best bet. "And I'm sure she didn't think you'd turn into a hit man for Rich."

Lenny smacked me hard in the face, and the car swerved. Daddy moaned in the backseat.

"Just drive," Lenny said angrily. "We're almost to the house. Then I'm dumping you and your daddy, too. You all can suffocate together."

"You know you can't get away with this. Killing four people?"

"You think your boyfriend will save you?" Lenny snapped.

"My boyfriend's in Kansas City," I said.

"I mean the reporter, with you at the party. You've probably told him everything," he said.

I felt a clenching in my stomach. Caleb was in danger, too. "I didn't," I said.

"Uh, huh. I'll take care of him, later."

"Look, he's really not my boyfriend—"

"Right," Lenny said with a sneering, mimicking tone. "I saw the way you looked at him."

I was shivering so hard that I had a hard time walking. And my hope—that when Lenny was preoccupied with trying to drag Daddy through the dark and cold, I'd have a chance to get the gun from Lenny—was ruined by the fact that Daddy had come back around when we'd jolted to a stop at the end of the long lane that led up to the Burkette house.

Lenny had held the gun on me while I untied Daddy's ankles and took the gag from his mouth. Daddy had immediately started to curse Lenny, but I'd shaken my head gently and he'd stopped. Then Lenny handed me a flashlight, and barked directions as we walked around the side of the house. He was behind us, the gun trained on us, of course.

And we were so far from the road, nobody would see the flashlight in the woods. If they did, they probably wouldn't think anything of it. Not only that, but it was unlikely anyone would drive by for hours. After all, only locals used these roads. And most of the locals were either at Rich's retirement party, or snugly in their homes sipping hot chocolate.

In other words, we were pretty much doomed.

"Don't talk," Lenny had told us as we started around the house. "If you do, I'll shoot. Don't run. If you do, I'll shoot. It's just as easy for me to shoot you now and dump your bodies in the cistern—but I'd rather think of you as dying cold and miserable in each other's company."

When we got to the cistern, I thought maybe I could attack him when he was pulling away the cistern lid.

But Lenny wasn't about to let himself get in a vulnerable position.

He ordered Daddy to pull away the lid, which was partially pulled back.

It was heavy and Daddy grunted and pulled, and finally got it off and to the side.

"Not as young as you used to be, huh, Henry," Lenny said. I could hear the grin in his voice. "Train the flashlight down there. Take a look."

Daddy and I crept to the edge, and I shone the flashlight down into the cistern.

At the bottom of the plaster-lined well was Mama. Her eyes were shut. She was still, her face tilted up. She had scrunched up in her fur coat, as far away as possible from the other thing in the bottom of the cistern.

A corpse that was mostly—but not completely—rotted away to the skeleton. A few rags were all that was left of the clothing.

I gagged.

Lenny laughed. "Take a look at your future."

I sat back, hard, on the cistern lid—and immediately felt it crack beneath me.

For the first time in my life, I was thanking the good Lord that I needed to lose twenty pounds—because the cracked lid gave me another idea.

I didn't react, though. My heart started thumping harder. What was a cistern lid, but gravel and mortar? And over time, even that would start to weaken. The old cistern lid had been pulled back and forth a lot lately, weakening it. How big of a piece had cracked off? Small enough to pick up and throw, but big enough to knock Lenny out? I prayed that maybe, yes, this was true.

"May? May?" Daddy was calling Mama's name anxiously.

I heard a barely audible, weak, "Henry?" Tears pricked my eyes.

"Oh good. Still alive. I was hoping she hadn't died of exposure just yet. That's why I left the cistern lid ajar. Leave her some air. Let her see you join her. Let her contemplate the choice she made—the wrong choice, years ago," Lenny said bitterly. "Get down there, Henry!"

I half expected Daddy to jump up, lunge at Henry, try to knock him off balance, but Lenny had anticipated that.

He released the safety, held the gun pointed down into the cistern. "Try anything Henry, and I'll pull the trigger and kill her. You won't even have your last minutes together."

Daddy stood up slowly, lowered himself down into the cistern using the ladder that was attached to the side.

"I tried to get out," Mama was saying. I could just hear her soft, dry voice. "But the lid was so heavy. I couldn't budge it. Henry, where's Josie . . ."

"Oh, she's coming, too, May," Lenny said. "Finally, your little family will be together again."

Daddy peered at me over the rim of the cistern. Our eyes met in the glow of the flashlight. His eyes said "I'm sorry." And mine said back, "It will be okay."

Then Daddy's head disappeared. Oh, Lord. I'd have to move fast . . . but I was so cold and shivering. How could I possibly aim with the chunk of cistern lid—assuming I could even lift it?

"Hand me that flashlight," Lenny said.

I held it up to him, not wanting to get up and have him see the cracked lid. He snatched it from me.

"There's still a chance, May. Come out. Tell me you love me like I know you always did. We can disappear together. You're good at that—disappearing. This time disappear with me. I saw the look in your eyes, May. I know you loved me all this time. You can undo your choice of Henry—"

There was silence, and then I heard my daddy saying, "May, oh May . . ." I could see them, somehow, in my mind's eye, and I knew they were holding each other.

"Shut up, damn you," shouted Lenny. "Or I'll shoot her now! Let her decide."

There was another silence. I scooted forward, shivering, shivering. Lenny knelt, leaned forward, peering into the cistern, waiting for my mother's answer.

I was waiting, too, because I knew all of Lenny's attention would be focused on her.

Finally, my mother spoke, her voice quivering but somehow still strong. "If I've learned anything in my life, Lenny, it's that you can't undo your choices. What you saw in my eyes was pity. Now, as before, and always, I choose Henry."

Lenny screamed, a long piercing, "nooooo!" and pointed the gun into the cistern, starting to pull the trigger . . .

I launched forward, grabbed the chunk of cistern lid—oh, Lord, it was too big for one hand . . . I grabbed it with both hands, threw it at Lenny.

I hit him in the shoulder.

He spun, still screaming "noooo!" and fell backward into the cistern as he finished pulling the trigger.

The bullet hit me in the shoulder, and I stumbled, losing my balance, and took an unfortunate step in the wrong direction as I gasped in pain and tried to keep from falling. But I fell anyway into the cistern. My head hit the side of the cistern wall and I plunged into sudden, consuming darkness before I hit the bottom.

Epilogue

"Am I dead?" I asked.

"Why would you think that?" Mrs. Oglevee asked sternly, frowning at me.

"You're not doing anything weird," I said.

Mrs. Oglevee was sitting behind her teacher's desk, looking like she always had back in junior high. I looked down at my arms, hands, outfit, feet.

I was wearing jeans with ripped knees, one of Uncle Horace's old sweatshirts—sleeves cut off, pulled to be off-shoulder to reveal my neon-green tank top—and tennis shoes with curly neon-green laces. The laces looked like curly fries.

Oh, my Lord. I had to be dead. I was dressed like I had in the 1980s, in junior high.

And if I was dead and back in junior high in the afterlife, I apparently hadn't lived as good a life as I thought I had. I gulped.

"Don't be impertinent, young lady," Mrs. Oglevee was saying. "Of course you're not dead. But you are, again, late with your assignment. Your essay about your family was due yesterday. Why didn't you write the assignment?"

Part of me knew this was a memory . . . part of me knew this wasn't real . . . but the same words came out of my mouth as I'd spoken years ago to Mrs. Oglevee, as I stared down at my green curly-fry laces.

"Everyone else was talking about how they were going to write about their mom or dad. But I can't do that," I mumbled. "I mean, I have Aunt Clara and Uncle Horace, and I love them, but the rest of my family . . ."

"Young lady, look at me!" Mrs. Oglevee barked.

I looked up at her. She was glaring across the table. "What do you think family is? Genetic coding? Bloodlines? A chart in the front of a Bible?" She leaned across the table, narrowed her eyes at me. "A real family is of the heart. And friends are the family the heart chooses."

She glared at me a little longer, then shook her head. "I reckon you'll understand someday, Miss Toadfern. At least, I hope so."

She started fading, Chesire-like as always. "Mrs. Oglevee!" I called. My clothes suddenly felt looser. I glanced down. My 1980s garb had changed to hospital wear. "Mrs. Oglevee!"

But she just smiled. "Remember! Friends . . . family the heart chooses . . ."

Then she disappeared completely, and I was left in a white fog . . .

And then my eyes were open and I was wincing from a light.

"Hey, look who's back from the dead!"

I tried to sit up, moaned.

"Take it easy," the voice said.

Sally, I realized. I opened my eyes.

She helped me sit up, pressed a call button. I was in a hospital room, I realized. Several nurses came in, checked me over.

After they bustled out, I focused on Sally. "Tell me," I said. She knew what I meant.

"You're in Masonville County Hospital," she said. "Room 53B." She jerked a thumb at the pulled-to curtain behind her. "Lady in the other bed is here with a broken leg. Car wreck. Anyway, you were shot in the shoulder and knocked out when your head hit the concrete as you fell into the cistern.

"Lenny Burkette died upon impact in the cistern. Broken neck. According to Uncle Henry and Aunt May, he landed the wrong way, right on top of his daddy's remains." Sally paused and shuddered. "With the cistern lid off, Aunt May was finally able to use her cell phone, called for help. You've been out for a few days. But you're going to be okay."

"But, if I fell in, too, why didn't I—"

Sally looked at me for a long moment, and then said, "Your parents moved to try to catch you. Even Aunt May, as weak as she was. They broke your fall, Josie, which may well have saved your life. Just as you saved theirs."

I took that in. Then said, "Guy?" I didn't like it that I had been out for a few days, unavailable for Guy.

"I've called Stillwater and let them know," Sally said. "Guy is okay."

"They didn't tell—"

"No," Sally said. "He was anxious two days ago—Sunday—when you didn't come for your regular visit, but he's okay. You may be okay to visit him next Sunday. Anyway, Chip Beavy's been running the laundro-mat for you since you've been gone. And Rich Burkette is in custody for aiding and abetting attempted murder. He and your parents explained everything. Caleb Lou-dermilk got quite a story. Had to have extra copies of the *Advertiser-Gazette* printed. He is expecting two columns, by the way, to make up for the fact you didn't get a chance to meet your deadline." Sally smiled when she made that last statement.

I took in everything she'd said, then asked for a sip of water. She helped me with that. My head was pounding and I felt weak. I also really didn't like all the IV lines coming into and out of my arms.

"Josie, I called Owen," Sally said. "He sent those—the yellow ones." I turned my head slowly. The ban-dage on my neck was stiff and thick. There was a gorgeous bouquet of yellow roses in the windowsill. And next to that, a purple and orange arrangement of fall flowers.

I looked back at Sally. My eyes pricked. "He's not coming back," I said.

Sally looked away for a second, then back at me with watering eyes. She shook her head. "I don't think so," she said, taking my hand.

"The other flowers?"

"From your mama and daddy," Sally said. "They . . . headed back to Arkansas, after they were treated and released—Aunt May, for exposure, and Uncle Henry, for a broken arm, which he got while saving you. They asked me to tell you that they're not going to pursue FleaMart here. They think they'll try to open one in the South. Something about keeping a promise to you, Aunt May said. But they said to tell you they wish you well."

I didn't even need to ask. They weren't coming back, either.

"Hey," I said. "You'd better get back to the boys."

Sally gave a pshaw-style laugh. "What are you talking about? They're out in the hallway—with the rest of your family. Want to see them?"

I perked up. "Of course."

She jumped up, opened the door, and in trooped my family.

Sally, of course. Harry, Barry, and Larry.

Cherry and Deputy Dean.

Mrs. Beavy.

Winnie, who started crying when she saw me, and hugged me so hard she almost pulled my IV loose. "You're supposed to be in Chicago," I said.

"I came back early," she said.

Rusty Wilton and Lorraine McMurphy, the antique store owners.

Luke and Greta Rhinegold, the Red Horse Motel owners.

Don Richmond and Mary Rossbergen, from Stillwater.

And even Caleb Loudermilk, although in this spiritual collection of siblings and nephews and cousins and aunts and uncles and parents and grandparents, I wasn't sure yet just where he fit in.

There were not enough seats for all of them, of course. But they stayed and chatted and talked and even laughed with me, fussing over me when the nurse brought in dinner for me: turkey slices and gravy and mashed potatoes and green beans and cranberries. At last, I was having my Thanksgiving meal.

Apparently, I was the only patient happy that the hospital was still serving Thanksgiving food. Although I have to say, Aunt Nora's cranberry sauce was much better. I wondered if she would ever give me the secret recipe and then decided that no, she probably wouldn't.

Finally the nurse came back in and shooed everyone out, and insisted on giving me another dose of pain-killer.

Sally was the last to leave. Before she went, she pulled a framed photo out of her big handbag, and handed it to me.

It was my photo of Guy with his pumpkins, the one I always kept on my nightstand. "Thought you'd want that," she said. "He's here in spirit, you know."

I nodded. "I know," I said.

Sally patted my arm and walked out, brushing the dividing curtain. In the swaying of the curtain, I thought I saw for just a brief second the fog thin images of Mrs. Oglevee, Aunt Clara, and Uncle Horace, all smiling at me.

I closed my eyes, heard the woman from the bed in 53A say, as I drifted off again, "That's some family you have."

"Sure is," I said.

PARADISE ADVERTISER-GAZETTE

Josie's Stain Busters

by Josie Toadfern
Stain Expert and Owner of Toadfern's Laundromat
(824 Main Street, Paradise, Ohio)

Vinegar solves an amazing number of life's problems. Just not heartache. Although I have heard of folks making a tonic of apple cider vinegar for various ailments.

But this is a column about stain removal, for which of course you only want to use pure WHITE vinegar.

In a spray bottle, mix up ⅔ water and ⅓ vinegar. Label the bottle and use it to pre-treat any number of stains (after blotting up as much of the spill as possible with a white absorbent cloth):

- Cranberry sauce (and other fruit-based stains)
- Spaghetti sauce (and other tomato-based stains)
- Deodorant and anti-perspirant stains
- Perspiration stains
- Pet stains (urine) or people stains of the same nature
- Cola stains

Wait at least 10 minutes before treating with enzymatic pre-treatment and washing as usual.

Remember, white vinegar is actually acetic acid, so if you want to use this solution on finer or fragile fabrics, test a hidden spot first, then apply just to the stain with an eyedropper.

You can also spray your knits with the solution before ironing if you want a sharper crease.

This vinegar/water solution is great outside the laundry, too. Use it to clean glasses (both the drinking and seeing kind), countertops, mirrors, windows, spigots, and sinks.

Full strength white vinegar is a good glue and gum dissolver.

Heated on the stove top or microwave, it works even better. (But be careful about using vinegar full-strength on wood—the acid can hurt wood.)

Add about a half cup of white vinegar to your rinse cycle to reduce lint, remove built-up detergent, reduce static cling, and prevent yellowing.

But never ever mix vinegar and chlorine bleach, or use vinegar on clothes that have been treated with bleach! The two chemicals will mix and may release a harmful gas. Clean clothes and linens are a joy in life but not worth harming yourself over.

Until next month, may your whites never yellow and your colors never fade. But if they do, hop on over and see me at Toadfern's Laundromat—Always a Leap Ahead of Dirt!

PERENNIAL DARK ALLEY

Men from Boys: A short story collection featuring some of the true masters of crime fiction, including Dennis Lehane, Lawrence Block, and Michael Connelly.
0-06-076285-3

Fender Benders: From **Bill Fitzhugh** comes the story of three people planning on making a "killing" on Nashville's music row.
0-06-081523-X

Cross Dressing: It'll take nothing short of a miracle to get Dan Steele, counterfeit cleric, out of a sinfully funny jam in this wickedly good tale from **Bill Fitzhugh.**
0-06-081524-8

The Fix: Debut crime novelist **Anthony Lee** tells the story of a young gangster who finds himself caught between honor and necessity.
0-06-059534-5

The Pearl Diver: From **Sujata Massey**, antiques dealer and sometime sleuth Rei Shimura travels to Washington D.C. in search of her missing cousin.
0-06-059790-9

The Blood Price: In this novel by **Jonathan Evans**, international trekker Paul Wood must navigate through the world of international people smugglers.
0-06-078236-6

The Reunion: A group of extremely disfunctional teenagers in a psychiatric hospital are forced to reconnect when two of them die unexpectedly in this thriller by **Sue Walker.**
0-06-083265-7

PERENNIAL
DARK ALLEY
An Imprint of HarperCollinsPublishers
www.harpercollins.com

Investigate the Hottest New Mysteries!

Sign up for the FREE HarperCollins monthly mystery newsletter,

The Scene of the Crime,

and get to know your favorite authors, win free books, and be the first to learn about the best new mysteries going on sale.

To register, simply go to www.HarperCollins.com, visit our mystery channel page, and at the bottom of the page, enter your email address where it states "Sign up for our mystery newsletter." Then you can tap into monthly Hot Reads, check out our award nominees, sneak a peek at upcoming titles, and discover the best whodunits each and every month.

Get to know the magnificent mystery authors of HarperCollins and sign up today!